GRANTA

9

Editorial Correspondence: Granta, 44a Hobson Street, Cambridge CB1 1NL. (0223) 315290.
All manuscripts are welcome but must be accompanied by a stamped, self-addressed envelope or they cannot be returned.

Subscriptions: £10.00 for four issues. Back issues are available for £2.50 including postage (issues 3 and 5) and £3.50 including postage (issues 6 to 8).

Granta is set by Lindonprint Typesetters, Cambridge, and is printed by Hazell Watson and Viney Ltd, Aylesbury, Bucks.

Granta is published by Granta Publications Ltd and distributed by Penguin Books Ltd, Harmondsworth, Middlesex, England; Penguin Books Australia Ltd, Ringwood, Victoria, Australia; Penguin Books Canada Ltd, 2801 John Street, Markham, Ontario, Canada L3R 1B4; Penguin Books (NZ) Ltd, 182–90 Wairau Road, Auckland 10, New Zealand.

Cover illustration by Ian Pollock.

Photographs of Chile are all from the John Hillielson Agency and are, in order, by S. Julienne, S. Julienne, C. Geretsen, David Burnett, David Burnett, David Burnett, C. Geretsen.

ISSN 0017–3231
ISBN 014–00–6880–5

Published with the assistance of the Eastern Arts Association

---

CONTENTS

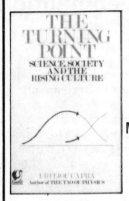

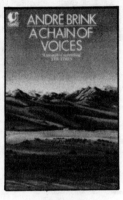

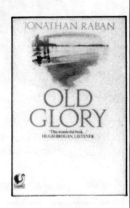

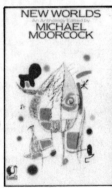

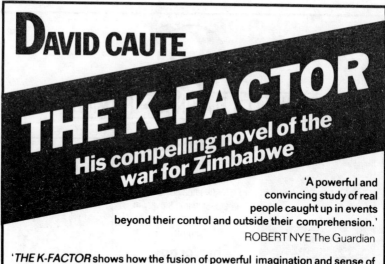

GRANTA

OBSERVATIONS

The Bird of Paradise Lost
G. Cabrera Infante

I first met William Henry Hudson in Havana many years ago. He was called Guillermo Enrique then, almost a namesake. It was Borges who introduced me to him. Borges praised him sky-high when he talked about Hudson's novel: '*The Purple Land* is perhaps unexcelled by any work of gaucho literature,' he said, looking at the horizon with his blank stare. 'It is essentially *criollo*,' he added, and then stopped short with some apprehension. Borges was afraid that I might translate *criollo* as creole, an Argentine anathema. 'Native to South America'—*that's* what he meant. Then he went on to quote Ezequiel Estrada on the subject—namely Hudson: 'Never before has there been a poet, a painter or an interpreter of things Argentine like Hudson. Nor will there be again.' I am not misquoting either, I think. If Don Ezequiel sounds excessive it's only because he was excessive. He always had been. He even died excessively.

Alastair Reid and E.R. Monegal were with Borges at the time, so the translation of his words is theirs. But all I remember about Estrada was when old Ezequiel saw the wheel on fire and the sun and the flaming stars as he fell from the top of the steps at the entrance of the Hotel Presidente in El Vedado, Havana. He then had an ugly gash in his forehead: blood was trickling from the invisible wound to daub his eyeglasses and his dark suit. I was in the lobby when the accident happened, talking to Baragano, the surrealist poet, who laughed the accident off, saying: 'Argentines bleed easy.' I became concerned for Don Ezequiel, a very old man even then. But he didn't notice my concern, only Baragano's scorn. It hurt him apparently more than the brass rail that had hit him. 'You are a callous young man!' yelled

Estrada to Baragano. He was furious now and bled even more: 'It's not funny to be an old man. It should happen to you!' It never did. Baragano died at twenty-nine from a cerebral aneurysm before Estrada was killed by chronic old age. Both Baragano and Ezequiel Estrada have been dead, together in death, for the past twenty years and all that is left of them is a book or two paving the road to the cold hell of oblivion. Only those slim or vast volumes are their password to posterity. That and the wake all ghosts leave behind: a sudden noise late at night that can easily be taken for the wind on the rafters. Or the unexplained rattling not of bones but of a lattice window—a pale face seen, unseen and obviously trying to sneak back from the grave—and bits and pieces of livid garment here and there. Rags, rags all.

But I was excitedly after the trail of Hudson, as hot then as the tropical day. A young sleuth, a tyro I was, a bookworm on my way to shedding all the books and being just a worm: a metamorphosis in reverse—first the butterfly. As if led by a bookhound, I crossed Belascoaín Street and, still favoured by the traffic light about to become red, I passed through a portal to enter a second-hand bookshop. It was called then, *ancien régime* usage, a *librería de viejo,* missing by only an *s* being a library for old people—which in fact it was: *librería de viejos.*

I had spent the luminous Havana afternoon (time for a *siesta a dos: l'après-midi d'un jeune fan*), brighter than the neon night, on my search for Hudson. Here I was, a man not yet thirty, with a dry mouth, looking for Hudson, any Hudson. To go on my quest I had left Miriam Gómez *en* Rada (or Revolutionary Academy of Dramatic Arts: the small letters are all mine), rehearsing a droll drama under a dubious *dramaturg.* The word, in German now, must be pronounced gutturally to enable one to hear Bertolt Brecht with an *eco in lontano,* as he transformed the theatre into Speakers' Stage. The director was an Argentine too, but from East Berlin. It is only a coincidence, I think, that both Borges and Hudson had praised the Banda Oriental of the River Plate as the land of adventure.

I had entered by now the old curiosa shop following Calvert Casey, who knew the place well. It was he who told me that I could perhaps find a book by Hudson here. Calvert was a lover of Nabokov and a committed writer, but a delicate dissenter who later became an exile in Rome, where he committed suicide (that's how committed he was) by taking an overdose of sleeping pills. But I can still hear the silent noise of his death: that's how dear he was to me. His friends in Rome chose an epitaph for him they deemed appropriate: 'He lived, he suffered: he was weak, he was destroyed.' But I never could agree with those infamous last words about Calvert Casey. He wasn't weak, only gentle. He was not destroyed. At least he still walks with me, beside me, in front of me now. That day, as I entered the bookshop with him, Calvert said, looking at the empty shelves that hit us like blanks: 'H–H–Hudson waswas here,' and he laughed at his own joke, a laughter I echoed like the words that always preceded him by a sound or two, an inverted echo: Calvert stammered badly all his life. But he was, I believe, a casualty of exile, the war with no truce. Determined on my quest, I followed him into the sombre recesses of the bookshop. Calvert had told me that before the revolution this particular shop was called *L'Infer,* after the hidden library at the Bibliothèque Nationale in Paris, where all the European erotica was kept. 'Beethoven's Erotica, too?' I asked him and Calvert almost choked on my joke. Or was it with his own words, wisely kept at bay by his silent stammer?

I didn't even ask myself then, for I was resolute on finding the sources of Hudson and I followed Calvert further into the dark, dusky domain, hoping against hope. *Mal d'estime.* The shop at the corner of Belascoaín and Reina, the street Calvert claimed, was selling the few second-hand books they had left as if *in articulo mortis.* Like a museum that has been successively and successfully plundered, in which looters had left only the slightly paler prints on the walls where paintings had hung for years, their present absence marked by the missing frames as familiar, friendly ghosts—on the shelves of the shop were the traces of long-kept books, older than old, now gone for ever but leaving their mark in decoration more than in literary history. *Impavidum ferient ruinae*: and rather than following Calvert I followed Horace: ruins will find me unmoved. As I moved towards the exit and the day, I saw near the door a title that needed no translation from its spaghetti Spanish: *Nostromo.* Then, next to it, as if hidden by the shadow of the door, I saw another book still extant in the *estante*: the self, as Calvert always pronounced shelf. It was just a title and a name—G.E. Hudson, *Allá lejos y hace tiempo*! Yes! *Far Away and Long Ago* translated! A coincidence? Perhaps. But chance then was to chance my arm to touch the book and thus force fate in my direction. I tend to believe now that it was the call of the literary wild, the lure of the open spaces of the mind, the romance of the pampas as an invitation to escape. Come with me to roam, said Calvert Casey then. Did he mean Rome?

I don't have to say what I did next. It was early in 1962 and even books were becoming scarce then and about to be rationed. I mean true books, literature, those that offer you adventures in reading. But if you were a pervert and you fancied Russian propaganda bound in leaders, then the whole city was *L'Infer.* The new names were everywhere in perverted commas: 'Gorky', 'Simonov', 'Sholokhov'. Ah Gogorky! Sisimonov had a novel titled *Night and Day* but it was no Porter, I tell you. Sholokhov's *Quiet Flows the Don* always made me laugh when I imagined a toga-ed tutor discreetly drowning in the Isis as Ophelia did in *Hamlet*: floating in his garments 'like a creature native into that element'. Nobody who has read more than two books (let's say three) can think that those names, titles and rank prose are literature. It was Soviet propaganda through and through. I tried to laugh it away, dismissing it as propagaganda. But it was all-pervasive in the once perversive city that was a *finca* and a bar and a tax haven for Hemingway, a male brothel and native cigars for Somerset Maugham and both brothel and gaming-house for our third man in Havana. Those were the days, my friends! Those were the writers then.

Before a faster customer could beat me to this volume written in exile by, as David Dewar says, an 'Argentine by birth, predominantly American by blood, who paid England the greatest compliment in his power by becoming a British subject by choice,' I made my move. Pawn to queen now. He lived in London once and here he starved and just before dying he was recognized as what he had always been, a great writer. But no knight's gambit for him. Now, lest any old-timer with reflexes quicker than his memories beats me to the nostalgia I never enjoyed or suffered until then—I finally managed to buy the book (colour cover, motley artwork, unnecessary embellishments) and when I had finally read it I was to feel vicariously, through the Argentine leaves, the remembrance of an uncommon past that would become a foliage *à deux.*

The book was actually barely in Spanish, translated in Argentina from Hudson's brand of English which, according to his friend Cunninghame Graham, was a written language thought in Spanish. 'To appreciate Hudson's book one must know Spanish.' I didn't know this, at the time anyway, and there I was reading Hudson in *Spanish,* almost. Be that as it may, I was successively delighted, enchanted and haunted by the timeless charm of the book that broke all barriers, from space to time to language. Hudson wrote of a time and a place that was for me doubly remote. Where was my pampa in the late nineteenth century? Far away and long ago indeed! But he made his time my own: that was my childhood in Gibara, my home town in Cuba's Oriente Province. 'On the second day of my illness,' writes Hudson in London—he never was a strong man, in spite of his life as a naturalist in La Plata and in England and he had had a bout of rheumatic fever as a child—'I fell into recollections of my childhood, and at once I had that far, that forgotten past with me again as I had never previously had it.' Now Hudson explained the Proustian mechanisms of memory, for him absolutely *avant la lettre:* 'It was not like that mental condition, known to most persons, when some sight or sound or, more frequently, the perfume of some flower, associated with our early life, restores that past suddenly and so vividly that it is almost an illusion.' This is the conclusion he reached: 'That is an intensely emotional condition and vanishes as quickly as it comes'—except, of course, when it becomes literature. That's what Hudson did with his recollections—and with mine.

Hudson had been a professional collector of birds in the pampas as a young man, employed first by the Smithsonian in the United States. He also sent stuffed birds to the Royal Zoological Society in London and later to the British Museum. He mailed to the Zoological Society specimens caught in Patagonia and one of Hudson's birds is still preserved in the British Museum. It bears the label 'Rio Negro 1871'—an old bird indeed. Says Cunninghame Graham of Hudson: 'He was himself a bird in London, caged in ill health and poverty, for the most part unable to escape, but at rare intervals, into his own world of light and air.' David Garnett, author of *The Man in the Zoo,* describes a photograph of Hudson from long ago and far away 'which shows him to have been an extremely handsome young man with dark curly hair, lively eyes, a short dark beard, and an expression of eager and friendly amusement.' Then adds Garnett: 'The querulous, embittered expression often to be seen in his later years was completely absent.' But Garnett regrettably fuses, confuses Hudson the writer of fiction with his hero: 'This early photograph makes it easy to understand why the women in *The Purple Land* felt towards him as they did.' Strangely enough Garnett, a critic, attributes Hudson's citric mien in old age to his success as a writer: it came too late, too little, while mediocrities everywhere had basked since early youth in neon lights, money and rave reviews. Hudson married a homely English lady many years his senior. They were poor together, for a time. Then she inherited an old house in Bayswater and she made it into a boarding house, a precarious enterprise that faded and finally failed utterly. They became poorer. Then Mrs Hudson, a funny name for a housekeeper in London at the time, died. 'It was in this gloomy eyrie,' says David Dewar, 'that Hudson died, aged eighty-one, in 1922'—four years after publishing *Far Away and Long Ago.* This was the man who wrote: 'For what soul, in this wonderful various world, would wish to depart before ninety!'

When exile finally came for me it was like death for W.H. Hudson: not sudden and dramatic but slow and sleazy, like a faint pain in the chest nobody could imagine was a coronary. It was nonetheless painful for that. Belgium, Spain, England were my *angina paulatim.* I first came to live in London with Miriam Gómez, actress, and my two young daughters in 1966. It was winter and I was as poor as Hudson, poorer even, for Hudson had no children. Nobody could say, though, that I had to sleep in Hyde Park, as some claimed Hudson did. I lived in the back of a basement flat in Trebovir Road, with the underground trains speeding next to our back yard (you couldn't call it a garden, could you?) and into Earls Court tube station like so many monsters slouching towards a Bethlehem of steel on time: every two minutes there was a second coming, then a third—and so on and on. It was in this dark, gloomy flat, that even Hudson would have refused as a dwelling-place, that I conceived the idea of making *The Purple Land* into a Western: I dreamed of the plains with Hudson again. He had been dead for decades then, but the rights to all his writings belonged to the Royal Society for the Protection of Birds. I wrote to them and they answered politely but to the point. It was obvious that the Society was humane enough: they were all for the protection of birds and copyrights but not for the protection of migratory men. They shoot mallards, don't they?

I moved to other things and to another address, in Gloucester Road, close to Kensington Gardens. Across the park Bayswater was near. But I became stranded on the Strand, on the banks of the tamed Thames, on the South Bank so far from the Banda Oriental: I drifted. Later I read *Far Away and Long Ago,* again and again, in Hudson's own brand of English, which for me, as the language of his friend Conrad, is good enough—even if Conrad pronounced it Godunov. Hudson and I came to share the past and pastures and the dreams of the pampa. As the Cuban poet Lezama Lima said of death: 'A dark and sombre prairie always invites me.' But Hudson's pampa was still, stiller yet for me. I dreamed of my moving Gulf Stream of consciousness: an exterior monologue, for ever in motion, endless. Like life. If time has a stop we will be into eternity in next to no time.

Hudson was nostalgic of the pampa, that vast space a visitor from France said to Borges that induces *le vertige horizontal.* But he was also nostalgic of the tiniest living creature of the plains—like the Argentine spider and the phosphorescent centipede. This scientific spirit linked Hudson to another exile into English, another lack-land naturalist: Vladimir Nabokov, who loved butterflies so much that he tried to keep them for ever, futilely, in the dubious immortality of a pin through the body and an eternal glass case. Nabokov hunted and caught and impaled butterflies literally and literarily. So much so that he could be known now as Vlad the Impaler by a posterity of moths.

Hudson loved birds and insects (and one Argentine arachnid or two), but he described them in freedom. He stuffed birds, naturally, but that was when he was young. Many years later, living in London then, he condemned the fashion of wearing exotic bird feathers pinned to ladies' hats. The fashion of feathers went as fashions go, fugitive fads, but Hudson stays with us yet. I only hope I'm not pinning him down now: the trapped naturalist.

Hudson flowed then, still flows, like the river of memories. I read as many books by him as I could at the time. I was very poor then, but I managed. There are many lending libraries in London (you can't miss them: they have three bronze balls over the door) and in each you can explore what you claim: Hudson found, Hudson sound. There are really wonderful things in every book of his, *trouvailles,* what he called *hallazgos.* Things that an exile from America such as he, and an exile from Europe or from Africa or even Asia, an exile from everywhere, anywhere, any exile can truly appreciate—true finds.

I remember a moment, just a glimpse, a fleeting instant in a book of his whose name I can't recall. But the title is not important, honestly, only the moment: only his moment in time. The writer, Hudson himself, as he goes down a street in London in summertime hears a bird sing. I don't remember the name of the borough either, nor the name of the street, and even the bird's name is unimportant. I don't remember the name of the bird and I forget the title of the book, but I'll always remember the moment. I remember Hudson walking through Chelsea and I am going, then or later, down the street after him. There was no trace at the time of the democratic asphalt, the leveller, so that we were both walking on the irregular cobblestones in Sloane Avenue, while the bird went on singing, seemingly for ever. Suddenly Hudson stops dead in his tracks. He appears to hesitate, then crosses the road without heeding the traffic. Anyway, there are no cars or trucks in the road and only once in a while a hansom cab is seen being dragged by a tired horse: a nag sweating, sweltering in the summer sun. What is he doing now? Hudson is actually knocking on a door across the street while the bird sings somewhere to summer or to whatever birds sing in summer. When the green door opens, the exile asks the woman who came to it if the bird he hears is singing in her back yard. She only nods. She is small and swarthy and does not seem to have any English. Hudson asks her if she speaks Spanish, but she says no: she is Italian. Hudson does not hesitate any more. 'Is that bird by any chance a South American bird, madam?' he asks. The woman says *sí.* She brought it with her on the boat all the way from Argentina. She lived in Buenos Ayres once. Ah! Hudson, so tall and so thin, his long white beard and his white hair flowing in the English summer breeze like an albino banner, remains silent for a while. It all seems like a long time, in fact. He stands in the doorway without crossing the threshold, but doesn't say anything. He doesn't move. He doesn't even blink. He just stands there, still but visibly moved. Is he crying? Now he nods. Suddenly Hudson has realized that this bird does not come from Argentina. It comes from his childhood and from his youth and from his dreams: out of the past. That Chelsea bird comes from remembrance and of course (now I remember) it's called nostalgia. That bird (from Hudson's pampas, from my savannahs and from Havana, from the prairies and the plains and even from the steppes) can be heard singing by every exile, anywhere. For you see, it's the emperor's nightingale that's come back.

The Boat Train
Russell Hoban

Liverpool Street at night is a darkling place; it darkles. Out of the dimness the red and yellow illuminated signs of the JAZZ BUFFET AND BAR, of CIGARETTES AND SWEETS assert themselves. In the dimness and against the fluorescent lights over the ticket barriers travellers manifest themselves halfway between chiaroscuro and silhouette. There is a general echoing of rattling and rumbling, there is a dark and stertorous clamour. The Harwich train will leave at 19.40 from Platform 9.

As the train pulled out, I was astonished to see how many illuminated clock-faces looked out from the station into the night.

I didn't count them; I was strongly satisfied by them—that in the hurrying past of the uncelebrated moment these heralds were yet present to trumpet silently with their luminous faces all departures, all arrivals.

The train wheels, now authorized to take up their song of distance, clacked and clattered their traditional shanty of miles. The unseen boat not yet arrived at, the dark sea waiting—these already lent significance to the travellers on our train; everyone looked interesting.

An ordinary mirror is silvered at the back, but the window of a night train has darkness behind the glass. My face and the faces of other travellers were now mirrored on this darkness in a succession of stillnesses. Consider this, said the darkness: any motion at any speed is a succession of stillnesses; any section through an action will show just such a plane of stillness as this dark window in which your seeking face is mirrored. And in each plane of stillness is the moment of clarity that makes you responsible for what you do.

Consider this, said the train wheels, repeating the message tirelessly moment after moment on the miles of cold iron that lay shining in the dark that led to Harwich and repeating face on face the faces reflected in the windows. Harwich attained, the windows became empty of faces.

Niagara
Frederic Prokosch

It was 1929. *Look Homeward, Angel* had just appeared and I was told that Thomas Wolfe was teaching English at NYU in Washington Square. I had some inner reservations about *Look Homeward, Angel,* but I was thrilled by the oceanic surge that swept through the pages.

And so one day I plucked up my courage and climbed the stairs and walked to his desk and said, 'Would you like to have lunch with me at Ruby Wang's, Mr Wolfe?'

Thomas Wolfe raised his damp, bulging face in my direction and said, 'Sure. Okay. Absolutely. Let's lunch at Ruby Wang's.'

Ruby Wang's was a Chinese restaurant in a dirty brick building just a block from the dust and decrepitude of Washington Square. There was an air of great fragility in the Ruby Wang restaurant. The chairs and tables were of a splintering bamboo, and the menu was scrawled on a cobweb-thin paper. The dishes were nearly weightless in their eggshell-like texture. Even the food had a flavour of dejected evanescence. Thomas Wolfe's enormous body and low, grumbling voice made the cutlery look like trinkets in a brittle Lilliput.

We ordered chow mein and drank some lukewarm beer. Tom Wolfe leaned over the table and muttered confidentially. 'This morning, one of my girls, a delightful child named Deirdre Rosebottom, asked me if I was a cousin or perhaps a nephew of Virginia Woolf. I explained about the *o*'s: she has two *o*'s as in *booby* whilst I have only one *o*, unfortunately, as in *whore.* She looked horribly shocked. Well, it isn't my fault, is it, that I am not a cousin or a nephew of Virginia Woolf? Maybe it was a blunder in the first place to have a name like Wolfe. There is Humbert Wolfe, the poet, who writes spindly little poems. There is Leonard Woolf, the novelist, who writes about jungles. There are other Wolves also, too many to be enumerated. What a relief to be Marcel Proust! No danger of losing one's identity!'

The waitress brought our lunch, along with some chopsticks.

'Would you like to use the chopsticks, gentlemen? Or would you boys prefer forks?'

'I'll try chopsticks,' said Wolfe after a sultry hesitation, during which his eyes were fixed on the rice with alarm.

The waitress brought the chopsticks and Wolfe attacked the rice, which eluded his chopsticks with insect-like dexterity. He kept poking at the rice with a feverish determination while small drops of sweat exploded on his forehead. His eyes rolled with horror as he tried to control the chopsticks. But the small grains of rice dribbled and darted from the chopsticks and lit on the floor, in the beer, on the butter.

'They say,' he said, 'that in every fat man there's a thin man trying to escape. I suspect that in a little man there is always a big one trying to escape. Take Napoleon. He was a little man with a big one trying to escape. Now take me. I'm a big man with a little one trying to get out. All my life I've felt this lousy little wretch screaming inside me. Max Perkins keeps telling me, "More delicacy, Tom, more delicacy." I quiver with horror, it's that little man inside me, he keeps wailing about delicacy and I'm incapable of delicacy. I feel like the Mississippi. Let it pour, let it pour! It's all I can do and to hell with the delicacy. Think of *Moby Dick*. It's been called the great American novel. Hitherto, that is to say. I insist on the hitherto. There are greater ones lurking in the offing. But consider *Moby Dick*. Where's the delicacy, now, I ask you? Virginia Woolf— *there's* the delicacy, if that's what you're looking for. Elinor Wylie has delicacy. Edith Sitwell has delicacy. But God Almighty, what can a man like me do with a thing like delicacy? I feel the grandeur sweeping through me, what a big howling flood of it! Don't laugh! I'm not joking, in spite of these chopsticks!'

He made a last despairing effort and rammed his chopsticks into the rice, which exploded from the plate and shot through the air like confetti.

He leaned back in his chair and plucked a grain from his eyelid. 'Absolutely devilish, these chopsticks. The Chinese must be sadists!'

The chair gave a crackle and sagged under his buttocks. He whisked it aside indignantly and grabbed a chair from the neighbouring table. The glasses danced and tinkled, the beer lurched over the tablecloth, and Wolfe glared at the waitress with a bubbling ferocity.

'Waitress, please! *Une fourchette*! *J'abandonne les chopsticks*!'

'That's *me,* you see,' he growled, gripping the fork with desolation. 'I'm too clumsy to use those instruments. They're too dainty and dandified. Max Perkins keeps telling me, "Subtlety, Tom! Deftness and discipline!" But I'm incapable of discipline. I'm like the Mississippi River. Does the Mississippi have subtlety? Does the Mississippi use chopsticks?'

His ravenous eyes roved over the plate with desperation. The sweat shone on his brow. His mouth began to quiver. He looked like a volcano on the verge of eruption.

'"Look at Hemingway," says Perkins. "Under the bluntness there's a discipline." But I don't want to turn into another god-damn Hemingway! Perkins says look at Fitzgerald. Under the glitter there's a delicacy. But by Jesus, I don't want to be another F. Scott Fitzgerald! I want to be a Niagara, not a dainty little trickle.

'Now, take Whitman,' he went on. 'He wasn't scared of the whirlpools. He did what he had to and there was no other way of doing it. There's plenty wrong with Whitman and I guess he was a pansy, but when it came to a crisis he had the true virility. Not the Hemingway virility, I mean the *real* virility. He wasn't scared of the Niagara! He wasn't frightened of the whirlpools!'

He placed his fists on the table, which trembled precariously, and the sweat on his face caught the light from the window. He gave a sudden gasp and clutched at the air triumphantly. He looked like a swimmer rising from the bottom of a whirlpool. His wild eyes, squeezed in fat, gleamed like a boar's, and the bubbles on his lips shone with a wild exultation.

I said goodbye to him at the doorway of New York University and he said, 'Thanks for the lunch, pal.'

'It was an honour, Mr Wolfe.'

His eyes grew dark with gratitude and he vanished in the hallway.

GRANTA

JOHN BERGER

BORIS

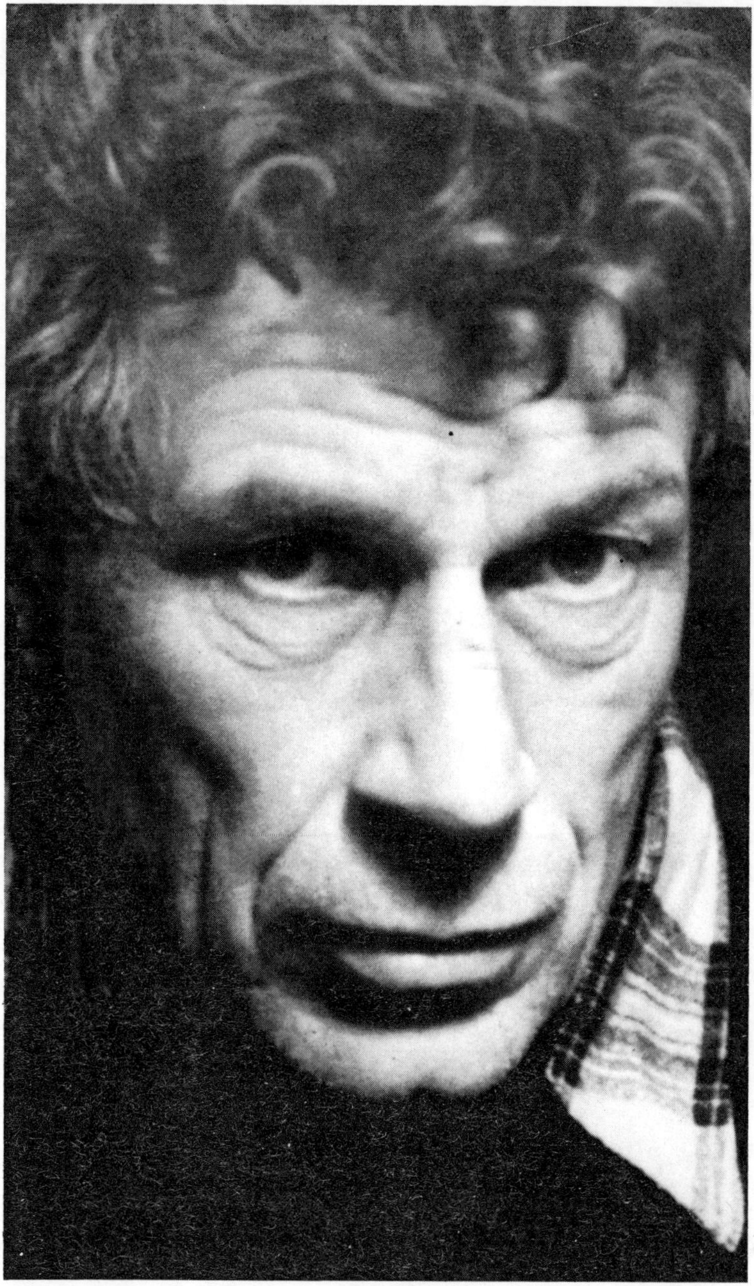

Sometimes to refute a single sentence it is necessary to tell a life story.

In our village, as in many villages in the world at that time, there was a souvenir shop. The shop was in a converted farm house which had been built four or five generations earlier, on the road up to the mountain. You could buy there skiers in bottles, mountain flowers under glass, plates decorated with gentians, miniature cow bells, plastic spinning wheels, carved spoons, chamois leather, sheepskins, clockwork marmots, goat horns, cassettes, maps of Europe, knives with wooden handles, gloves, T-shirts, films, key rings, sunglasses, imitation butter-churns, my books.

The woman who owned the shop served in it. She was by then in her early forties. Blond, smiling but with sharp eyes, she was buxom with small feet and slender ankles. The young in the village nick-named her the Goose—for reasons that are not part of this story. Her real name was Marie-Jeanne. Earlier, before Marie-Jeanne and her husband came to the village, the house belonged to Boris. It was from him that they inherited it.

Now I come to the sentence that I want to refute.

Boris died, said Marc, leaning one Sunday morning against the wall that twists (like the last letter of the alphabet) through our hamlet, Boris died like one of his own sheep, neglected and starving. What he did to his cattle finally happened to him: he died like one of his own animals.

Boris was the third of four brothers. The eldest was killed in the War, the second by an avalanche and the youngest emigrated. Even as a child Boris was distinguished by his brute strength. The other children at school feared him a little and at the same time teased him. They had spotted his weakness. To challenge most boys you bet that they couldn't lift a sack of seventy kilograms. Boris could lift seventy kilograms with ease. To challenge Boris you bet him that he couldn't make a whistle out of a branch of an ash tree.

During the summer, after the cuckoos had fallen silent, all the boys had ash whistles, some even had flutes with eight holes. Having found and cut down the little branch of wood, straight and of the right diameter, you put it in your mouth to moisten it with your tongue, then tapped on it, all round, briskly but not too hard with the wooden handle of your pocket knife. This tapping separated the bark from the wood so that you could pull the white wood out, like an arm from a sleeve. Finally you carved the mouth piece and reinserted it into the bark. The whole process took a quarter of an hour.

Boris put the little branch into his mouth as if he was going to devour the tree of life itself. And his difficulty was that he had invariably struck too hard with his knife handle, so that he had damaged the bark. His whole body went tense. He would try again. He would cut another branch and when it came to tapping it, either he would hit too hard, or, with the concentrated effort of holding himself back, his arm wouldn't move at all.

Come on, Boris, play us some music! they teased him.

When he was fully grown, his hands were unusually big and his blue eyes were set in sockets which looked as though they were meant for eyes as large as those of a calf. It was as if, at the moment of his conception, every one of his cells had been instructed to grow large; but his spine, femur, tibia, fibula had played truant. As a result, he was of average height but his features and extremities were like those of a giant.

One morning in the alpage, years ago, I woke up to find all the pastures white. One cannot really talk of the first snow of the year at an altitude of 1600 metres, because often it snows every month, but this was the first snow which was not going to disappear until the following year, and it was falling in large flakes.

Towards midday there was a knock on the door. I opened it. Beyond, almost indistinguishable from the snow, were thirty sheep, silent, snow on their necks. In the doorway stood Boris.

He came in and went over to the stove to thaw out. It was one of those tall stoves for wood, standing free in the centre of the room like a post of warmth. The jacket over his gigantic shoulders was white as a mountain.

For a quarter of an hour he stood there silent, drinking from the glass of gnole, holding his huge hands over the stove. The damp patch on the floorboards around him was growing larger.

At last he spoke in his rasping voice. His voice, whatever the words, spoke of a kind of neglect. Its hinges were off, its windows broken, and yet, there was a defiance in it, as if, like a prospector living in a broken-down shack, it knew where there was gold.

In the night, he said, I saw it was snowing. And I knew my sheep were up by the peak. The less there is to eat, the higher they climb. I drove up here before it was light and I set out. It was crazy to climb by myself. Yet who would come with me? I couldn't see the path for the snow. If I'd lost my foothold, there was nothing, nothing at all, to stop me till I reached the church-yard below. For five hours since daybreak I have been playing against death.

His eyes in their deep sockets interrogated me to check whether I had understood what he was saying. Not his words, but what lay behind them. Boris liked to remain mysterious. He believed that the unsaid favoured him. And yet, despite himself, he dreamed of being understood.

Standing there with the puddle of melted snow at his feet, he was not in the least like the good shepherd who had just risked his life for his flock. St John the Baptist, who crowned the Lamb with flowers, was the very opposite of Boris. Boris neglected his sheep. Each year he sheared them too late and they suffered from the heat. Each summer he omitted to pare their hooves and they went lame. They looked like a flock of beggars in grey wool, Boris's sheep. If he had risked his life that day on the mountain, it wasn't for their sake, but for the sake of their market price.

His parents had been poor, and from the age of twenty Boris boasted of the money he was going to make one day. He was going to make *big* money—according to the instructions received at his conception and inscribed in every cell of his body.

At market he bought cattle that nobody else would buy, and he bought at the end of the day, offering a price which twelve hours earlier would have appeared derisory. I see him, taciturn beside the big-boned animals, pinching their flesh with one of his immense thumbs, dressed in khaki and wearing an American army cap.

He believed that time would bring him nothing: and that his cunning must bring him everything. When he was selling he never named his price. 'You can't insult me,' he said, 'just tell me what you want to offer.' Then he waited, his blue, deep-set eyes already on the brink of the derision with which he was going to greet the price named.

He is looking at me now, with the same expression. I told you once, he says, that I had enough poems in my head to fill a book, do you remember? Now you are writing the story of my life. You can do that because it's finished. When I was still alive, what did you do? Once you brought me a packet of cigarettes whilst I was grazing the sheep above the factory.

I say nothing. I go on writing.

The uncle of all cattle dealers once told me: 'A ram like Boris is best eaten as meat.'

Boris's plan was simple: to buy thin and sell fat. What he sometimes underestimated was the work and time necessary between the two. He willed the thin cattle to become fat, but their flesh, unlike his own, was not always obedient to his will. And their bodies, at the moment of conception, had not received the same instructions.

He grazed his sheep on every scrap of common land and often on land which wasn't common. In the winter he was obliged to buy extra hay, and he promised to pay for it with lambs in the spring. He never paid. Yet he survived. And his herd grew bigger: in his heyday he owned a hundred and fifty sheep. He drove a Land Rover which he had recuperated from a ravine. He had a shepherd whom he had recuperated from an alcoholic's clinic. Nobody trusted Boris, nobody resisted him.

The story of his advancement spread. So too did the stories of his negligence—his unpaid debts, his sheep eating off land which belonged to other people. They were considered a scourge, Boris's sheep, as if they were a troop of wild boar. And often, like the Devil's own, his flock left and arrived by night.

In the Republican Lyre, the café opposite the church, there was sometimes something of the Devil about Boris too. He stood at the bar—he never sat down—surrounded by the young from several villages: the young who foresaw initiatives beyond the comprehension of their cautious yet wily parents, the young who dreamed of leisure and foreign women.

You should go to Canada, Boris was saying, that's where the future belongs. Here, as soon as you do something of your own, you're mistrusted. Canada is big, and when you have something big, you have something generous!

He paid for his round of drinks with a fifty thousand note, which he placed on the counter with his wooden-handled knife on top of it, so that it wouldn't blow away.

Here, he continued, nothing is ever forgiven! Not this side of death. And, as for the other side, they leave it to the curé. Have you ever seen anyone laughing for pleasure here?

And at that moment, as though he, the Devil, had ordered it, the door of the café opened and a couple came in, the woman roaring with laughter. They were strangers, both of them. The man wore a weekend suit and pointed shoes, and the woman, who, like her companion, was about thirty, had blond hair and wore a fur coat. One of the young men looked out through the window and saw their car parked opposite. It had Lyons number plates. Boris stared at them. The man said something and the woman laughed again. She laughed shamelessly, like a cock crowing.

Do you know them?

Boris shook his head.

Shortly afterwards he pocketed his knife, proffered the fifty thousand note, insisted upon paying for the two coffees the couple from Lyons were drinking, and left, without so much as another glance in their or anybody else's direction.

When the strangers got up to pay, the patronne simply said: It's already been settled.

Who by?

By the man who left five minutes ago.

The one in khaki? asked the blond. The patronne nodded.

We are looking for a house to rent, furnished if possible, said the man. Do you happen to know of any in the village?

For a week or a month? queried the patronne.

No, for the whole year round.

You want to settle here? asked one of the youths, incredulous.

My husband has a job in A———, the blond explained. He's a driving instructor.

The couple found a house. And one Tuesday morning, just before Easter, Boris drew up in his Land Rover and hammered on the door. It was opened by the blond, still wearing her dressing gown.

I've a present for you both, he said.

My husband, unfortunately, has just gone to work.

I know. I watched him leave. Wait!

He opened the back of the Land Rover and returned with a lamb in his arms.

This is the present.

Is it asleep?

No, slaughtered.

The blond threw her head back and laughed. What should we do with a slaughtered lamb? she sighed, wiping her mouth with her sleeve.

Roast it!

It still has its wool on. We don't know how to do such things and Gérard hates the sight of blood.

I'll prepare it for you.

It was you who bought us the coffee wasn't it?

Boris shrugged his shoulders. He was holding the lamb by its hind legs, its muzzle a few inches from the ground. The blond was wearing mules of artificial leopard skin.

Come in then, she said.

All this was observed by the neighbours.

The hind legs of the lamb were tied together and he hung it like a jacket on the back of the kitchen door. When he arrived, the blond had been drinking a bowl of coffee which was still on the table. In the kitchen there was the smell of coffee, of soap powder and of her. She had the smell of a buxom, plump body without a trace of the smell of work. Work has the smell of vinegar. He put out a hand to touch her hips as she passed between the table and the stove. Once again she laughed, this time quietly. Later he was to recall this first morning that he found himself in her kitchen, as if it were something he had swallowed, as if his tongue had never forgotten the taste of her mouth when she first bent down to kiss him.

Every time he visited her, he brought her a present; the lamb was only the first. Once he came with his tractor and trailer and on the trailer was a side-board. He never disguised his visits. He made them in full daylight before the eyes of his neighbours who noticed that each time, after about half an hour, the blond closed the shutters of the bedroom window.

And if one day her husband should come back unexpectedly? asked one of the neighbours.

God Forbid! Boris would be capable of picking him up and throwing him over the roof.

Yet he must have his suspicions?

Who?

The husband.

It's clear you've never lived in a big town.

Why do you say that?

The husband knows. If you'd lived in a big town, you'd know that the husband knows.

Then why doesn't he put his foot down, he can't be that cowardly?

One day the husband will come back, at a time agreed upon with his wife, and Boris will still be there, and the husband will say: What will you have as an aperitif, a pastis?

And he'll put poison in it?

No, black pepper! To excite him further.

Boris had been married at the age of twenty-five. His wife left him after one month. They were later divorced. His wife, who was not from the valley, never accused him of anything. She simply said, quietly, that she couldn't live with him. And once she added: perhaps another woman could.

The blond gave Boris the nickname of 'Little Humpback'.

My back is as straight as yours.

I didn't say it wasn't.

Then why—

It's what I like to call you.

Little Humpback, she said one day, do you ski?

When could I have learned?

You buy the skis and I'll teach you.

I'm too old to start, he said.

You're a champion in bed, you could be a champion on the ski slopes!

He pulled her towards him and covered her face and mouth with his huge hand.

This too he was to remember later when he thought about their two lives and the differences between them.

One day he arrived at the house carrying a washing machine on his shoulders. Another day he came with a wall-hanging, as large as a rug, on which were depicted, in bright velvet colours, two horses on a mountainside.

At that time Boris owned two horses. He'd bought them on the spur of the moment because he liked the look of them and he'd beaten down their price. In the spring I had to deliver a third horse to him. It was early morning and the snow had melted the week before. He was asleep in his bed and I woke him. Above his bed was a Madonna and a photograph of the blond. We took a bale of hay and went out to the field. There I let the horse go. After a long winter confined to the stable, she leapt and galloped between the trees. Boris was staring at her with his huge hands open and his eyes fixed. Ah Freedom! he said. He said it in neither a whisper nor a shout. He simply pronounced it as if it were the name of the horse.

The blond hung the tapestry on the wall in the bedroom. One Sunday afternoon, when Gérard was lying on the bed watching television, he nodded at the tapestry where the horses' manes were combed by the wind as if by a hairdresser and the horses' coats gleamed like polished shoes and the snow between the pine trees was as white as a wedding dress, and he said:

It's the only one of his presents I could do without.

I like horses, she said.

Horses! He made a whinnying noise.

Your trouble is that horses scare you!

Horses! The only thing to be said about a picture—and that's a picture even if it is made out of cotton—

Velvet!

—same thing, the only thing to be said about that picture there—is that in a picture horses don't shit.

She laughed, her shoulders and bosom shaking.

Have you talked to him about the house yet? Gérard asked.

How difficult it is to prevent certain stories becoming a simple moral demonstration! As if there were never any hesitations, as if life didn't wrap itself like a rag round the sharpest blade!

One midday, the following June, Boris arrived at the blond's house, covered in sweat. His face, with his hawk-nose and his cheekbones like pebbles, looked as if he had just plunged it into a water trough. He entered the kitchen and kissed her as he usually did, but this time without a word. Then he went to the sink and put his head under the tap. She offered him a towel which he refused. The water from his hair was running down his neck to the inside of the shirt. She asked him whether he wanted to eat; he nodded. He followed her with his eyes wherever she went, not sentimentally like a dog, nor suspiciously, but as though from a great distance.

Are you ill? she asked him abruptly as she put down his plate on the table.

I have never been ill, he replied.

Then what is the matter?

By way of reply he pulled her towards him and thrust his head, still wet, against her breast. The pain she felt was not in her chest but in her spine. Yet she did not struggle and she placed her plump white hand on the hard head. For how long did she stand there in front of his chair? For how long was his face fitted into her breast like a gun into its case lined with velvet? On the night when Boris died alone, stretched out on the floor with his three black dogs, it seemed to him that his face had been fitted into her breast ever since he first set eyes on her.

Afterwards he did not want to eat what was on his plate.

Come on, Humpback, take your boots off and we'll go to bed.

He shook his head.

What's the matter with you? she screeched. You sit there, you say nothing, you eat nothing, you do nothing, you're good for nothing!

He got to his feet and walked towards the door. For the first time she noticed he was limping.

What's the matter with your foot?

He did not reply.

For Christ's sake have you hurt your foot?

It's broken.

How?

I overturned the tractor on the slope above the house. I was flung off and the fender crushed my foot.

Did you call the doctor?

I came here.

Where's the jeep?

I can't drive, the ankle is blocked.

She started to untie the boots. She began with the unhurt foot. He said nothing. The second boot was a different matter. His whole body went rigid when she began to unlace it. His sock was drenched in blood and the foot was too swollen for her to remove the boot.

She started to snivel. He, now that the boot no longer gave his foot support, could not stand up. Her head hanging, her hands limp by her side, she sat on the kitchen floor at his feet, sobbing inconsolably.

His foot had eleven fractures. The doctor refused to believe that he had walked the four kilometres from his farm to the blond's. He said it was categorically impossible. The blond had driven Boris down to the surgery, and, according to the doctor, she had been at Boris's house all morning but for some reason didn't want to admit it. This is why, according to the doctor, the two of them had invented the implausible story of his walking four kilometres. The doctor, however, was wrong and the blond knew it. Of all the many times that Boris visited her, this was the only one which she never once mentioned to Gérard. And when, later, she heard the news of Boris's death, she immediately asked whether he was wearing boots when they found him.

No, was the surprising reply, he was barefoot.

Boris, when young, had inherited three houses, but all of them, by the standards of the towns, were in a pitiable condition. In the house with the largest barn he himself lived. There was electricity but no water. The house was below the road and the passer-by could look down its chimney. It was in this house that the three black dogs howled all night when he died.

The second house, the one he always referred to as the Mother's house, was the best situated of the three and he had long-term plans for selling it to a Parisian—when the day and the Parisian arrived.

In the third house, which was no more than a cabin at the foot of the mountain, Edmond, the shepherd, slept when he could. Edmond was a thin man with the eyes of a hermit. His experience had led him to believe that nearly all those who walked on two legs belonged to a species named Misunderstanding. He received from Boris no regular salary but occasional presents and his keep.

One spring evening, Boris went up to the house under the mountain, taking with him a cheese and a smoked side of bacon.

You're not often at home now! was how Edmond greeted him.

Why do you say that?

I have eyes. I notice when the Land Rover passes.

And you know where I go?

Edmond deemed the question unworthy of a reply, he simply fixed his unavailing eyes on Boris.

I'd like to marry her, said Boris.

But you can't, said Edmond.

She would be willing.

Are you sure?

Boris answered by smashing his right fist into his left palm. Edmond said nothing.

How many lambs? asked Boris.

Thirty-three. She is from the city isn't she?

Her father is a butcher in Lyons.

Why hasn't she any children?

Not every ram has balls, you should know that. She'll have a child of mine.

How long have you been going with her?

Eighteen months.

Edmond raised his eyebrows. City women are not the same, he said, and I ought to know. I've seen enough. They're not built the same way. They don't have the same shit and they don't have the same blood. They don't smell the same either. They don't smell of stables and onions and vinegar, they smell of something else. And that something else is dangerous. They have perfect eyelashes, they have unscratched legs without varicose veins, they have shoes with soles as thin as pancakes, they have hands white and smooth as peeled potatoes and when you smell their smell, it fills you with a god-forsaken longing. You want to breathe them to their dregs, you want to squeeze them like lemons until there is not a drop or a pip left. And shall I tell you what they smell of? Their smell is the smell of money. They calculate everything for money. They are not built like our mothers, these women.

You can leave my mother out of it.

Be careful, said Edmond, your blond will strip you of everything. Then she'll throw you aside like a plucked chicken.

With a slow blow to the face Boris knocked the shepherd over. He lay spread-eagled on the ground.

Nothing stirred. The dog licked Edmond's forehead.

Only somebody who has seen a battlefield, can imagine the full indifference of the stars above the shepherd spread-eagled on the ground. It is in face of this indifference that we seek love.

Tomorrow I will buy her a shawl, whispered Boris, and without a glance behind him, took the road back to the village.

Next morning the police came to warn him that his sheep were a public danger, for they were encumbering the motorway. Edmond, the shepherd, had disappeared and he was not seen again until after Boris's death.

The month of August was the month of Boris's triumph. Or is glory a better term? For he was too happy, too self-absorbed, to see himself as a victor who had triumphed over others. It had become clear to him that the instructions inscribed at the moment of his conception had involved more than the size of his bones, the thickness of his skull or the power of his will. He was destined, at the age of forty, to be recognized.

The hay had been brought in, his barn was full, his sheep were grazing high in the mountains, without a shepherd but God would preserve them, and every evening he sat on the terrace of the Republican Lyre overlooking the village square, with the blond in a summer dress, her shoulders bare, her feet in high-heeled silver sandals, and, until nightfall, the pair of them were the colour-television picture of the village.

Offer drinks to every table, he said, leaning back in his chair, and if they ask what's happened, tell them that Boris is buying horses!

Humpback, not every night, you can't afford it!

Every night! My balls are swollen.

He placed one of his immense hands on the bosom of her red polka-dot dress.

His energy made her laugh.

It's true about the horses, he said, I'm going to breed horses—for you! Breed riding horses that we'll sell to the idiots who come for weekends.

What should I do with horses? she asked, I can't ride.

If you have a child of mine—

Yes, Humpback.

I'll teach the child to ride, he said. A child of ours will have your looks and my pride.

The last word he had never uttered before concerning himself.

If we have a child, she whispered, the house where we live now is too small. We'd need at least another room.

And how many months have we got to sort out the question of a house? asked Boris with his cattle-dealer's canniness.

I don't know, Humpback, perhaps eight.

A bottle of champagne, Boris shouted, pour out glasses for everybody.

Are you still buying horses? asked Marc, who, with his pipe and blue overalls, is the sceptic of the Republican Lyre, the perennial instructor about the idiocy of the world.

That's none of your business, retorted Boris; I'm buying drinks.

I'll be tipsy, said the blond.

I'll get you some nuts.

On the counter of the Republican Lyre is a machine where you put in a franc and a child's handful of peanuts comes out. Boris fed coin after coin into the machine and asked for a soup plate.

When the men standing at the bar raised their glasses of champagne and nodded towards Boris, they were each toasting the blond: and each was picturing himself in Boris's place, some with envy, and all with that odd nostalgia which everyone feels for what they know they will never live.

Beside Marc stood Jean who had once been a long-distance lorry-driver. Now he kept rabbits with his wife and was seventy. Jean was in the middle of a story.

Guy was pissed out of his mind, Jean was saying; Guy slumped down on to the floor and lay there flat out, as if he were dead. Jean paused and looked at the faces around the bar to emphasize the impasse. What should we do with him? It was then that Patrick had his brainwave. Bring him round to my place, said Patrick. They got Guy into the car and they drove him up to Patrick's place. Bring him in here, lay him on the work bench, said Patrick. Now slip off his trousers.

The blond started to laugh.

You're not going to harm him? Slip off his trousers I tell you. Now his socks. There he lay on the work bench, as naked as we'll all be when the Great Holiday starts. What now? He's broken his leg, announced Patrick. Don't be daft. We're going to make him believe he broke his leg, Patrick explained. Why should he believe it? Wait and see. Patrick mixed up a bathful of plaster and, as professionally as you'd expect from Patrick, he plastered Guy's leg from the ankle to half-way up the thigh. Jean paused to look round at his listeners. On the way home in the car Guy came round. Don't worry, mate, said Patrick, you broke your leg, but it's not bad, we took you to the hospital and they've set it in plaster and they said you could have it off in a week, it's not a bad fracture. Guy looked down at his leg and the tears ran down his cheeks. What a cunt I am! he went on repeating. What a cunt I am!

The blond broke out into laughter, her head flung back, her chest out, her red-spotted dress stretched tight.

What happened afterwards, she asked, her mouth still open.

He was a week off work, watching the telly, with his leg up on a chair!

Boris put the back of his hand against her throat—for fear that the palm was too calloused—and there he could feel the laughter which began between her hips, gushing up to her mouth. Systematically he moved the back of his immense hand up and down the blond's throat.

Jean, the lorry-driver who now kept rabbits, watched this action, fascinated, as if it were more improbable than the story he had just told.

I couldn't believe it, he recounted to the habitués of the Republican Lyre later that night: there was Boris, over there, bone-headed Boris caressing the blond like she was a sitting-up squirrel, and feeding her nuts from a soup plate. And what do you think he does when the husband comes in? He stands up, holds out his hand to the husband and announces: What do you want to drink? A white wine with cassis? I'm taking her to the ball tonight, Boris says. We shan't be back till morning.

The ball was in the next village. All night it seemed to Boris that the earth was moving past the plough of its own volition.

Once they stopped dancing to drink. He beer, and she lemonade.

I will give you the Mother's house, he said.

Why do you call it that?

My mother inherited it from my father.

And if one day you want to sell it?

How can I sell it if I've given it to you?

Gérard will never believe it.

About our child?

No. About the house, he won't agree to move in, unless it's certain.

Leave Gérard! Come and live with me.

No Humpback, I'm not made for preparing mash for chickens.

Once again, by way of reply, Boris thrust his massive head against her breast. His face fitted into her breast like a gun into its case lined with velvet. For how long was his face buried between her breasts? When he raised it he said: I'll give you the house formally, I'll see the notary, it'll be yours, yours not his, and then it'll go to our child. Do you want to dance again?

Yes, Humpback.

They danced until the white dress with red polka-dots was stained with both their sweats, until there was no music left, until her blond hair smelled of his cows.

Years later, people asked: how was it possible that Boris, who never gave anything away in his life, Boris, who would cheat his own grandmother, Boris, who never kept his word, how was it that he gave the house to the blond? And the answer, which was an admission of the mystery, was always the same: a passion is a passion.

Women did not ask the same question. It was obvious to them that, given the right moment and circumstances, any man may be manipulated. There was no mystery. And perhaps it was for this reason that the women felt a little more pity for Boris than the men.

As for Boris, he never asked himself: Why did I give her the house? He never regretted this decision, although—and here all the commentators are right—it was unlike any other he had ever taken. He regretted nothing. Regrets force one to relive the past, and, until the end, he was waiting.

The flowers which grew in the mountains had brighter, more intense colours than the same flowers growing on the plain; a similar principle applied to thunderstorms. Lightning in the mountains did not just fork, it danced in circles; the thunder did not just clap, it echoed. And sometimes the echoes were still echoing when the next clap came, so that the bellowing became continuous. All this was due to the metal deposits in the rocks. During a storm, the hardiest shepherd asked himself: What in God's name am I doing here? And next morning, when it was light, he might find signs of the visitations of which, fortunately, he had been largely ignorant the night before: holes in the earth, burned grass, smoking trees, dead cattle. At the end of the month of August there was such a thunderstorm.

Some of Boris's sheep were grazing just below the Rock of St Antoine on the far slopes facing east. When sheep are frightened they climb, looking to heaven to save them; and so Boris's sheep moved up to the screes by the rock, and there they huddled together under the rain. Sixty sheep, each one resting his drenched head on the oily drenched rump or shoulders of his neighbour. When the lightning lit up the mountain—and everything appeared so clear and so close that the moment seemed endless—the sixty animals looked like a single giant sheepskin coat. There were even two sleeves, each consisting of half-a-dozen sheep, who were hemmed in along two narrow corridors of grass between the rising rocks. From this giant coat, during each lightning flash, a hundred or more eyes, glistening like brown coal, peered out in fear. They were right to be frightened. The storm centre was approaching. The next forked lightning struck the heart of the coat and the entire flock was killed. Most of them had their jaws and forelegs broken by the shock of the electrical discharge, received in the head and earthed through their thin bony legs.

In the space of one night Boris lost three million francs.

It was I, thirty-six hours later, who first noticed the crows circling in the sky. Something was dead there, but I didn't know what. Somebody told Boris and the next day he went up to the Rock of St Antoine. There he found the giant sheepskin coat, discarded, cold, covered with flies. The carcasses were too far from any road. The only thing he could do was to burn them where they were.

He fetched petrol and diesel oil and started to make a pyre, dragging the carcasses down the two sleeves and throwing them one on top of another. He started the fire with an old tyre. Thick smoke rose above the peak, and with it the smell of burned animal flesh. It takes very little to turn a mountain into a corner of hell. From time to time Boris consoled himself by thinking of the blond. Later he would laugh with her. Later, his face pressed against her, he would forget the shame of this scene. But more than these promises which he made to himself, it was the simple fact of her existence which encouraged him.

By now everybody in the village knew what had happened to Boris's sheep. No one blamed Boris outright—how could they? Yet there were those who hinted that a man couldn't lose so many animals at one go unless, in some way, he deserved it. Boris neglected his cattle. Boris did not pay his debts. Boris was having it off with a married woman. Providence was delivering him a warning.

They say Boris is burning his sheep, said the blond, you can see the smoke over the mountain.

Why don't we go and watch? suggested Gérard.

She made the excuse of a headache.

Come on, he said, it's a Saturday afternoon and the mountain air will clear your head. I've never seen a man burning sixty sheep.

I don't want to go.

What's niggling you?

I'm worried.

You think he could change his mind about the house now? He'll certainly be short of money.

It's not a flock of sheep that's going to make him change his mind about the house.

We shouldn't count our chickens—

Only one thing could make him go back on his word about the house.

If you stopped seeing him?

Not exactly.

What then?

Nothing.

Has he mentioned the house recently?

Do you know what he calls it? He calls it the Mother's house.

Why?

She shrugged her shoulders.

Come on, said Gérard.

Gérard and his wife drove up the mountain to where the road stopped. From there, having locked the car, they continued on foot. Suddenly she screamed as a grouse flew up from under her feet.

I thought it was a baby! she cried.

You must have drunk too much. How can a baby fly?

That's what I thought, I'm telling you.

Can you see the smoke? Gérard asked.

What is it that's hissing?

His sheep cooking! said Gérard.

Don't be funny.

Grasshoppers.

Can you smell anything?

No.

I wouldn't like to be up here in a storm, she said.

He wasn't here often either.

It's all very well for you to talk, you've never lifted a shovel in your life, she said.

That's because I'm not stupid.

No. Nobody could call you that. And he's stupid, Boris is stupid, stupid, stupid!

He was encouraging the fire with fuel, whose blue flames chased the slower yellow ones. He picked up a sheep by its legs, and swung it back and forth, before flinging it high into the air so that it landed on top of the pyre, where, for a few minutes longer, it was still recognizable as an animal. The tear-stains on his cheek were from tears provoked by the heat, and, when the wind turned, by the acrid smoke. Every few minutes he picked up another carcass, swung it to gain a momentum, and hurled it into the air. The boy, who had never been able to tap the ash-bark gently enough, had become the man who could burn his own herd single-handed.

Gérard and the blond stopped within fifty yards of the blaze. The heat, the stench and something unknown prevented them approaching further. This unknown united the two of them: wordlessly they were agreed about it. They raised their hands to protect their eyes. Fires and gigantic waterfalls have one thing in common. There is spray torn off the cascade by the wind, there are the flames: there is the rock-face dripping and visibly eroding, there is the breaking up of what is being burned: there is the roar of the water, there is the terrible chatter of the fire. Yet at the centre of both fire and waterfall there is an ungainsayable calm. And it is this calm which is catastrophic.

Look at him, whispered Gérard.

Three million he's lost, poor sod! murmured the blond.

Why are you so sure he isn't insured?

I know, she hissed, that's why. I know.

Boris, his back to the fire, was bent over his haversack drinking from a bottle of water. Having drunk, he poured water on to his face and his black arms. Its freshness made him think of how he would strip in the kitchen this evening and wash before going to visit the blond.

When Boris turned back towards the fire he saw them. Immediately a gust of smoke hid them from view. Not for a moment, however, did he ask himself whether he had been mistaken. He would recognize her instantly whatever she was doing, anywhere. He would recognize her in any country in the world in any decade of her life.

The wind veered and he saw them again. She stood there, Gérard's arm draped over her shoulders. It was impossible that they had not seen him and yet she made no sign. They were only fifty yards away. They were staring straight at him. And yet she made no sign.

If he walked into the fire would she cry out? Still holding the bottle, he walked upright, straight—like a soldier going to receive a medal—towards the fire. The wind changed again and they disappeared.

The next time the smoke cleared the couple were nowhere to be seen.

Contrary to what he had told himself earlier, Boris did not come down that night. He stayed by the fire. The flames had abated, his sheep were ashes, yet the rocks were still oven-hot and the embers, like his rage, changed colour in the wind.

Huddled under the rock, the Milky Way trailing its veil towards the south, he considered his position. Debts were warnings of the ultimate truth, they were signs, not yet insistent, of the final inhospitality of life on this earth. After midnight the wind dropped, and the rancid smell, clinging to the scree, was no longer wafted away; it filled the silence, as does the smell of cordite when the sound of the last shot has died away. On this inhospitable earth he had found, at the age of forty-one, a shelter. The blond was like a place: one where the law of inhospitality did not apply. He could take this place anywhere with him, and it was enough for him to think of her, for him to approach it. How then was it possible that she had come up the mountain on the day of his loss and not said a word to him? How was it possible that on this rock, far above the village, where even the church bells were inaudible, she should have come as close as fifty yards and not made a sign? He stirred the embers with his boot. He knew the answer to the question and it was elementary. He pissed into the fire and on the stones his urine turned into steam. It was elementary. She had come to watch him out of curiosity.

Before he saw her, he was telling himself that, after all, he had only lost half his sheep. As soon as he saw her with his own eyes, and she made no sign to him, his rage joined that of the fire: he and the fire, they would burn the whole world together, everything, sheep, livestock, houses, furniture, forests, cities. She had come out of curiosity to watch his humiliation.

All night he hated her. Just after sunrise, when it was coldest, his hatred reached its zenith. And so, four days later he was asking himself: could she have had another reason for coming up to the Rock of St Antoine?

Boris decided to remain in the mountains. If he went down to the village, everyone would stare at him to see how he had taken his loss. They would ask him if he was insured, just in order to hear him say No. This would give them pleasure. If he went down he might start breaking things, the windows of the mayor's office, the glasses on the counter of the Republican Lyre, Gérard's face, the nose of the first man to put an arm round the blond's waist. The rest of his sheep were near Peniel, where there was a chalet he could sleep in. Until the snow came, he would stay there with his remaining sheep. Like that, he would be on the spot to bring them down for the winter. If she had really come to see him for another reason, she would come again.

A week passed. He had little to do. In the afternoons he lay on the grass, gazed up at the sky, occasionally gave an order to one of the dogs to turn some sheep, idly watched the valleys below. Each day the valleys appeared further away. At night he was obliged to light a fire in the chalet; there was no chimney but there was a hole in the roof. His physical energy was undiminished, but he stopped plotting and stopped desiring. On the mountainside opposite the chalet was a colony of marmots. He heard the marmot on guard whistle whenever one of his dogs approached the colony. In the early morning he saw them preparing for the winter and their long sleep. They lifted clumps of grass with roots attached, and carried them, as if they were flowers, to their underground hide-out. Like widows, he told himself, like widows.

One night, when the stars were as bright as in the spring, his anger returned to galvanize him. So they think Boris is finished, he muttered to the dogs, but they are fucking well wrong. Boris is only at the beginning. He slept with his fist in his mouth, and that night he dreamed.

The following afternoon he was lying on his back looking up at the sky, when suddenly he rolled over on to his stomach in order to look down the track which led through the forest to the tarred road. His hearing had become almost as acute as that of his dogs. He saw her walking towards him. She was wearing a white dress and blue sandals, around her neck a string of beads like pearls.

How are you, Humpback?

So you've come at last!

You disappeared! You disappeared! She opened her arms to embrace him. You disappeared and so I said to myself: I'll go and find Humpback, and here I am.

She stepped back to look at him. He had a beard, his hair was tangled, his skin was dirty and his blue eyes, staring, were focused a little too far away.

How did you get here? he asked.

I left the car at the chalet below.

Where the old lady is?

There's nobody there now, and the windows are boarded up.

They must have taken the cows down, he said, what date is it?

September 30th.

What did you come for, when I was burning the sheep?

How do you mean?

You came up to the Rock of St Antoine with your husband.

No.

The day I was burning the sheep, I saw you.

It must have been somebody else.

I'd never mistake another woman for you.

I was very sorry to hear about what happened to your sheep, Boris.

Grandma used to say that dreams turned the truth upside down. Last night I dreamed we had a daughter, so in life it'll be a son.

Humpback, I'm not pregnant.

Is that true?

I don't want to lie to you.

Why did you come to spy on me? If you're telling the truth, tell it.

I didn't want to.

Why didn't you come over and speak to me?

I was frightened.

Of me?

No, Humpback, of what you were doing.

I was doing what had to be done, no more. Then I was going to come and visit you.

I was waiting for you, she said.

No, you weren't. You had seen what you wanted to see.

I've come now.

If he's conceived today, he'll be born in June, he said.

He took her arm and led her towards the crooked chalet whose wood had been blackened by the sun. He pushed open the door with his foot. The room was large enough for four or five goats. On the earth floor were blankets. The window, no larger than a small transistor radio, was grey and opaque with dust. There was a cylinder of gas and a gas-ring, on which he placed a black saucepan with coffee in it.

I'll give you whatever you want, he said.

He stood there in the half light, his immense hands open. Behind him on the floor was a heap of old clothes, among which she recognized his American army cap and a red shirt which she had once ironed for him. In the far corner something scuffled and a lame lamb hobbled towards the door where a dog lay. The floor of beaten earth smelled of dust, animals and coffee grounds. Taking the saucepan off the gas, he turned down the flame, and its hissing stopped. The silence which followed was unlike any in the valley below.

If it's a boy, I'll buy him a horse—

Ignoring the bowl of coffee he was holding out to her, without waiting for the end of his sentence, her eyes bulging, she fled. He went to the door and watched her running, stumbling downhill. Occasionally she looked over her shoulder as if she thought she were being pursued. He did not stir from the doorway and she did not stop running.

In the evening it began to snow, tentatively and softly. Having brought all three dogs into the chalet, Boris bolted the door, as he never usually did, lay down beside the animals and tried to sleep, his fist in his mouth. The next morning, beneath the white pine trees and through the frozen brambles and puddles of water, he drove his flock of miserable grey sheep towards the road which led down to the village.

When Corneille the cattle dealer drew up in his lorry before Boris's house and walked with the slow strides of the fat man he was, through the snow to tap on the kitchen window, Boris was not surprised; he knew why Corneille had come. He swore at his dogs who were barking, threatened them with being salted and smoked if they were not quieter, and opened the door. Corneille, his hat tilted towards the back of his head, sat down on a chair.

It's a long time since we've seen you, said Corneille. You weren't even at the Fair of the Cold. How are things?

Quiet, replied Boris.

Do you know they are closing the abattoir at Saint-Denis. Everything has to be taken to A——— now.

I hadn't heard.

More and more inspections, more and more government officials. There's no room for skill anymore.

Skill! That's one way of naming it!

You've never been short of that sort of skill yourself, said Corneille. There I take my hat off to you!

In fact he kept his hat on and turned up the collar of his overcoat. The kitchen was cold and bare, as if it had shed its leaves like the beech trees outside, its leaves of small comfort.

I'll say this much, continued Corneille, nobody can teach me a new trick, I know them all, but there's not one I could teach you either. All right, you've suffered bad luck—and not only last month up on the mountain, the poor bugger Boris we said, how's he going to get out of this one—you've suffered bad luck, and you've never had enough liquid cash.

From his right-hand overcoat pocket he drew out a wad of fifty-thousand notes and placed them on the edge of the table. One of the dogs sniffed his hand. Fuck off! said Corneille, pushing the dog with one of his immense thighs, the overcoat draped over it so that it advanced like a wall.

I'm telling you, Boris, you could buy the hindlegs off a goat and sell them to a horse! And I mean that as a compliment.

What do you want?

Aren't you going to offer me a glass? It's not very warm in your kitchen.

Gnole or red wine?

A little gnole then. It has less effect on Old King Cole.

So they say.

I hear you swept her off her feet, said Corneille, and the husband under the carpet!

Boris said nothing but poured from the bottle.

Not everyone could do that, said Corneille, that takes some Old King Cole!

Do you think so? What are you showing me your money for?

To do a deal, Boris. A straight deal, for once, because I know I can't trim you.

Do you know how you count, Corneille? You count one, two, three, six, nine, twenty.

The two men laughed. The cold rose up like mist from the stone floor. They emptied the little glasses in one go.

The winter's going to be long, said Corneille, the snow has come to stay. A good five months of snow in store for us. That's my prediction and your uncle Corneille knows his winters.

Boris refilled the glasses.

The price of hay is going to be three hundred a bale before Lent. How was your hay this year?

Happy!

Not your woman, my friend, your hay.

Happy, Boris repeated.

I see your horses are still out, said Corneille.

You have sharp eyes.

I'm getting old. Old King Cole is no longer the colt he once was. They tell me she's beautiful, with real class.

What do you want?

I've come to buy.

Do you know, said Boris, what the trees say when the axe comes into the forest?

Corneille tossed back his glass, without replying.

When the axe comes into the forest, the trees say: Look! The handle is one of us!

That's why I know I can't trim you, said Corneille.

How do you know I want to sell? Boris asked.

Any man in your position would want to sell. Everything depends upon the offer, and I'm going to mention a figure that will astound you.

Astound me!

Three million!

What are you buying for that? Hay?

Your happy hay! said Corneille, taking off his hat and replacing it further back on his head. No, I'm willing to buy everything you have on four legs.

Did you say ten million, Corneille?

Boris stared indifferently through the window at the snow.

Irrespective of their condition, my friend. I'm buying blind. Four million.

I've no interest in selling.

So be it, said Corneille. He leaned with his elbows on the table, like a cow getting up from the stable floor, rump first, forelegs second. Finally he was upright. He placed his hand over the pile of bank notes, as if they were a screaming mouth.

I heard of your troubles, he said very softly in the voice that people use in a sick room. I have a soft spot for you, and so I said to myself, this is a time when he needs his friends and I can help him out. Five million.

You can have the horses for that.

Corneille stood with his hand gagging the pile of money.

If you take my offer, if you have no animals during the winter, my friend, you can sell your hay, you can repair the roof of your barn and when the spring comes, you'll have more than enough to buy a new flock. Five million.

Take everything, said Boris. As you say, it's going to be a long winter. Take everything and leave the money on the table. Six million.

I don't even know how many sheep I'm buying, muttered Corneille.

On this earth, Corneille, we never know what we're buying. Perhaps there's another planet where all deals are straight. All I know is that here the earth is peopled by those whom God threw out as flawed.

Five and a-half, said Corneille.

Six.

Corneille lifted his hand from the pile and shook Boris's hand.

Six it is. Count it.

Boris counted the notes.

If you want a tip from a very old King Cole, Corneille spoke evenly and slowly, if you want a tip, don't spend it all on her.

For that you'll have to wait and see, Corneille, just as I am going to do.

There followed the correspondence between Boris and the blond. This consisted of two letters. The first, with the postmark of October 30th, was from him:

My darling,
I have the money for our fares to Canada. I am waiting for you— always your Boris.

The second, dated November 1st, was from her:

Dearest Humpback,
In another life I might come—in this one forgive Marie-Jeanne.

There were no longer any sheep to feed. The horses had gone from the snow-covered orchard. When the lorry had come to fetch them, there was half a bale of hay lying on the snow and Boris had thrown it into the lorry after his horses. On one small point Marc was right when he said that Boris died like one of his own beasts. Not having to feed his animals gave him the idea of not feeding himself.

In the icy trough in the yard he lay down a bottle of champagne, ready to serve cold. The water detached the label and after a week it floated to the surface. When the police opened the kitchen cupboard, they found a large jar of cherries in *eau-de-vie* with a ribbon round it, and a box of After Eight chocolates, open but untouched. Most curious of all, on the kitchen floor beneath the curtainless windows, they found a confectioner's cardboard box with golden edges, and inside it were rose-pink sugared almonds such as are sometimes distributed to guests and friends after a baptism. On the floor too were blankets, dog-shit and wet newspapers. But the dogs had not touched the sugared nuts.

In the house during the unceasing period of waiting he did not listen to the sounds which came from outside. His hearing was as unimpaired as is mine now, registering the noise of my pen on the paper—a noise which resembles that of a mouse at night earnestly eating what its little pointed muzzle has discovered between its paws. His hearing was unimpaired, but his indifference was such that the crow of a neighbour's cock, the sound of a car climbing the road from which one looks down on to the chimney of his house, the shouts of children, the drill of a chain-saw cutting in the forest beyond the river, the klaxon of the postman's van—all these sounds became nameless, containing no message, emptier, far emptier than silence.

If he was waiting and if he never lost for one moment, either awake or asleep, the image of what he was waiting for—the breast into which his face at last fitted—he no longer knew from where it would come. There was no path along which he could look. His heart was still under his left ribs, he still broke the bread into pieces for the dogs with his right hand, holding the loaf in his left, the sun in the late afternoon still went down behind the same mountain, but there were no longer any directions. The dogs knew how he was lost.

This is why he slept on the floor, why he never changed a garment, why he stopped talking to the dogs and only pulled them towards him or pushed them away with his fist.

In the barn when he climbed a ladder, he forgot the rope, and, looking down at the hay, he saw horses foaling. Yet considering his hunger, he had very few hallucinations. When he took off his boots to walk in the snow, he knew what he was doing.

One sunny day towards the end of December, he walked barefoot through the snow of the orchard in the direction of the stream, which marks the boundary of the village. It was there that he first saw the trees which had no snow on them.

The trees form a copse which I would be able to see now from the window, if it were not night. It is roughly triangular, with a linden tree at its apex. There is also a large oak. The other trees are ash, beech, sycamore. From where Boris was standing the sycamore was on the left. Despite the December afternoon sunlight, the interior of the copse looked dark and impenetrable. The fact that none of the trees was covered in snow, appeared to him to be improbable but welcome.

He stood surveying the trees as he might have surveyed his sheep. It was there that he would find what he awaited. And his discovery of the place of arrival was itself a promise that his waiting would be rewarded. He walked slowly back to the house but the copse was still before his eyes. The night fell but he could still see the trees. In his sleep he approached them.

The next day he walked again through the orchard towards the stream. And, arms folded across his chest, he studied the copse. There was a clearing. It was less dark between the trees. In that clearing she would appear.

She had lost her name—as the champagne bottle which he was keeping for her arrival had lost its label. Her name was forgotten, but everything else about her his passion had preserved.

During the last days of the year, the clearing in the copse grew larger and larger. There was space and light around every tree. The more he suffered from pains in his body, the more certain he was that the moment of her arrival was approaching. On the second of January in the evening he entered the copse.

During the night of the second, Boris's neighbours heard his three dogs howling. Early next morning they tried the kitchen door which was locked on the inside. Through the window they saw Boris's body on the floor, his head flung back, his mouth open. Nobody dared break in through the window for fear of the dogs, savagely bewailing the life that had ended.

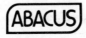

GRANTA

GABRIEL GARCÍA MÁRQUEZ

THE SOLITUDE OF LATIN AMERICA

Antonio Pigafetta, a Florentine navigator who travelled with Magellan on the first voyage around the world, wrote on his passing through our southern America, a strictly factual account that nonetheless seems like a work of fantasy. In it he tells of seeing hogs with navels on their haunches, birds without legs whose hens laid eggs on the backs of their mates, and other birds still who, resembling tongueless pelicans, had beaks that looked like spoons. He tells of seeing a creature born with the head and ears of a mule, the body of a camel, the legs of a deer and the whinny of a horse. He tells of how they, on encountering their first native in Patagonia, confronted him with a mirror, whereupon the impassioned giant lost his senses to the terror of his own image.

Pigafetta's short and fascinating book, which even then contained the seeds of our present-day novels, is by no means the most staggering account of our reality in that age. The chroniclers of the Indies left us countless others. Eldorado, our so avidly sought and illusory land, figures on a number of maps for many, many years, shifting its place and form to suit the fantasy of cartographers. In his search for the fountain of eternal youth, the mythical Alvar Núñez Cabeza de Vaca explored the north of Mexico for eight years, on a deluded expedition whose members devoured each other and from which, of the six hundred who had undertaken it, only five returned. Another of the many mysteries which have still not been explained is that of the eleven thousand mules, each loaded with one hundred pounds of gold, that left Cuzco one day bearing the ransom of Atahualpa but never reached their destination. Later the hens, that had been raised on alluvial land and were sold in Cartagena de Indias, were discovered to have gizzards containing tiny lumps of gold. This golden delirium of our founders has persecuted us until very recently. As late as the last century, a German mission appointed to study the possibilities of constructing an interoceanic railroad across the Isthmus of Panama concluded that the project was feasible on one condition: that the rails be made not of iron, which was scarce in the region, but of gold.

Our independence from Spanish domination did not put us beyond the reach of madness. General Antonio López de Santana, three times dictator of Mexico, held a magnificent funeral for the right leg he had lost in the so-called Pastry War. General Gabriel

García Moreno ruled Ecuador for sixteen years as an absolute monarch; his corpse, dressed in full military uniform and covered with medals, attended its own wake, seated on the presidential chair. General Maximiliano Hernández Martínez, the theosophical despot of El Salvador who had thirty thousand peasants slaughtered in a savage massacre, invented a pendulum to detect poison in his food, and had streetlamps draped in red paper to combat an epidemic of scarlet fever. The statue of General Francisco Morazán erected in the main square of Tegucigalpa is actually a statue of Marshal Ney, purchased in Paris at a warehouse of second-hand sculptures.

Eleven years ago, the Chilean Pablo Neruda, one of the outstanding poets of our time, made his visit to Stockholm. Since then, Europeans of good will—and sometimes of bad as well—have been struck, with ever greater force, by strange unearthly tidings from Latin America: that boundless realm of haunted men and historic women, whose unending obstinacy blurs into legend. We have not had a moment's rest. A Promethean president, entrenched, alone, in his burning palace, died fighting an entire army; and two suspicious airplane accidents, still to be explained, took the lives of another great-hearted president and of a democratic soldier who had restored the dignity of his people. Since Pablo Neruda made his visit, there have been five wars and seventeen military coups; a diabolic dictator has emerged who is now carrying out, in God's name, the first Latin American ethnocide of our time. In the meanwhile, twenty million Latin-American children have died before the age of one—more than the children born in Europe during the same period. *Los desaparecidos,* those missing because of repression, number nearly one hundred and twenty thousand—it is as if suddenly no one were able to account for all the inhabitants of the city of Uppsala. Numerous women arrested while pregnant have given birth in Argentinian prisons; but nobody knows the whereabouts and identity of their children, who were furtively adopted or sent to orphanages by order of the military authorities. Nearly two hundred thousand men and women have died throughout the continent, because they, fighting, wanted not to see their world continue, unchanged. And over one hundred thousand have lost their lives in three small and ill-fated countries of Central America: Nicaragua,

El Salvador and Guatemala. If this had happened in the United States, the proportional figure would be one million six hundred thousand violent deaths in four years.

From Chile, a country with a tradition of hospitality, one million people have fled: ten per cent of its population. In Uruguay, a tiny nation of two and a half million inhabitants who consider themselves the most civilized population on the continent, one out of every five citizens is in exile. Since 1979, the civil war in El Salvador has produced one refugee almost every twenty minutes. The country that could be formed of all the exiles and forced emigrants of Latin America would have a population larger than that of Norway.

I dare to think that it is this monstrous reality, and not just its expression in literature, that has deserved the attention of the Swedish Academy of Letters. A reality not of paper, but one that lives within us and that determines each instant of our countless daily deaths, and that sustains the source of the insatiable creativity, full of sorrow and beauty, of which this roving and nostalgic Colombian is but one cipher more, singled out by fortune. Poets and beggars, musicians and prophets, warriors and scoundrels, all creatures of that unbridled reality, we have had to ask very little of the imagination, as our greatest problem has been the inadequacy of a convention or a means by which to render our lives believable. This, my friends, is the crux of our solitude.

And if this problem, which is of our very essence, makes us clumsy, it is understandable that the rational talents on this side of the world, exalted in the contemplation of their own cultures, should have found themselves without a valid means by which to interpret us. It is only natural that they insist on measuring us with the same yardstick that they use for themselves, forgetting that the ravages of life are not the same for all, and that the quest for an identity is as arduous and bloody for us as it was for them. Interpreting our reality with foreign terms serves only to make us ever more unknown, ever less free, ever more solitary. Venerable Europe would perhaps be more perceptive if it tried to see us in its own past: if it recalled that London took three hundred years to build its first city wall, and three hundred years more to acquire a bishop; that Rome laboured in a gloom of uncertainty for twenty centuries, until an Etruscan king anchored it in history; and that the peaceful Swiss of today, who feast us with their mild cheeses and formidable watches, bloodied Europe as soldiers of fortune as late as the sixteenth century. Even at the height of the Renaissance, twelve thousand mercenaries in the pay of the imperial armies sacked and devastated Rome and put eight thousand of its inhabitants to the sword.

I do not mean to embody the illusions of Tonio Kröger, whose dreams of uniting a chaste north to a passionate south were exalted in Stockholm fifty-three years ago by Thomas Mann. But I do believe that those clear-sighted Europeans who struggle for a more just and humane world can help us by reconsidering their way of seeing us. Solidarity with our dreams will not make us feel less alone—as long as this solidarity is still not expressed in acts of legitimate support for the people who want it most: those who still believe in the illusion that they will one day lead a life enjoying its fair share of the world.

Latin America neither wants, nor has any reason, to be a pawn without a will of its own; nor is it merely wishful thinking that its quest for independence and originality shouldn't also become an aspiration of the west. However, the navigational advances that have narrowed the distances between our Americas and Europe seem, conversely, to have accentuated our cultural remoteness. Why is the originality so readily granted us in literature so mistrustfully denied us in our difficult attempts at social change? Why think that the social justice sought by progressive Europeans in their own countries cannot also be a goal in Latin America, with different methods for dissimilar conditions? No: the immeasurable violence and pain of our history result from age-old inequities and untold bitterness, and not from a conspiracy plotted three thousand leagues from our home. But many European leaders and thinkers have believed this, with the childishness of old men who have forgotten the fruitful excesses of their youth: as if it were impossible to live by any other destiny than that which places us at the mercy of the two great masters of the world. This, my friends, is the very scale of our solitude.

Nevertheless, in the face of oppression, plundering and abandonment, we respond with life. Neither floods nor plagues, famines nor cataclysms, nor even the eternal wars of century upon century, have been able to subdue the persistent advantage that life enjoys over death. An advantage that grows and quickens: every year, there are seventy-four million more births than deaths, a sufficient number of new lives to multiply each year the population of New York sevenfold. Most of these births occur in the countries of least resources—including, of course, those of Latin America. Conversely, the most prosperous countries have succeeded in accumulating powers of destruction to annihilate, a hundred times over, not only all the human beings that have existed to this day, but also the totality of all living beings that have ever drawn breath on this planet of misfortune.

On a day like today, my master William Faulkner said, 'I decline to accept the end of man.' I would feel unworthy of standing in this place that was his, if I were not fully aware that the colossal tragedy he refused to recognize thirty-two years ago is now, for the first time since the beginning of humanity, nothing more than a simple scientific possibility. Faced with this awesome reality that must have seemed a mere utopia through all of human time, we, the inventors of tales, who will believe anything, feel entitled to believe that it is not yet too late to engage in the creation of a utopia of a very different kind. A new and sweeping utopia of life, where no one will be able to decide for others how they die, where love will prove true and happiness be possible, and where the races condemned to one hundred years of solitude will have, at last and forever, a second opportunity on earth.

Translated from the Spanish by Marina Castañeda

GRANTA

Mario Vargas Llosa

The Story of a Massacre

On January 25 1983, a group of journalists met in the city of Ayacucho, situated in the Andes in Peru. They wanted to travel to Huaychao, a village in the mountains of the Huanta Province, 12,000 feet high, and had booked a taxi for the following morning. The driver, Salvador Luna Ramos, had agreed to take them to Yanorco—an hour from Ayacucho on the Tambo highway—for 30,000 *soles.*

The group consisted of reporters from Lima as well as a number from Ayacucho itself: Félix Gavilán, the local correspondent for *Diario de Marka,* and Octavio Infante, the managing editor of Ayacucho's daily newspaper *Noticias.* Infante's mother lived in Chacabamba—a small village down the mountain from Huaychao and a short distance from the place at which their taxi would leave them. Infante suggested that they should stop first at his mother's house, where they could ask his half-brother to be their guide. Nevertheless, the way to Huaychao would be dangerous: the mountain slopes were steep and the paths were narrow, and there was always the possibility of meeting either members of the guerrillas who dominated the region or the *sinchis,* the anti-subversive police force who sought to protect it. But among the group of journalists—the first journalists to have ventured into the region since the troubles had begun—only Félix Gavilán appeared to appreciate the extent of the danger they faced: while the others bought shoes, pullovers and plastic ponchos for the rain, Gavilán packed a white sheet to be used as a flag in case of difficulties.

What was the attraction of a village so small that it does not even appear on any map? And how had the name Huaychao become so important that everyone in Peru appeared to be talking about it? Because of an unprecedented announcement made in Ayacucho three days before by General Clemente Noel, Chief of the Political Military Command in the Emergency Zone: that the Huaychao *comuneros,* peasants from the Indian community, had captured seven guerrillas of the *Sendero Luminoso,* the 'Shining Path', and, after taking their weapons, their ammunition, their red flags, and their propaganda, had killed them.

The General's evident delight in his announcement was largely because it was the first good news that he was able to offer since assuming command of the campaign against the *Sendero Luminoso* five weeks before. Although he had, until then, spoken of various skirmishes with the *senderistas,* he had been unable to diffuse the sense that the guerrillas had succeeded in eluding the military's attempts to stop them. The guerrillas' success was evident in the fact that they had continued, apparently without inhibition, to blow up bridges and power pylons, blockade roads, and occupy villages where they were known to beat or execute thieves and spies or the officials who had taken office in the municipal elections of 1980. The seven dead men in Huaychao were, in a sense, the General's first success, even though it was a success for which he could not claim responsibility. It was also the first incident, since the insurrection had begun two years ago, that suggested that the *Sendero Luminoso* was not able to rely entirely on the support—or at least the tolerance—of the peasant community.

Nevertheless, the General was evasive when pressed for details. He knew—or seemed to know—only that a number of peasants had shown up at the police station in Huanta to report the incident and that a patrol, led by a lieutenant from the Civil Guard, had made the twenty-hour climb to Huaychao to confirm the killings.

Many felt that General Noel knew much more than he was saying and that his evasiveness merely confirmed what was already suspected: that the General was afraid of the free press and that he, like so many from the military, had come to resent the newspapers and television and radio stations that had been expropriated by the dictatorship but had been returned to their former owners when the Belaúnde government came to power. Moreover, many of the newer papers—like the leftist *El Diario de Marka* and the right-wing *La República* which was founded by many of the officials from the dictatorship itself—were especially critical of the military, and the General did not know how to deal with their questions and their scepticism. After twelve years of military dictatorship, the General was simply not trained for democracy.

In fact the General was being reasonably straight-forward: he had to speak in generalities because generalities were all he knew. Not even the lieutenant in charge of the patrol really understood what had happened; he, like the Civil Guards under his command, was from another region: only one of them spoke Quechua.

On the way to Huaychao the lieutenant reported that they saw great masses of Indians assembled on the mountain tops, carrying white flags. The peasants, obviously agitated, alarmed them, but there were no incidents. In Huaychao they came upon the corpses of the seven guerrillas. The *comuneros* there wanted to retain the weapons, but General Noel had ordered that none be left behind as, according to him, they would attract the return of the 'subversive delinquents' even more than the desire for revenge which the peasants obviously feared. The community leaders, the *varayocs,* stated, through an interpreter, that they had used trickery to kill the *terrucos*: as they approached Huaychao the people came out to greet them, waving red flags and cheering for the Communist Party and its armed struggle. Chanting the slogans and songs of 'the militia', they escorted the guerrillas to the community meeting hall, where, once they had surrounded them completely, they attacked and killed them in a few seconds with the axes, knives and stones that they carried under their ponchos. Only one *senderista* managed to escape, badly wounded. That was all General Clemente Noel knew at his jubilant press conference on January 21. He did not even know that three of the seven murdered guerrillas were boys of fourteen and fifteen, students at the Colegio Nacional in Huanta, who had run away from home several months earlier. Nor did he realize that the Huaychao incident was only one very small representation of what was taking place in the Peruvian highlands.

Throughout Peru, news of the murders in Huaychao was largely received with a sense of relief: it suggested that the peasants were starting to fight not with but against the terrorists. Perhaps it marked the end—or at least the decline—of *Sendero Luminoso.* But the left was sceptical, and many of its representatives declared, in both Parliament and *El Diario de Marka,* that the real killers had to be the *sinchis* or possibly even paramilitary troops disguised as peasants. But in one respect, the left and the right were agreed: everyone was united in their dissatisfaction with information that was so obviously inadequate. They wanted to know more. And so dozens of reporters travelled to Ayacucho. And, on the morning of January 26, eight of them found themselves squeezed together in the taxi of Salvador Luna Ramos.

Who were the reporters? Except for Amador García—the photographer for *Oiga,* a pro-government weekly—the other seven journalists worked for opposition papers. Two of them—Willy Retto and Jorge Luis Mendívil—were with *El Observador,* which was moderate to left-of-centre. Willy Retto was twenty-seven and the son of a well-known photographer; Jorge Luis Mendívil was only twenty-two. Both were from Lima: for them, the Indians they passed—dressed in sandals and coloured ponchos and herding flocks of llamas—were as exotic as they would be to any tourist. Willy Retto had spent only a few days in Ayacucho, during which time the police had already confiscated a roll of his film. The night before the trip he scribbled a few lines to a girl in Lima:

> Things happen here that I never thought I would see and to which I never believed I would come so close. I've seen the poverty of the people, the fear of the peasants, and the tension that exists among the PIP [investigative police], the GC [Civil Guard], the army, as well as among the *Senderos* and the innocent people.

Retto was not a political activist, but Mendívil belonged to the UDP, an organization of the left, and he was in Ayacucho because he had insisted that his paper send him there. He had just been transferred from the international section of *El Observador* to the Sunday supplement: his report on Ayacucho was meant to be his debut.

Jorge Sedano was also from Lima and a stranger to the world of the Sierra. He was the oldest of the group, fifty-one, and the heaviest, weighing almost seventeen stone. He was the distinguished photographer for *La República* and a popular journalist famous for his pictures of car races, his overwhelming good humour, and his Rabelaisian appetite. He was also an excellent cook, and claimed to have invented an irresistible feline stew—the meat was from the cats he raised—called *seco.*

Eduardo de la Piniella, Pedro Sánchez and Félix Gavilán were from *El Diario de Marka,* a paper published cooperatively by the various branches of Peruvian Marxism. De la Piniella, the most militant of the three, was thirty-three, tall, fair, athletic, and was active in the Maoist Revolutionary Communist Party. Pedro Sánchez spent much of his time in Ayacucho photographing the homeless children of the city. Unlike the other two, Félix Gavilán, a member of the MIR (Movement of the Revolutionary Left), was familiar with the Andes. He was from Ayacucho, had been a student at the School of Agriculture, and had a radio programme in which he broadcast to the peasants in Quechua. He had spent a good part of his life working with the Indian communities as a journalist and as a specialist in stockbreeding. Octavio Infante, editor of the Ayacucho daily paper, was also from the region; before working on *Noticias* he had been a labourer, a rural school teacher, and a government employee. He was also of the left, but seems to have been the least enthusiastic about the expedition. It is not impossible that he joined it only to be with his friends.

Regardless of their respective backgrounds and aims all of the reporters disbelieved—or else dismissed completey—the military's claim that the peasants had executed the seven *senderistas.* They assumed that the *sinchis* were responsible or possibly that the seven dead men were not guerrillas at all but innocent peasants murdered by drunken or overbearing Guards. Such cases were not uncommon. The journalists, that is, were going to Huaychao to confirm beliefs that, while varying from individual to individual according to his particular political prejudice, nevertheless seemed to be self-evident truths: that the police and the military were committing atrocities in the Andes, and the government was lying to cover up what had happened in the country near Ayacucho.

But according to the taxi-driver, Salvador Luna Ramos, the burden of their journey was not evident in the way they conducted it. He recalls that the journalists were constantly laughing and joking, and that although they were very uncomfortable—with five in the back and four in the front—they were so amusing that Luna Ramos enjoyed what would otherwise have been a very long and hard drive. They took the Tambo road, climbing to an altitude of 12,000 feet along a narrow edge that overlooks a sheer drop. As they drove, the trees grew sparse; the land around them consisted of black rocks and cactus. They began to see the red flags with the hammer and sickle that were placed on the hilltops or suspended by long cords over the ravines. The small farmers along this road had been attacked by *Sendero Luminoso,* and their detachments often stopped vehicles whose drivers were asked to pay their 'revolutionary share'. There was very little traffic.

An hour from Ayacucho they stopped for something to eat in Paclla—a half-dozen huts scattered between the highway and the stream—and then drove on past the Tocto Lagoon. There they told the taxi driver to stop. Luna Ramos was paid and turned the car around and headed back toward Ayacucho. The last time he saw the journalists, they were carrying their cameras and bags and had begun to climb the mountain in single file. He wished them good luck; the area into which they were going had been declared a 'liberated zone' by *Sendero Luminoso.*

Most Peruvians first heard of *Sendero Luminoso* in 1980, during the last days of the dictatorship, when its members suspended dogs from the street lamps in Lima. The animals were all wearing placards that accused Deng Tsiao Ping of having betrayed the Revolution. *Sendero Luminoso* had arrived.

At the time *Sendero Luminoso* was merely a small group of political fanatics. It had few followers in either Lima or any of the other sections of Peru, with the exception of one place in the southeastern Andes: Ayacucho. Ayacucho is a city of 80,000 inhabitants, and is the capital of the region with the fewest resources, the greatest unemployment, and the highest rates of illiteracy and infant mortality in the country. It is also the area in which *Sendero Luminoso* is best established. Part of its success there can be attributed to the economic conditions of the region of its origins. But part of its success is also in the charismatic leader who was born in Arequipa in 1934, and who graduated from the Faculty of Letters at the University of Ayacucho with a thesis on 'The Theory of Space in Kant', and became a full professor by 1963. His name, Abimael Guzmán, with its resonances in Hebrew, has suggestions of a biblical prophet.

The ideologue of *Sendero Luminoso* is withdrawn, plump, mysterious, and perpetually inaccessible; since the 1950s he has been a militant member of the Communist Party; in 1964, he was among the disciples of Mao who formed the Red Flag Communist Party. In 1970 he and his followers broke with Red Flag and founded the organization that would be known as *Sendero Luminoso,* although its members only recognize the official name, the Communist Party of Peru. The term *Sendero Luminoso* is taken from a statement by an earlier ideologue, José Carlos Mariátegui, who said: 'Marxist-Leninism will open the shining path to revolution.'

Sendero Luminoso developed in Ayacucho through the labours of this professor and the middle-class Ayacuchan woman he married, Augusta La Torre, and together they turned her small house into a salon for groups of fascinated students. The professor is now difficult to find, however: no one has ever seen him give a speech or take part in the street-demonstrations organized by his followers: it is not even known if he is still in Peru. He was arrested once, in 1970, but spent only a few days in prison. He went into hiding in 1978, and has not been seen since. What is certain, however, is that Comrade Gonzalo—his *nom de guerre*—is the indisputable leader of *Sendero*. The *senderistas* call him the 'Fourth Sword of Marxism' (the first three are Marx, Lenin and Mao), arguing that he has given back to ideology the purity it lost in the revisionist betrayals of Moscow, Albania, Cuba, and now Peking. Unlike other insurrectionist groups, *Sendero Luminoso* avoids publicity; it holds the bourgeois media in contempt. No reporter has ever interviewed Comrade Gonzalo.

According to Guzmán, José Carlos Mariátegui's description of Peru in the 1930s is true of Peru today: it is a 'semifeudal and semicolonial society'. It will achieve liberation, therefore, only by following a strategy identical to that of Mao's: a strategy of prolonged war, with the peasantry as its backbone, that will 'assault' the cities. *Sendero's* models of socialism are Stalinist Russia, the Cultural Revolution of 'The Gang of Four', and the Pol-Pot Regime in Cambodia—models that are not only extreme and uncompromising but also, it appears, reasonably popular. In Ayacucho and especially the other Andean provinces, *Sendero* has attracted many followers among students, perhaps because it provides such an immediate outlet for the frustrations felt among young people who are unable to sustain any hope for the future. In the interior the young know that there will be no jobs for them in the saturated markets of their home towns; they also know that what future they do have is in emigrating to the capital, where they face the prospect of living with the other provincials stuck in the slums.

In 1978 the *senderistas* left the University of Ayacucho, and a few months later the sabotage and terrorism began. The first, in May 1980, was the burning of the ballot boxes in the community of

Chuschi during the presidential election. Nobody paid much attention to the first explosions in the Andes: modern European Peru—in which half of the country's eighteen million inhabitants live—was euphorically celebrating the end of the dictatorship and the re-establishment of democracy. Belaúnde Terry, deposed by the Army in 1968, returned to the presidency with a strong majority, and his Popular Action Party, in a coalition with the Popular Christian Party, won an absolute majority in the Parliament.

The new government was reluctant to recognize what was happening in Ayacucho. During his previous term (1962-1968) Belaúnde Terry had been forced to take a stand against the insurrectionist activities of MIR and ELN (Army of National Liberation); in 1965 and 1966, guerrilla bases were established in the Andes and in the jungle. The government entrusted the suppression of the rebels to the Army, and the military then crushed the rebellion with brutal efficiency, summarily executing most of the people who participated in it. But the same military commanders who directed the anti-guerrilla operations then went on to overthrow the government in the coup of October 3 1968: the regime that emerged lasted twelve years. When Belaúnde Terry returned to office, he tried at all costs to keep the Armed Forces from assuming the responsibility of the fight against the *Sendero Luminoso.* He was afraid of a military campaign: its excesses and its consequences.

For the first two years of *Sendero Luminoso,* the government buried its head in the sand. It said that the press was exaggerating the importance of the movement; that it wasn't a matter of 'terrorism' but of 'petardism', and, as all the incidents were confined to an area that constituted less than five per cent of the country's territory, there was no reason to divert the Armed Forces from their primary function of national defence. The incidents were ordinary crimes, and the police could control them.

A battalion of Civil Guard *sinchis*—the word means *valiant* and *daring* in Quechua—was sent to Ayacucho. Their ignorance of the region and of the ways of the peasants, their inadequate training and poor equipment made their efforts ineffectual if not embarrassing. More important, the police, who had enjoyed more than a little freedom under the regime, were slow to renounce the expediencies of dictatorship: they had not really readjusted to democratic rule. The *sinchis*, therefore, had almost no effect on the *senderistas,* but at the same time committed abuses on a scale that simply could not be ignored: arbitrary arrests, torture, rape, theft, accidents involving injuries and deaths. They generated a fear and resentment among the poor that served to work in *Sendero Luminoso*'s favour, neutralizing the possible negative response that the violence of the *senderistas* might otherwise have provoked.

The tactics of the *senderistas,* on the other hand, demonstrated 'technological' efficiency and a cold, unscrupulous mentality. Besides blowing up pylons and raiding mining camps for explosives, *Sendero Luminoso* devastated the small farms in Ayacucho (the large ones had been redistributed in the Agrarian Reform of 1960) and killed or wounded the owners. Dozens of police stations in the rural areas were attacked. In August 1982, *Sendero Luminoso* boasted that it had carried out '2,900 successful operations'.

Many of these were murders; eighty civilians and forty-three police had been killed by December 31 1982. In the first four months of 1983 the figure rose to more than two hundred civilians and one hundred soldiers and police. Guards and police were shot down in the streets; political officials, especially the elected mayors, were also targets. The Mayor of Ayacucho, Jorge Jáuregui, miraculously survived two bullets in the head after an attempted assassination on December 11 1982. In the peasant communities the 'people's courts' sentenced real or supposed enemies of the guerrillas to beatings or execution.

The insurrectionists' tactics led to the collapse of civil authority in the interior of Ayacucho: mayors, subprefects, lieutenant governors, judges and other officials fled *en masse.* Even the priests ran away. The police stations that had been blown up were not reopened. The Civil Guard, convinced that it was too risky for squads of three or five men to be in the villages, re-grouped their forces in the cities where they could defend themselves more easily. And what would happen to the peasant settlements left to the mercy of the guerrillas? It is senseless to ask if they received *senderista* indoctrination willingly or unwillingly, since they had no choice but to support, or at least coexist with, those who had assumed real power.

It was, of course, through one of these areas that the eight journalists were walking—through brambles and clumps of *ichu*—towards Chacabamba. The region is divided into lowlands—the more prosperous and modern villages—and highlands in which some twenty scattered peasant communities are populated by a single ethnic group, the Iquichans: their lands are poor, their isolation is almost absolute, and their customs are archaic. The lowlands had been the victim of continual raids in 1980 and 1981, and all of its police stations—in San José de Secce, Mayoc, and Luricocha—had been abandoned. In mid-1982, *Sendero Luminoso* declared it a 'liberated zone'.

This process had gone almost unnoticed in the Peru from which the reporters came. They knew more about the operations of *Sendero Luminoso* in the cities. Their papers had been primarily concerned with incidents in Lima, or, for example, the daring dawn attack on the Ayacucho Prison on March 3 1982, when *Sendero* liberated two hundred and forty-seven prisoners and demonstrated to the government that 'petardism' had grown considerably. But they were ignorant of the mountain regions where no reporter ever goes and where little news ever gets out.

Doña Rosa de Argumedo, Octavio's mother, goes barefoot. She is a woman in her sixties with a rudimentary knowledge of Spanish, and has spent her whole life in the region. Doña Rosa would have known just by looking at the men accompanying her son that most of them were not from the mountains. The fat one, Jorge Sedano, could scarcely speak because of fatigue and altitude sickness: he wore a summer shirt, and was suffering from the cold. The young one, Jorge Luis Mendívil, had torn his trousers. They were irritable and thirsty. Doña Rosa invited them in—her small house is made of mud, wood and zinc—and offered them lemons so they could fix something to drink. They were joined by her children, and while they rested the reporters talked with the family, who lent Jorge Sedano a coat and Mendívil a pair of trousers. Eduardo de la Piniella tried to find out about conditions in the village, and he asked Julia Aguilar how she got her children to school, jotting down her replies in his notebook.

Meanwhile Infante, the managing editor of *Noticias,* asked his half-brother, Juan Argumedo, to be their guide and to rent them animals to carry their bags, cameras, and the fat Jorge Sedano, who otherwise would obviously not make the climb to Huaychao. Juan Argumedo agreed and said he would guide them about two-thirds of the way, as far as Uchuraccay, where he would leave them and return with the horse and mule.

There are no visible trails between Chacabamba in the lowlands and Huaychao in the highlands, but the Argumedos would have known the way. They usually climbed to highland villages in October, for the Feast of the Virgen del Rosario, or in July for the Feast of the Virgen del Carmen, to sell *aguardiente,* clothing, medicine and coca.

Within the strange social structure of the Andes, the Argumedo family, although poor and uneducated, is privileged, even wealthy, compared to the Indians in poverty-stricken communities like Uchuraccay and Huaychao in the highlands. Valley farmers like the Argumedos, with their *mestizo* culture and their ability to speak Quechua with the peasants and Spanish with the city people, have been the traditional link between the Iquichans and the rest of the world. But their contacts are limited to fairs or those occasions when the highland peasants pass through Chacabamba on their way to market. In the past relations had been peaceful. But the advent of both *Sendero Luminoso* and the *sinchis* changed all that. Communications between the valley and the highlands had been destroyed: there was tension and hostility. The Argumedo family, for instance, had not gone up to sell their products at the Feasts of Rosario and Carmen for the past two years.

Perhaps this explains the enormity of our ignorance. In the Sierra information is transmitted orally, and during this period no one was speaking. It is possible that the Argumedo family would have known as little about the highlands as General Noel, the government in Lima, and the eight reporters.

Doña Rosa said that Octavio Infante had asked her to prepare some blankets in the barn and some food, because they would try to get back that same night. Amador García was the reason for their hurry: he was supposed to send his photographs back to Lima on the Thursday plane. Their plans were optimistic. It is some fifteen kilometres from Chacabamba to Uchuruccay, and another eight from there to Huaychao. It would be difficult for them to get back the same day, and Doña Rosa gave them the name of a friend in Uchuraccay. Félix Gavilán wrote her name in his notebook.

It was not yet noon when they started out on the last stage of their journey. The sun was shining and there was no threat of rain.

The Iquichans are among the most destitute inhabitants in the depressed region of Ayacucho. Without roads, medical care, or technology, without water or electricity, on the inhospitable lands where they have lived since pre-Hispanic times, they have only known the exploitation of the landowner, the demands of the tax collector and the violence of civil war since the establishment of the Republic. Although Catholicism is deeply rooted among the *comuneros,* it has not displaced the old beliefs. They continue, for instance, in their worship of the *Apus* (god-mountains) and of *Rasuwillca* (in whose belly a horseman with light skin and a white horse is meant to live) whose cult still dominates the entire region. Most of these men and women are illiterate and speak only Quechua. They live on a limited diet of beans and potatoes, and have become accustomed to the daily threat of starvation, disease or simple natural catastrophe.

The eight journalists, led by Juan Argumedo, were journeying towards an encounter with another time, for life in Uchuraccay and Huaychao has not changed in almost two hundred years. In the houses of Huanta, for instance, families still talk nervously about the possibility that the Iquichan Indians of Uchuraccay and Huaychao will come down out of the highlands, as they did in 1896 when they captured the city and murdered a government official in a rebellion against the salt tax. Throughout history, the Iquichan communities have never left their lands—except to fight. And there is one feature true of every outbreak of violence: it is the fear that their way of life will be disturbed; they fight the threat of change. During the Colonial period, they fought not with the Indians but with the royalists. Their complete independence from the other ethnic groups in the Andes has always been evident but especially in their resistance to Independence: between 1826 and 1839, for instance, they actively opposed the Republic and fought for the King of Spain. In every uprising during the nineteenth century, the Iquichans fought for their regional sovereignty. The Iquichans, that is, are zealous defenders of the customs and mores which, although archaic, are all they have.

Relations between the Iquichans and the more modern, westernized villages in the valley have always been strained. This is common in the Andes. The *mestizo* settlers in the lowlands are contemptuous of the upland Indians, calling them *chutos* (savages), and the Indians, in turn, despise the *mestizos.*

This was the situation when *Sendero Luminoso* began its operations in the region. In 1981 and 1982 the guerrillas were strong throughout the lowlands, but they apparently made no effort to win over the Iquichans. And no one understands why. For two years the highlands served as only a passage that permitted the guerrillas to move from one end of the province to the other.

The Iquichans would usually hear the *Sendero* 'militias' passing through their highland villages at night. And when the *comuneros* talk about those strange, disturbing apparitions, they seem to take on for them a phantasmagoric quality, suggestive of unconscious terrors. The fact that their rivals in the lowlands help *Sendero Luminoso,* willingly or unwillingly, is cause enough to prejudice the Iquichans against them. But there are other reasons as well. The guerrillas hunt for shelter and food on their marches, and when the *comuneros* try to protect their animals there is violence. Invariably, the theft of animals among communities with minimal resources causes resentment; when the *comuneros* of Uchuraccay talk of *Sendero,* for instance, they call them *terrorista-sua*: terrorist-thief. In Uchuraccay, just a few weeks earlier, a *Sendero* detachment had killed two shepherds.

But the final break between the Iquichans and *Sendero Luminoso* was precipitated by the revolutionaries' attempt to apply a policy of 'economic self-sufficiency' and controlled production in the 'liberated zones'. The objective was simple: to cut off all supplies to the cities and to inculcate in the peasants a mode of production that conformed to *Sendero*'s ideological model. The communities were ordered to plant only enough for their own needs, to avoid surpluses, and to stop all urban trade. Each community was meant to be self-sufficient so that the money economy would disappear. *Sendero Luminoso* imposed this policy, however, by violent means. In the beginning of January its members closed the Lirio Fair at gunpoint, dynamited the highway, and then cut off all traffic between the two main towns of the region, Huanta and Lirio. The Iquichan *comuneros* who come down to Lirio to sell their surplus and to buy provisions of coca, macaroni and corn, discovered that all trade had ceased—and, perhaps most important, had ceased for reasons that seemed incomprehensible: their regional sovereignty was being threatened.

In mid-January the leaders, the *varayocs,* of the Iquichan communities held meetings in Uchuraccay and Carhuaurán—the same villages at which they had gathered one hundred and fifty years before to declare war on the new Republic. They agreed to oppose *Sendero Luminoso.*

The government, the police and the military knew nothing of these events. Belaúnde Terry had ordered the army to take charge of operations only at the end of December 1982, and General Clemente Noel was just beginning to realize how complicated his job was going to be. A company of marines, a battalion of infantry and a group of Army commandoes had just arrived in Ayacucho to back up the Civil Guard, but so far only the *sinchis* had been up to Uchuraccay in the highlands.

Alejandrina de la Cruz, a school teacher, saw the first patrol of *sinchis* arrive in May 1981. In Uchuraccay there were no incidents between the Guards and the *comuneros,* although in one of the nearby highland villages the troops had abused one of the peasants. In 1981 the *sinchis* came through Uchuraccay about every two months in their unsuccessful search for *senderistas.* But Alejandrina de la Cruz, the school teacher, saw no patrols in 1982; she left Uchuraccay on December 18. The villagers, however, insist that after she left the *sinchis* came one more time in helicopters. When the peasants asked them to stay to protect the village, they said they couldn't; they told the *comuneros* that if the *terrucos* appeared they should 'defend themselves and kill them.'

This was, in any case, precisely what the Iquichans had decided to do at their meetings. And their decision was implemented almost immediately—and in several villages at the same time. Detachments of *senderistas* and their real or presumptive accomplices were hunted down, tortured and executed throughout the Iquicha district. The seven deaths at Huaychao which General Noel announced at his press conference represented only a small part of the massacres that the Iquichans had carried out. But unlike the dead at Huaychao, the other victims were not shown to the authorities. It is difficult to learn of the actual extent of the slaughter. Some of the massacres are known. Five *senderistas,* for instance, had been killed in Uchuraccay on January 22, and at least twenty-four *terrucos* had been murdered in the other nearby villages—although the real number of victims may be significantly higher.

The journalists knew none of this; neither, apparently, did their guide: but the district they approached was in turmoil. The *comuneros* were in a state of extraordinary hysteria, a state for which they have their own word: *chaqwa,* a state of disorder and chaos. They were convinced that at any moment the *senderistas* would return to avenge their dead. And they felt threatened: they had no firearms and had no longer the element of surprise that had permitted the earlier killings. This was the mood in Uchuraccay, where some three hundred *comuneros* were holding a council meeting, when the shepherds, or sentinels, came to warn them that a group of strangers was approaching the community meeting hall.

In Chacabamba that night the journalists' guide, Juan Argumedo, was expected by his mother Doña Rosa, his sister Juana Lidia and his wife Julia Aguilar. But he did not return. Doña Rosa had prepared food and blankets for Octavio Infante and the other journalists. They were not particularly surprised that the reporters did not turn up, but that Juan should not return was a mystery.

The next morning—Thursday, January 27—a boy, Pastor Ramos Romero came into Chacabamba shouting that something terrible had happened, that in Uchuraccay they'd killed the men who had left with Juan. Doña Rosa and her daughter left in terror for Uchuraccay, grabbing on their way out a small sack of potatoes and coca leaves. Juan's wife was ahead of them.

Juan's wife reached the outskirts of Uchuraccay around noon. As soon as she saw the outlying huts with their straw roofs and their little stone corrals, she knew that something was wrong. Large numbers of Indians were standing on the hills; they were armed with slingshots, sticks and axes, and among them were *comuneros* from all the nearby villages: Huaychao, Cunya, Pampalca, Jarhuachuray and Paria. Some were waving white flags. A group surrounded her, and, without giving her a chance to ask about her husband, its members began accusing her of collaborating with the *terrucos.* They said they would kill her just like they had killed them. They were excited, frightened, violent. Julia tried to talk to them, to explain that the strangers weren't terrorists and neither was her husband, but the peasants, growing increasingly hostile, called her a liar. They listened to her inasmuch as they did not kill her, but they did take her prisoner and brought her to the community hall of Uchuraccay. As they entered the village she saw the community in a 'frantic state', and it seemed to her that there were 'several thousand' peasants from other villages.

Her sister-in-law and mother-in-law were also prisoners in the community hall. Their experience had been similar to hers, but they had been able to find out something about what had happened the night before. On the outskirts of the village they had talked for a moment to Roberta Huicho, a *comunera.* She told them that the peasants had killed some terrorists, but that Juan Argumedo was not with them at the time. He had fled Huachhuaccasa Hill with his animals. *Comuneros* had chased him on horseback, caught up with him in a village called Yuracyaco, and taken him prisoner. Doña Rosa and Juana Lidia had seen Juan's dead horse and mule on the road to Uchuraccay. But they couldn't ask any more because they were suddenly surrounded by furious *comuneros* who called them *terrucas.* On their knees, the women swore that they weren't terrorists. In an effort to pacify the Indians they gave them some of the potatoes and coca they had brought with them.

They were held prisoner until the following afternoon. Thirteen other prisoners, all badly beaten, were in the dark hall that served as their jail: all charged with collaborating with *Sendero Luminoso.* One of them was Julian Huayta, the Lieutenant Governor of the region, who was bleeding from head wounds. They had tied a red flag around his neck and accused him of having raised that flag in Iquicha. That afternoon, that evening, and the following morning, Doña Rosa, her daughter and her daughter-in-law watched the *comuneros* from Uchuraccay and other communities—they say there were 'four or five thousand', but the number seems exaggerated—try the thirteen prisoners in an open Council meeting, in accordance with ancient custom. Nine were found innocent of the charge of helping the *terrucos.* Were the four others sentenced to death? The Argumedos don't know; they only know that the Uchuraccayans turned the prisoners over to people from another community, who took them away. But it seems likely that the previous night's killing would continue after the Council meeting.

The Argumedos were tried on Friday afternoon. Over and over again they heard that the *comuneros* had killed some terrorists, and nobody listened when they explained that the victims were not terrorists but reporters on their way to Huaychao. Do the Iquichan *comuneros* know what a 'reporter' is? If a few of them do, it is with dim understanding at best.

Why this insistence on treating the women as if they were accomplices of the *terrucos?* Didn't many of the *comuneros* know the Argumedo family from Chacabamba? A persistent but unverified rumour accused Juan Argumedo of being a protector and friend of the *senderistas.* His family denies it. But they do in fact live in an area controlled by *Sendero,* where the villagers, in solidarity or in fear, collaborate with the guerrillas. Perhaps Juan Argumedo didn't, but it doesn't matter. For the highland peasants he might very well have appeared as the leader of the *senderist* detachment that the village had been expecting. Was Juan Argumedo the determining factor in the misunderstanding that provoked the killing? No one will ever know: to this day the *comuneros* of Uchuraccay claim that they didn't know him, that they never saw him, and, despite all the searching, his body has not been found. The three women were luckier. The *varayocs* finally succumbed to their pleading. Before letting them go, the Council made them solemnly swear on a staff with a crucifix (it belonged to the leader) that they would remain absolutely silent about what they had seen and heard since the moment they entered Uchuraccay.

When the women returned to Chacabamba Friday night, two military patrols were combing the area searching for the reporters. After a ten-hour march, in a torrential rainstorm, one of the patrols finally reached the village. The *comuneros* were in their houses, and wouldn't speak until the following day, when they told the patrol through an interpreter that they had killed 'eight terrorists who came into Uchuraccay waving a red flag and shouting death to the *sinchis.*' They showed the patrol the graves and handed over a red flag, a telephoto lens, twelve rolls of unused film and some identity cards. 'And their weapons?' asked one of the officers. 'They didn't have any.'

And on Saturday night the authorities in Ayacucho and Lima learned of the deaths of the reporters. On Sunday all of Peru watched on television as the corpses were exhumed, saw the gruesome sight of the eight bodies mutilated by sticks, slingshots, stones and knives. There were no bullet wounds.

The government appointed a commission to investigate the massacre; I was one of the members. It was not difficult, after on-site visits and the review of official documents and the interrogation of dozens of people, to reconstruct the essential facts, although some details were not clarified. It was not difficult to conclude that the reporters, exhausted after their five-hour climb, were murdered in Uchuraccay by a mob of men and women whom fear and anger had armed with a ferocious brutality. And there was no doubt that the Iquichans had killed them because they thought they were *senderistas.*

The peasants of Uchuraccay spoke to us at a hearing we held there on March 14. They spoke naturally—without any sense of guilt—and were intrigued and surprised that people had come from so far away, and that there was so much excitement, because of one little incident. Yes, they had killed them. Why? Because they had made a mistake. Isn't life full of errors and deaths? They were 'ignorant'. They were concerned not about the past but about the future—that is, the *senderistas.* Could we ask the *sinchis* to come and protect them? Could we ask the 'Honourable Mr Government' to send them at least three rifles? At the start of the hearing, instructed by the anthropologists who were advisers to the commission, I had spilled *aguardiente* on the ground and drunk in homage to the tutelary god-mountain *Rasuwillca*; after then scattering coca leaves on the ground I tried, through an interpreter, to explain to the dozens and dozens of *comuneros* gathered around us that the laws of Peru prohibit murder, that we have judges to try cases and sentence the guilty, that we have police to make sure that everyone obeys the law. And while I was saying these things and looking at their faces, I felt as absurd and unreal as if I were teaching them the authentic revolutionary philosophy of Comrade Mao, betrayed by that counter-revolutionary dog Den Tsiao Ping.

The Uchuraccayans refused to give us the details of the actual murder. We assumed that they had come down from the hills and had attacked the journalists suddenly, before anyone could speak. We supposed that they used *huaracas* (slingshots). We thought that there was no dialogue because the Iquichans believed that the *senderistas* were armed and because, if given the chance, the Quechua-speaking reporters—Octavio Infante, Félix Gavilán and Amador García—could have tempered the hostility of their attackers.

But the facts were different. They came to light four months later when a patrol, escorting the judge in charge of the investigation, found Willy Retto's camera in a cave on the hilltop near Uchuraccay. It had been uncovered by *vizcachas* digging in the earth where the *comuneros* had hidden it. The young photographer for *El Observador* had the presence of mind to take pictures in the moments just before the massacre, perhaps when the lives of some of his friends had already been taken. The photographs show the reporters surrounded by *comuneros.* In one of them Jorge Sedano is on his knees next to the bags and cameras that someone, possibly Octavio Infante, has just placed on the ground. In another Eduardo de la Piniella is raising his arms, and in another young Mendívil is gesturing with his hands as if he were asking everybody to calm down. In the last picture Willy Retto, who had fallen down, photographed the Iquichan who was attacking him. The horrifying document proves that talk did no good, that although the Iquichans saw they were unarmed, they attacked the strangers convinced they were their enemies.

The massacre had magical and religious overtones as well. The hideous wounds on the corpses were arranged in such a way as to suggest ritualistic killing. The eight bodies were buried in pairs, face down—the form of burial used for those whom the *comuneros* consider 'devils', or for those who are believed to make pacts with the Devil. They were buried outside the community boundaries to emphasize the fact that they were strangers: in the Andes the image of the Devil is assimilated within the image of the stranger. The bodies were conspicuously mutilated around the mouth and eyes, expressing the belief that the victim, deprived of sight, will not then be able to recognize his killers, and, deprived of his tongue, will not be able to denounce them. Their ankles were broken so they could not return for revenge. And finally the *comuneros* stripped the bodies, washed the clothes and then burned them in a ceremony of purification known as *pichja.*

The crime at Uchuraccay was horrifying; knowing the circumstances does not excuse the crime, but they do make it more comprehensible. The violence, extraordinary in our lives, stuns us. For the Iquichans, that violence is present in their lives from the time they are born until the time they die. Scarcely a month after we had been in Ayacucho, another tragedy confirmed that the Iquichans' terror of reprisals by *Sendero Luminoso* was justified. In Lucanamarca, a village about two hundred kilometres from Uchuraccay, the *comuneros* had cooperated with *Sendero Luminoso* but later disputes emerged concerning food supplies. On April 23 four detachments of *Sendero Luminoso,* leading hundreds of peasants from a rival community, attacked Lucanamarca in a retaliatory raid. Seventy-seven people were murdered on the village square, some with bullets but most with axes, machetes and stones. There were four children among the decapitated, mutilated bodies.

When the hearing had ended and, overwhelmed by what we had seen and heard—the graves of the reporters were still open—we prepared to return to Ayacucho, a tiny woman from the community suddenly began to dance. She was singing quietly a song whose words we couldn't understand. She was an Indian as tiny as a child, but she had the wrinkled face of a very old woman and the scarred cheeks and swollen lips of those who live exposed to the cold of the highlands. She was barefoot and wore several brightly-coloured skirts and a hat with ribbons, and as she sang and danced she tapped us gently on the legs with brambles. Was she saying goodbye to us in an ancient ritual? Was she cursing us because we belonged to the strangers—*senderistas,* 'reporters', *sinchis*—who had brought new fears to their lives? Was she exorcizing us? For the past few weeks I had been living in a state of extraordinary tension as I interviewed soldiers, politicians, policemen, peasants, and reporters, and reviewed dispatches, evidence and legal testimony, trying to establish what had happened. At night I lay awake, attempting to determine the truth of the testimony and the hypotheses, or I had nightmares in which the certainties of the day became enigmas again. And as the story of the eight journalists unfolded—I had known two of them, and had been with Amador García just two days before his trip to Ayacucho—it seemed that another more terrible story about my own country was being revealed. But at no time had I felt as much sorrow as in Uchuraccay on that late afternoon with its threatening clouds, watching the tiny woman who danced and tapped us with brambles and who seemed to come from a Peru different from the one in which I live, an ancient archaic Peru that has survived in these sacred mountains despite centuries of isolation and adversity. That frail little woman had undoubtedly been one of the mob who threw rocks and swung sticks. The Iquichan women are no less warlike than the men. In the posthumous photographs of Willy Retto you can see them at the front of the crowd. It wasn't difficult to imagine that community transformed by fear and rage. We had a presentiment of it at the hearing when, after too many disturbing questions, the passive assembly, led by the women, suddenly began to roar '*chaqwa, chaqwa,*' and the air was filled with evil omens.

The peasants killed some strangers because they thought the strangers were coming to kill them. The reporters believed that the *sinchis* and not the peasants had murdered the *senderistas.* It is possible that the journalists never knew why they were attacked. A wall of disinformation, prejudice and ideology separated one group from the other and made communication impossible.

The guerrilla movements in Latin America are not 'peasant movements'. They are born in the cities, among intellectuals and middle-class militants who, with their schematic rhetoric, are often as foreign and incomprehensible to the peasant masses as *Sendero Luminoso* is to the men and women of Uchuraccay. The outrages committed by those other strangers—the forces of counter-insurgency—tend to win peasant support for the guerrillas. Put simply, the peasants are coerced by those who think they are the masters of history and absolute truth. The fact is that the struggle between the guerrillas and the armed forces is really a settling of accounts between 'privileged' sectors of society, and the peasant masses are used cynically and brutally by those who say they want to 'liberate' them. And it is the peasants who always suffer the most: in the first six months of 1983, seven hundred and fifty of them have been killed in Peru.

The story of the eight journalists reveals how vulnerable democracy is in Latin America and how easily it dies under dictatorships of the right and the left. Democracy will never be strong in our countries as long as it is a privilege for one sector of society and an incomprehensible abstraction for the others. The double threat—the Pinochet model or the Fidel Castro model—continues to haunt our few democratic governments.

Translated from the Spanish by Edith Grossman

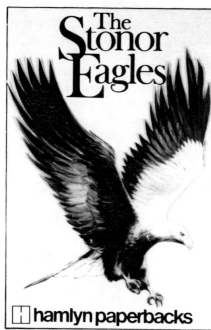

GRANTA

Patrick Marnham

The Border

> By indolence and recalcitrance the Spaniard has preserved his individuality, a creature unashamedly himself, whose only notion of social obligation is what old custom dictates.
>
> V.S. Pritchett

I crossed into El Salvador from Guatemala at the Anguiatú border post, on a quiet road linking the Guatemalan backwater of Esquipulas with the Salvadoran backwater of Metapán. There were once silver mines in this part of Salvador, but the metal ran out as it did in all the precious mines of Mexico and Central America. It was a Saturday afternoon. It was very hot. The bus dropped us on the Guatemalan side of the border, and we carried our bags through the heat towards the luxuriant blue and gold uniforms of the Salvadoran border guards.

The town I had left, Esquipulas, is one of those places famous to Central Americans and ignored by the rest of the world. It is a little town, almost a one-street town, which lives off the 'Black Christ' guarded there since it was carved in 1594. My guide book described Esquipulas as 'a tourist centre'. In fact it is a place of pilgrimage, a rather different matter. Walking up the main street I met a lawyer who said that he had seen two Italians in Esquipulas eight months before, otherwise no Europeans or *gringos* in three years. He was from Guatemala City but had come to Esquipulas 'to get away from the death squads.' It was safe in this part of Guatemala. 'There are few Indians, so few *comunistas*.' He was speaking humorously. The lawyer lived with a beautiful girl. He introduced her as his wife, and then told me, rather proudly, that they were not yet married, they were 'living-in-sin'. It seemed the sort of sin that might escape God's attention on the Guatemalan-Salvadoran border.

Earlier I had watched the pilgrims, whom the lawyer distinguished from tourists, at work in the Benedictine church. At six-thirty in the morning the monks sat on chairs scattered along the nave hearing confessions amid the bustle of family groups arriving from all over Guatemala, as well as from El Salvador and Honduras. There were Indians kneeling on the flagged floor setting up little shrines with candles and rosaries. Some knelt holding a candle in each hand, others returned from the communion rail wearing a smile. The women's costumes showed that they came from all the villages of the Highlands. Having travelled up there I recalled that it had been hard to think of the Indians as anything but political people. Whose side were they on? Where they sheltering guerrillas? Would they join the Civil Guard? How could one persuade them to talk about the army? Here, out of journalistic context, they were just people on pilgrimage, excited and happy. Some of them had babies, carried in white cloths across their backs from head bands, but suspended horizontally so that the babies lay as though in hammocks. To soothe them the mothers, many of whom were teenagers, tossed their babies in the air, swinging them from the hips in semi-circles. This did not soothe the babies. The noise of children crying during Mass was extraordinary but not distracting. It was not urgent, it just drifted up to the roof of the church like incense, and failed to rebound.

After Mass there was a benediction, a local rite. The Indians lined up outside the church, and the monks, mostly from Louisiana, walked past them carrying large brushes and plastic buckets full of holy water. Something similar used to happen at High Mass before the Church reformed its liturgy. There was a chant taken from Psalm 50—'*Asperges me:* Thou shalt sprinkle me with hyssop, Lord, and I shall be cleansed; Thou shalt wash me, and I shall be whiter than snow.' At school we used to duck to avoid being soaked. But at Esquipulas the monks had to give each pilgrim and all their belongings—which were spread out on the ground in front of them—a thorough dousing. The Indians became agitated if anything remained dry. To them the holy water was a medicine: it had to be administered in the correct dose.

The previous evening I had watched as the shrine, abandoned by the monks for the night, was enthusiastically taken over, like shrines all over the world, by the faithful. The blaze of candles around the 'Black Christ' could be seen for half a mile down the street, framed in the gloom of the nave. The family parties arrived, knelt across the west doorway, and started singing the shrine's hymn. The old women wailed it like *muezzins*, then advanced on their knees into the building. Inside some wandered around chatting, others made directly for the ramp behind the altar which led up to the silver and crystal casket around the image. This they touched and kissed and emptied their pockets before. When they left it after a few moments of prayer, patiently observed by those to come, they walked backwards down the ramp, eyes still fixed on the *Cristo Crucificado.* Such devotion can be seen all over Latin America—a region which, according to its priests, contains a church in crisis.

It happened that the bus to the border carried a number of pilgrims, not Guatemalan Indians but Salvadorans returning after one night in Esquipulas. El Salvador has only ten per cent pure Indian people and less than ten per cent pure white. Its eighty per cent *mestizo* majority is by far the largest in Central America. Its present troubles are said to be due to its recent history. The country seceded from Guatemala in 1849 shortly after coffee was introduced to the region I was about to pass through. At that time the population was only a few hundred thousand. But the coffee led to prosperity and the population, that is the *mestizo* population, grew fast. By 1930 there were one and a half million people, by 1966 three million, by 1979 nearly four and a half million. There are now one hundred and fifty-seven people to the square kilometre, which makes El Salvador the most densely populated country on the American continent. Furthermore, the land is mountainous and much of it is useless. Traditionally the country has been owned and run by fourteen families. It is not hard to see how the trouble started.

At the border I lost my pilgrims. They were waved through and on to another bus, leaving me to face Salvadoran immigration for the second time in twelve months. On my previous journey I had entered El Salvador not by a back door but from Honduras by the Pan American Highway and—though I did not know this at the time—by a customs post which had been destroyed on the previous day. The few soldiers on duty had fled into Honduras when the guerrillas attacked. Eight border guards had stayed at their posts and had all been killed. The buildings and the bridge had been blown up. All traffic along the Pan American Highway had ceased; it had been one of the guerrillas' most spectacular coups for many months. The Honduran army had opened up with artillery from their side of the river. Later it was rumoured that most of the Salvadoran troops detailed to guard the bridge had been absent rehearsing a parade for the national 'Day of the Soldier'. For members of the immigration service it must have been their worst experience for many years. Quite unaware of any of this, I approached a burly female who started to search my baggage.

If you ask experienced observers of Salvador how *not* to travel through the country, they will tell you not to travel by bus. For some

reason this advice never reached me until I had crossed the country twice by bus. One was told that the main danger on these buses came not from the guerrillas but from the army. I was eventually issued with a *laisser passer* by the Ministry of Defence. It was a fine piece of typing addressed to *Señores Comandantes y Jefes de Cuerpos Militares.* It identified me as a correspondent for the *Spectator,* London, and said that as long as I did not breach military security I should be assisted in my journalistic labours. It was signed not 'yours sincerely' but 'God, Unity, Liberty', and it was stamped with the military motto 'TODO POR LA PATRIA, JUNTOS, PUEBLO Y FUERZA ARMADA'. I showed it to the correspondents based in El Salvador and suggested that this would see me safely off the bus. They laughed quite a lot.

The Ministry of Defence nearly did not give me the *laisser passer* because my press card was 'out of order'. It was out of date by one year. I thought of the National Union of Journalists, their office in the Grays Inn Road called Acorn House, their fidgety demands for my subscription, their confident proclamation of the recognition of the Association of Chief Police Officers of England and Wales. I talked about the matter for quite a long time with Captain P.A. Luis Mario Aguilar Alfaro. I pointed out that my subscription arrears were usually only cleared in June, two months away. He replied that my credentials were out of order. Then he was distracted by the arrival of an assistant press officer who wanted to show off her new khaki uniform, so I got my *laisser passer.* It carried one of those little passport photos, several years out of date, which to the writer abroad in an interesting part of the world always look a little ominous.

'How do you intend to leave our country?' The customs woman was not very friendly.

'By San Miguel.'

'You can't. That road is closed.'

'But that is the Pan American Highway.'

She explained the events of the previous day. She began to go through my books and papers. *Anna Karenina* passed, despite a reported prejudice against Russian authors. She opened *Donne.* 'Poemas,' she said.

'Yes,' I said, 'about love.'

A dry look. 'You are here simply as a tourist?'

'Yes.'

She looked through the piles of books, notebooks, newspapers, photocopies, the usual working junk of a journalist. *Viva Mexico!* by Charles Macomb Flandrau, *The Catechism of Christian Doctrine, Scarlet and Black, The Country Between Us* by Carolyn Forché, *Il Principito* by Saint-Exupéry, *Guatemalan Indian Costumes.*

'Your profession?'

'Barrister.'

'You understand our situation?'

She began to flick through a notebook, *libreta espiral*, marked No. 8 on the cover: 'Heads too decomposed to know the sex. Many died. Sixty cadavers one morning.' This was only page two.

'You know our condition?'

'Yes.' It was not clear whether she repeated the question because she was concerned about my lack of information or because she was emphasizing her suspicions. But she remained courteous. She was bound, as so many people are in Latin America, by the hispanic tradition of courtesy, by social obligation.

'Enjoy yourself.'

I was free to go. As I climbed up the slope, carrying my books, I looked back to the desk beneath the high roof. The woods and slopes pressed down around the customs post. She was still standing there, staring after me. There was no one else to attend to. The *abogado* from England would be remembered for a while. I was reminded looking at her as she stood alone of how lightly Salvadorans accept danger.

From Anguiatú I drove to Metapán in the back of an open pick-up. By now it was late afternoon. Long shadows lay on the hills, chilling the collected heat that rose from the tarmac. There was no sign of the teeming population. The hills looked quite empty. In the truck there was a woman dressed in red with her husband and a small girl, and another woman, a stray pilgrim from Esquipulas. After a while the empty hills began to give the impression that they were looking on; one was being watched. This impression was supplied simply by the knowledge that I was in El Salvador. This was not Mexico or Panama.

Uniformed men with guns stopped the pick-up and demanded to see papers. Their shoulder flashes said Border Police. As we drove on they started to insult each other roughly. One snatched a cigarette from the other's mouth. The open hostility was unusual. I wondered what was making them so irritable.

The pick-up stopped again to let a country woman clamber up. She was brown-skinned and blue-eyed. She had a kind face, although I did not notice it for a while for fear of looking at her too closely. Beneath the face she had two throats. The original throat was pushed to one side. Beside it a lump had formed which had grown in time parallel to her original throat and which, from her chin to her shoulder, was just as thick. It must have been the world's largest goitre. We all avoided her gaze. She did not mind. Her expression remained kind. She was accustomed to being ignored by strangers. She said nothing. Perhaps she could not speak.

The stray pilgrim, a heavy elderly woman, was perched on the wheel hub. There were no seats in the pick-up. Twice she refused my offer of a seat on my case. We talked about her pilgrimage, about Santa Ana, about my journey. Nobody mentioned 'the situation'. Away from the hills, the wind rushing over the edge of the truck grew hot again. The woman in red crouching opposite me allowed her foot to touch mine. She had gold teeth and thick black hair. She would have been beautiful but for her jaw which was large and slack. Her husband leaned forward and noticed her foot and suddenly stopped smiling at me. Our feet separated. Then her daughter fell over and we all laughed. There was an innocence and happiness in her face when she saw that I admired her child—which was quite different from the calculating friendliness there before. It made her look five years younger.

In the boredom of riding day after day on a crowded, uncomfortable bus, watching the behaviour of the women and children of Central America became more and more of a pleasure. The children were frequently polite, obedient and curious, at first alarmed by the sight of a *gringo*, later trusting. I remember two of them on an evening ride in Guatemala playing some version of 'I-Spy' for an hour. The girl—quick-witted, younger, the dominant partner—evaded the sharp nudges of her larger brother which were directed at her whenever she broke the rules. She broke the rules at

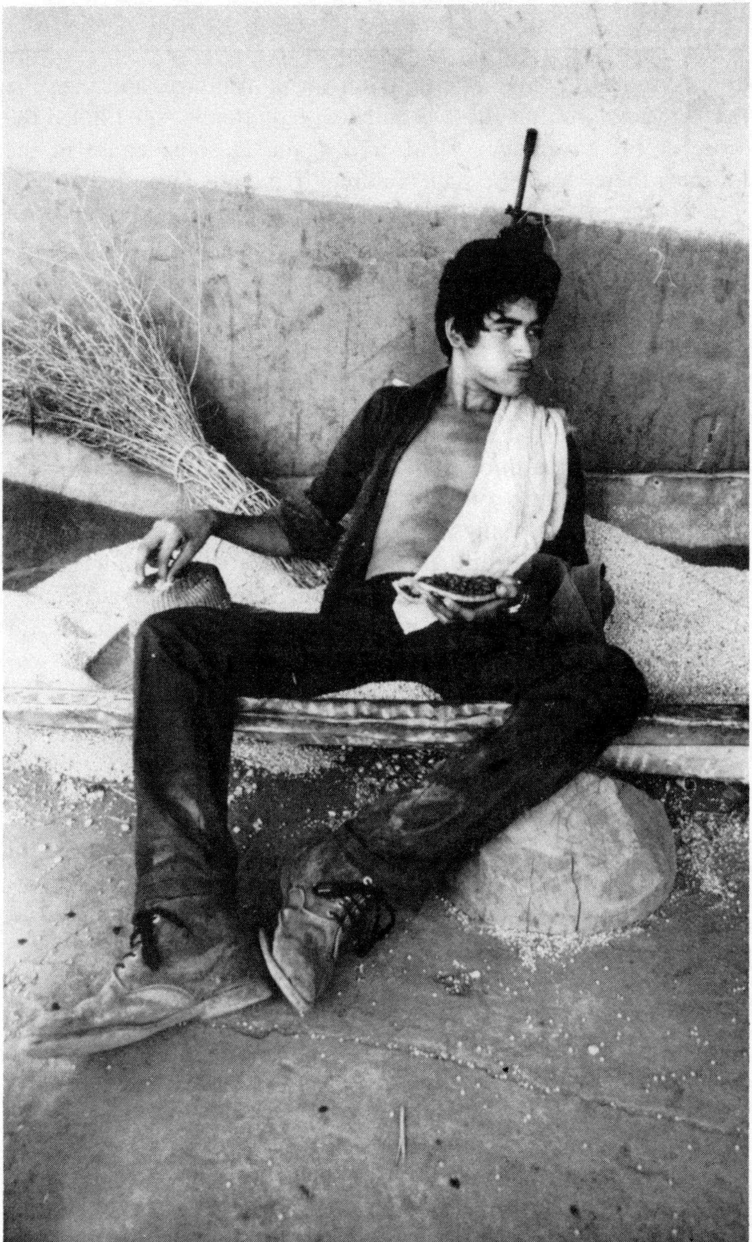

every opportunity and always to her own advantage, and then she fiddled the score. But she was quick-witted after all: she fiddled the score to his advantage. Again and again, at some pause in the journey, there would be such children, frequently looked after by a thin woman in a thin cheap dress whose graceful movements were a constant solace in solitude. I grew to love the cheap colours and materials which these women wore so well, their large eyes and modesty and nervous strength, their endless pride and care of their appearance however tired they might be, and their remarkable lack of self-consciousness. While quite aware of their easy power to attract, they also seemed aware of its unimportance. They played the game very well, to win, and then got on with life. Life, after some years, altered their appearance. Equally lovable were the slatternly, fat women, their bulging rolls of tummy barely contained by the same cheap materials that clung so sparely to the thin women, their breasts hanging out carelessly for their children to take, their confidence that they could impose the necessary area of privacy with a single glance. The thin women were usually aunts or mothers of one child. The fat women were the same women three children later.

At Metapán the pick-up stopped at a bus station. I crossed the road and people called out in English, amused to see a *gringo* in this part of the world. 'Not many *gringos* in town,' they said mockingly. The newspaper seller, an intelligent-looking European, though unshaven and unkempt, made a joke of selling me a Spanish paper. The news that a *gringo* had arrived from Anguiatú spread up and down the street. Things must be looking up. 'The situation' was improving. The bus from Metapán to Santa Ana was an express and only stopped when ordered to do so by the heavily-armed soldiers dug in at every road bridge.

I spent that night at Santa Ana's best hotel. The war which has wrecked the economy of El Salvador has done so more obviously in this once pleasant town than in other parts of the country. Paul Theroux visited it in 1978 and described Santa Ana as 'a perfect place . . . perfect in its slumber, its coffee-scented heat, its jungly plaza, and in the dusty elegance of its old buildings.' Five years had changed all that. The hotel was run by a family of Spanish refugees from General Franco. They were from Bilbao but had not seen the city since 1938. They had locked their hotel up like a fortress, and it remained locked up like that all day. I rang the bell in the steel door, and eventually a very, very old man in a greyish-white starched jacket opened it a crack.

'Do you have a room?'

'*Securo.*'

I dined alone in a dining-room that seated seventy-five. The building had been handsomely planned with stone floors and vaulting and a spacious arcade to cool the rooms. But the money had long since run out. There was little money in Santa Ana. The dust and the insects were breaking through every chip in the plaster.

The Basques accustomed themselves eventually to the unexpected presence of a visitor in their hotel. The mother spoke of Franco—'You will never know how many bottles of champagne we drank in this room the night he died.'

Their daughter admired England. Why? 'Because it stood alone in the war against Hitler for one year. And because it is always raining there. The same weather as Bilbao.' She had never left Salvador but she wore a tee-shirt with the Basque word *Euzkadi* printed on it. She read a lot about Europe. They asked me what I was doing and I said I was a tourist. I could see the daughter did not believe me.

Her mother talked of Barcelona when *los rojos* defended it. Their friends now appeared to be of the right—businessmen, officials. They had a hotel. They were against the *subversivos.* The mother said, 'When we came here we never dreamed that one day Spain would be the safe country.' She could not go back. 'My life is here now.' She did not say it but she could hardly have dreamed when she left Spain that *los rojos* would become as much of a threat to her as Franco had been.

They told me it was safe to go out at night. I had heard of a casino in Santa Ana and I thought that I might spend a few *colones* there. There was very little lighting in the streets around the Plaza Mayor. Eventually I found a bar which had not closed and sat down to write my notebook. I was vaguely aware of several men at another table, watching me. The beer, added to the wine at dinner, made me feel rather sleepy. I started to wander back across the plaza in what I regarded as the probable direction of the hotel.

'Venga! Venga!' Outside the heavily-defended police station on one side of the plaza, which was now quite deserted, the three men

from the bar were sitting in the back of a truck. One of them snapped his fingers impatiently. They were dressed as civilians. They were quite confident that I would obey them. Somewhere in the darkness beyond the edge of the plaza there was a single shot. 'Papers,' they said. 'Who are you?' Something seemed to have happened to the

hispanic tradition of courtesy. I remembered that I carried no papers.

'You're not a member of the press are you?' said one.

'The *international* press?' said another. They asked again for my papers. I tried to look helpful. There was a small plastic wallet in my pocket. I pulled it out. It contained the record slip for my travellers' cheques. At least it was typed. The light outside the police station was not very good. I handed the wallet over and said it was my English identity card. One of them began to study it carefully.

'It is dangerous here at night,' said another. 'There is a curfew. Why are you out? Where are you staying?'

I tried without success to remember the name of the hotel.

'Where is it?'

I pointed in what I hoped was the right direction.

The first man brandished the wallet at me. 'If this is your identity card, where is your name?' I peered at the record slip. Ah yes, my name. He read it out carefully. 'Thomas . . . Cook. Very well, *Señor* Cook must return at once to his hotel.' He was behaving very foolishly. I agreed and set off in the wrong direction. They called me back. They had to redirect me. My behaviour could hardly have been more conspicuous.

There were more shots as I left the plaza. A file of police started to walk past me. They kept close to the wall and checked the bolts of their rifles. They were stalking along the street as though it were a jungle. Is this what Paul Theroux had meant? Their behaviour seemed to me rather exaggerated. Then there was a blaze of light ahead. An armoured car had come round a corner and was now lighting up the wall of a house. The police stopped moving. Seeing a lighted doorway to the right I decided to take refuge, passed through and found myself happily in 'the Casino'. A waiter came forward to welcome me, everything was reassuringly normal at last. At the end of a long corridor I could see palm trees, a bar, men dressed in well-cut suits sitting on stools, more waiters. There was music playing somewhere.

Then it all started to go wrong. The welcoming waiter, another very old man, was not so welcoming.

'What do you want?' he said.

'A drink.'

'But not here, *señor.* This a club.'

'This *is* the casino?'

'Yes, *señor,* the *Casino,* a private club.' He looked quite distressed. I should not have been allowed to pass the door. 'Please, *señor,* you must leave.' Outside the firing had started again.

'Of course,' I said. Who did he think I was? A private club, just like in London. Rules, waiters, old customs. One never entered a private club uninvited. I was concerned to reassure the waiter. No one had noticed me come in. He looked so grateful as I stepped back into the darkness and disturbance outside.

I read later that four soldiers had been killed in *un ataque terrorista* that night. Three decapitated bodies had been recovered and subsequently recognized. Three other corpses had been taken to the Santa Ana mortuary and named.

When I got back to the hotel the Basques also looked relieved. They had heard the firing. 'Most unusual,' they said, as they locked us all in yet again. I slept badly that night. It was terribly hot but I did not want to open the window. And so the day which had started amid the candles and hymns of the Indian shrines ended in a sealed bedroom with the noise of army lorries changing gear, occasional shouts and, when there was no other sound, the sound of running feet.

Photographs of El Salvador are by Don McCullin.

GRANTA

Manlio Argueta

A Day in the Life in El Salvador

6.00 a.m.

We're from Chalatenango, in a place about ten blocks from town. That's why we call it the Kilometre. The people here like to sing. And laugh over nothing. Almost all of us are poor but we don't consider poverty a disgrace. Nor is it something to be proud of. It never mattered to us that life has been the same for many years. No major changes. We all know each other and treat each other as equals. Someone who owns a cart is no different from the man who owns nothing but a machete.

José is my husband. He plays guitar and sings *rancheras,* popular political songs that are so good they drive you a little crazy. Or else he sings love songs; for instance, 'Look how I yearn for your love' is his favourite. Or maybe it's merely the one he knows best.

We like the *rancheras* because they have pretty lyrics and everyone can understand them. It wasn't so long ago that we started singing the new songs: around the time that the boys arrived, the ones who used to accompany the priest. Those songs were called protest songs.

Yes, but lately everything has changed.

Once upon a time the priests would come and hold Mass in the Detour's chapel, giving us hope: 'Hang on,' they would say, 'hang on just a little longer.' They'd tell us not to worry, that heaven was ours, that on earth we should live humbly but that in the kingdom of heaven we would be happy. That we shouldn't care about worldly things. And then when we'd tell the priests that our children were dying from worms, they'd recommend prayer or else claim that we hadn't given them their yearly purge. But despite the purges we gave them, the children would die. The worms—so very many of them—would eat the children from within and then would have to be expelled through their noses and mouths. The priest would tell us to be patient. And when we took our children to him—when we brought the skeletons with eyes—he'd remind us that we mustn't forget to bring our little offerings.

One of my children died on me that way—from dehydration and from being eaten up by worms. We were fortunate, though, in having lost only one because of disease.

'Well, what's the matter with your baby?'

'Ay, look dear Father. All of a sudden he shits water.'

'Maybe the milk you gave him was bad.'

'No, Father, he never drinks milk.'

'Well?'

'It's worms, Father.'

'You need to give him a purge quickly and then feed him properly. What are you giving him to eat?'

'During the day he has a little drink made from corn flour and at night sugar water.'

'And how old is your baby, Lupe?'

'Nine months already, Father.'

'You ought at least to give him cheese; if you don't have milk, cheese is a good substitute.'

'In the shop at the Detour you can buy some milk, which is the same thing, but we can't afford such luxuries. Besides, José's boss has told him—which we know to be true—that it isn't good for them to get accustomed to drinking milk or eating meat.'

'Did the landowner tell you that?'

'Yes, and it's something everyone knows.'

'Well, what is there to do? May God's will be done.'

'It would be good of you to sprinkle him with holy water, Father.'

'But, my dear child, you forgot to bring his godfather.'

'Tomorrow there'll be plenty of time to find him, Father. I thought you could recommend some medicine, you see. I would have wanted to give him a purge made from the *altamiza* plant but I'd have to go to the gully for it and José isn't here.'

'My dear child, I'd get the *altamiza* for you, but I know it isn't going to cure him. In cases like this only worm-medicine helps.'

'And where can we get the medicine, Father?'

'That's your business, my child. But why don't you bring his godfather tomorrow and we'll baptize the baby, just in case....'

And the priest would tell me to keep the faith, and that if the child was not saved it would be because of someone's carelessness. And that Christ had died this way, and that he would sprinkle holy water on the child so that he'd go straight to heaven without having to pass through purgatory.

Then all of a sudden the priests began to change. They started urging us to join cooperatives. To help each other, to share profits. It's wonderful to help someone, to live in peace with everyone, to get to know each other, to wake up before sunrise and go to work with the children, herding pigs and selling eggs for a good price. We started taking the eggs to town instead of to Don Sebas's shop because Don Sebas pays next to nothing. Everything was starting to get better.

They also changed the sermons and stopped saying Mass in a jargon that nobody understood. Mass became a serious affair: the priests were starting to open our eyes and ears. One of them would always repeat to us: 'To get to heaven first we must struggle to create a paradise on earth.' We began to understand that it was better this way. And we would ask them why the priests before them forced us to conform. Forget the previous ones, the younger priests would say.

What matters is that our children don't die. To let a child die is the worst sin one can commit. At the first sign of illness we were told to look for the priest. And so we started being less afraid.

A meeting was held once—I don't know where, I'm not even sure when—but after it the young priests, who began visiting our own houses, told us that religion was no longer the same. The priests arrived in working clothes, and we saw that they, like us, were people of flesh and blood—only better dressed. They'd descend to the Kilometre and would come to see how we were living. How are you doing? How many children do you have? How much are you earning? They even taught us to manage money and how to get a good price for our eggs, chickens or pigs.

We knew how to manage money—we weren't stupid—but as we never had any surplus, we had no money to manage. Now at the end of the year we had something left over for toys: a car, a plastic ball or marbles.

Back then, something else occurred that had never happened before: the Guards started appearing in our neighbourhood. When we saw them we'd spread the word: because the Guards are very strict, and you can't walk around with, say, a machete strapped to your wrist because it's certain you'll then get a whipping or else be fined more than any poor person could ever pay.

But now, if we were caught carrying a machete, it wasn't enough for us to show our identification papers: the Guards wanted to know if we were going to Mass. And they wanted to know what the priests were saying at Mass. And at first we didn't understand anything. Why recount every detail?

Yes, we'd say, we're going to Mass and you should see how good this priest is, Officer. He isn't like the others.

But they weren't really interested. They didn't like the priests and they only wanted to frighten us from seeing them. They'd call the priests names: bastards, fairies in robes, teaching us disobedience. And then they'd point their guns at us, and tell us that we'd better stay away from the chapel.

Although the Guards hated the priests, they wouldn't dare touch one, of course, because deep down they were afraid of them. Like us, the Guards are Catholics, and almost all of them are peasants, except that they've had education and we haven't. They've had schooling, because to be a Guard requires training.

They were also afraid of the priests because the priests wouldn't stay quiet; they scolded the Guards. Why did they go around doing cruel things along the roads? They weren't getting paid to give people a hard time. But it always went in one ear and out the other. And a few days later they'd be up to their old tricks again, treating people badly.

One day they dared the worst. Something that made us feel like dying: the priest was found half dead on the road to the Kilometre. They had disfigured his face, had beaten him all over. Someone was passing that way and saw a naked man moaning in a ditch. They'd stuck a stick up his anus and it was there still. The priest's voice could barely be heard. A little farther up the road, his robe was hanging all ripped. When they came to tell us we all went together. Right there we lifted him on to the road to wait for a vehicle that would pick him up. And there I realized we had become hardened, because no one grieved or cried. We said 'poor thing' only because he was a priest; something had happened that we had never imagined. It was a nightmare. We noticed that the saints could descend from heaven, that they too could be toppled. After that, nothing shocked us: all that remained was for it to rain fire and for cats to chase dogs. They found the priest's jeep farther up the road, burned, in another ditch. As if it had ignited itself. That's all we needed in this life. From that moment on, any sin was going to seem petty.

Still it must be said that those young priests had accomplished a great deal. With them, we began to change, and the change was exciting. We learned a number of new words, new ideas. Like rights: the right to health care, to food, and to schooling for our children. And if it hadn't been for the priests, we wouldn't have found out about these things. They opened our eyes, nothing more. Later we were on our own. We had to rely on our own resources.

We learned to look out for ourselves. The young priest who had been wounded in the anus didn't come back. Later we learned that he'd gone abroad because he feared so much for his life. But he had already helped us: we had managed to grow a little in stature. Our eyes had been opened. And José, my husband, became good friends with all the other young priests. And it was because of them that we joined the cooperatives, for which we had to be better at raising chickens; every egg laid had to be hatched—and forget about eating the little pigs. We had to let them grow. And that was how we came to have four dozen chickens—and thus more eggs to sell to the cooperative—and good, meaty pigs.

Sometimes people would come from the city to sing at the church—songs about poverty. And there was always something about those songs that reminded us of the young priest who had almost been killed.

6.30 a.m.

I am happy today, and it's because my husband José stayed home last night to sleep, even though he had to leave around five in the morning. And maybe that's why I woke up thinking about these things.

I remember snuggling up to him, hugging him. The warmth of José. Being next to him without talking, close to him, to the sweat of his shirt, my face against it, his wet shirt. There's a humidity that clings to clothes after a hard day's work.

Usually José doesn't come home: he sleeps in the bush, like almost all the men from our region. And I also don't see him during the day because he's working. The plantation during the day, the bush at night: it was because of the murder of our son, Justino. After

Justino's death they then came to threaten José, and it was clear that if he didn't leave and go into hiding he, too, would be a dead man.

What was the poor man to do? He didn't want to go. He wanted to remain with the rest of the people because already so many of the men were going into the bush. But they convinced him. So did I. 'Do it for your children,' I told him. 'The three little ones we have.'

But last night he did come to sleep. Taking precautions, he appeared in the back garden. Pijiriche, our dog, first discovered him. And I thought the dog was playing with the chickens. And he left just after coffee.

'The tortillas are from noon yesterday,' I told him, serving him a little frying pan of beans.

'Don't worry. Don't go to the trouble of making them by hand so early in the morning just to please me.'

'I'm sorry that you don't have fresh tortillas to eat, especially now that you can't come home for lunch or even for supper.' While I talked he was looking at me in the candlelight. Because it wasn't dawn yet. At this time of the year the sun rises late: at five you still can't see your own fingers. You have to light a candle because it's hard to talk in the dark. Not to see another person's mouth moving, not to see their eyes: it's like talking with the dead.

'I wonder where I've left the matches.'

'Forget it. Daylight is coming soon,' he said.

'I'm still going to make a fire so you can leave all warm inside. I'm going to make coffee and you're not going to eat cold beans.'

'Don't worry about it. You have enough work during the day.' That's how he is: he won't get upset about anything any more. He used to be a little difficult, but now he's changed. And while I watched him eating in the candlelight, I kept quiet, not saying a word. It was time to say goodbye.

'I won't be back for three days,' he said. And then, 'That's why I came home to sleep last night.'

And I didn't ask him anything. Because right at the moment when I was about to ask him something, our youngest child began to cry.

Life gets harder and harder. They say that there are many of us in this country. Hordes of poor people everywhere. But what can we do? What are we guilty of? It's important to be aware that we are poor, José tells me repeatedly. 'And what good is that?' I ask him. And he replies that only that way will we become strong enough to claim what we deserve. Everything else is a farce. We must always insist on our rights.

José, I must admit, has opened my eyes. I don't complain as much as before, because I have that awareness of being poor that José talks about. No one is so hardened as to pretend not to understand.

Lately, José has learned many things. The poor man is interested in the problems of the community. I say it that way, because with all the work he has to do, he is still interested in others. 'One has to help people, so that they themselves will recognize their own problems,' he tells me.

And I like this quality in him. Others also like it. They know he's looking out for the good of everyone. All the time. For instance, when I say: 'I pray that nothing happens to you, José. It's enough that I've lost Justino....' He says to me, 'Don't worry, if we failed to act, then we would all be in real trouble.'

'Yes, I won't worry,' I tell him.

But, as I say, one is not made of stone. Justino's death destroyed me, why should I lie? It left me feeling like a piece of wood. It was not a matter of being cowardly, not in the least. But after the blood of our son was spilled, we felt so much fright. I told myself: this is too much, I have lost Justino. I know why he joined the struggle. He used to talk to me about those things in a way that perhaps not even José can. So I told myself: forget this blood of my blood, even though I'd get a lump in my throat saying it. But I'm not the one who's going to cry; I'm not going to give our enemies the satisfaction of seeing any tears fall from my eyes. They'll pay. That's what I told myself. Sooner or later. They'll pay. That's what I told myself. No human being must suffer what those assassins did to my son. And no one who is a human being would do it. That's what I told myself.

9.30 a.m.

Pijiriche, our dog, has seemed nervous. He runs underneath the stool, and in a little while he jumps up again and darts desperately all over the place. I know it's not fleas, because only a few days ago I washed him with DDT.

And then the authorities appeared. Pijiriche had got their scent. These sad people don't even ask permission. I hear the crash of the door and all of a sudden they're inside.

'What do you want?'

'Does Adolfina Guardado live here?' they ask me. 'We want to know if this is the house of Adolfina Guardado. We're looking for her.'

'No Adolfina Guardado lives here. My name is Guadalupe Fuentes. It is Guadalupe Fuentes who lives here. What can I do for you?'

These men have high leather boots, halfway up their calves, and bandolier belts. But the worst are those monsters they carry on their shoulders. The famous automatics. These people are very serious. They're studying to be President. And how can they fail, with monsters that shoot a ton of lead a minute, as José says. If they hit you in the leg, they rip the leg right off; if they hit you in the arm, the arm is blown away—they tear the arm right off. So how can they fail?

'The person we're looking for is a relative of yours—we know that—and her name is Adolfina.'

Adolfina is my granddaughter. It would be better to pretend I don't understand: maybe they've made a mistake. How could these people be asking about my granddaughter? She's only a child. Why weren't they asking for me or José? Because, after all, adults can be bad but children can't. When did they decide to start punishing innocent children?

But they tell me that there is no mistake: it's definitely Adolfina whom they want.

'She's over at the Detour buying salt and a little cheese for the baby.'

'Which Detour?'

'At the shop of Don Sebas.'

How to talk to them? I can see them sweating from the hot sun. The sun is oppressive. And they've come on foot from who knows where. They always leave their jeep far away: it's a custom they have. They love to walk because that way the people can see them better, showing off their tall bodies, their uniforms the colour of cow dung, and their big automatic monsters. They're all tall and strong. Not by

ESCUADRON

chance: they're well fed. And they always travel in pairs.

'We'll wait for her, then.'

And they stand waiting in the little hallway. One of them wipes his brow. The other looks at the banana trees outside, searching through the bunches of bananas.

'Sit down if you want.'

They say no.

Something sticks in my throat. They always claim self-defence. They kill and that's the end of it, then and there. Self-defence. This is serious business.

'Perhaps you would like a little drink of water?' They pretend not to hear me. 'It's cool. You can even see the red jug sweating. Water, full of life. Fresh, cool water from the well.'

These people always bring bad luck. That's why I've offered them water, to drive a little of the bad luck away. Besides, one shouldn't refuse water to anyone. But they don't say a word.

'That woman hasn't come yet.'

I hear them speaking in low voices. I explain: 'She has three children with her and the youngest is still a babe in arms. She must be having trouble getting here.'

José has advised me many times about the authorities: you must be respectful. You must never show that you think they are our enemies. Don't provoke them. Don't run from them, or else they'll shoot. Especially if they want something. They scrutinize you so as to take advantage of you. Don't fall into their traps. You can achieve all this without hurting yourself, that's what José tells me.

12 noon

Along the road, Adolfina appears. She is singing, and is followed by Benjamin, Ester and Moncho.

'At last, she's here.'

'They're looking for you,' I shout to her before they can surprise her. 'Hurry up,' I tell the children who have remained behind.

Pijiriche leaps.

'There comes my granddaughter,' I say. Talking to myself. Nothing more because there she is, opening the door, with a pile of tortillas on her head. Balancing tortillas on her head.

'Hurry up, girl.'

The official takes out his notebook.

Asking: What's your name, both paternal and maternal last names? Who is your father? What do you do for a living? Where have you come from? How did you get to the Kilometre? Are you in the Federation of Christian Farmworkers? Since when? How old are you? What have you come to do at your grandmother's place?

'You're Private Martínez, aren't you?'

'Can you believe this child?'

And the other agent: 'Didn't I tell you about these people?'

'My mother and grandmother have told me about you. You went to my old grandfather's house.'

And he: 'I've heard enough from you. You have confused me with someone else. We're the ones asking questions: next thing you'll be pulling out a notebook and taking notes.'

The other: 'It's just that these people aren't interested in working things out anymore.'

And he: 'Stop tempting me because already I'm capable of zapping this child on her dirty face. Isn't it true that you don't even bathe? Isn't it true that you fuck Communists?'

And I: 'Sergeant, up to now we've been respectful. Although we're humble, we know how to be polite. I would like you to respect us, to finish whatever it is you are doing without insults. You must take into account that if the child questions you, it's because she has suffered much. Her father has been imprisoned, her mother almost lost an eye from a whack the authorities gave her, and then they go to the child's grandfather's house. Imagine what she has had to put up with.'

And Adolfina: 'You people don't put too fine a point on anything. Look how you kicked my mother, and I know that you, Mr Private, had something to do with that. I know it very well, and what's more, I know your mother, Doña Patricia. Don't try to tell me it's a lie. I am the daughter of Helio Hernández. Where is he?'

And I, grabbing her by the hand, press her against me: 'Child, don't be impudent, respect the gentlemen and answer their questions. You understand, Mr Sergeant, she's just a child and still feeling her tragedy. We aren't made of stone, and sometimes we behave badly....

You must tell us the purpose of your visit. Since you've been here you haven't told us anything, and, well, that's what creates problems. Because she is, as you know, just a child, still in the care of her family. Be understanding, Mr Sergeant.'

And he: 'Be reasonable and you'll soon see that you won't be any the worse for it. Tell your granddaughter to cooperate with us for everyone's sake. We'll do our job and then you'll have a good time of it.'

'Well, then, tell me what you want from me.'

And it seems to me that their intentions aren't bad. Even though one can never know with these people.

12.10 p.m.

We want to talk to you alone.

'We have found the body of a wounded man, and as you passed that road earlier, we thought you may have noticed him.'

'I haven't seen anyone.'

'You passed that place at nine o'clock.'

'Which place?'

'Where we found the wounded man. They told us that you were on that road. And then the wounded man mentioned a name that sounded like Adolfina.'

'But I don't know what you're talking about.'

'The wounded man will not tell us his name and it turns out that he doesn't even have identification papers. And so we said, well, let's look for the Adolfina he mentioned, and as you are the only one with that name around here...'

'But you say you're not very sure?'

'There you are. We're not very sure, otherwise we wouldn't be asking you. Everything would have been cleared up at once.'

'And you, what do you want?'

'To see if you will go with us, in case you know him.'

'Wouldn't it be better to take him to the hospital, if he is as wounded as you say?'

'We came to get you. Leave those tortillas you're carrying and let's go.'

And I tell them: 'No, what for? If that wounded man knows Adolfina he must know me too. It would be better if I went and she remained with the children. In fact, better if we all went.'

And they: 'Don't get involved. We don't have time for this and the man is several miles away and why do you want to involve these children in such a serious legal affair.'

And I, knowing them, say Adolfina is not leaving this house, is not going to take even one step alone. You will understand that she is a child and that she has been entrusted to me: 'She's my granddaughter. I can't let anything happen to her while she's in my care. Take me. I can walk long distances as well as you and I will leave the children with my neighbour. I could recognize the man if he is from around here. I know everyone—unless he's from some other place, in which case he isn't our problem and there's been some mistake. You yourselves admit that possibility. You must understand my reasons: I'm in mourning, as you can see: not long ago a loved one of mine died, and that's why I'm nervous and I won't let the child leave. I'd rather you shot me, if that's what makes you happy, but my granddaughter will not budge from here. You will have to kill us all.'

I didn't even know what I was saying. I could only hear the voice of Adolfina: 'Wait, Grandmother, maybe we can all go together. Don't get that way. We're all going. Isn't that right gentlemen? Isn't that right—that all of us can go?'

Meanwhile I was gathering strength, because I wasn't going to allow her to be taken from me after what happened to Justino, by men who didn't seem well-intentioned to me at that moment. They, not budging an inch, were looking at me strangely, thinking perhaps this old woman is crazy—what's the matter with her? But nothing would stop me. My granddaughter is not going anywhere, I shouted until even Pijiriche began barking at me. Adolfina started hugging me, still without putting down the pile of hot tortillas. 'Don't be like this, Grandmother'—she was on the verge of tears. 'Don't be like this.'

Justino would condemn me if I were to let her go with those men. And thinking of him, I gathered more strength. They will have to kill me first; they will have to kill all of us.

Until finally they spoke: 'This old woman is going to have a fainting fit.'

'What a scandalous old woman.'

And the man took out a little radio, pulled out the antenna and began talking with numbers, asking if it were possible to bring the wounded man. Speaking into the strange gadget, asking if the jeep could come this way with the man.

2 p.m.

Right then we saw a cloud of dust over the fences. 'Here comes the jeep with the man,' Private Martínez says—well, that's what Adolfina told me his name was. And it stopped in front. Four guardsmen got out dragging the man, pulling him as if he were a sick animal. He was so disfigured, you couldn't even see what he looked like because of all the blood covering his face and drenching his shirt and trousers. 'Bring him over here to see if they know him.'

It wasn't until I got close that I realized it was you, that it was your face covered with blood. And I could see that one of your eyelids was tattered, because the eye was showing. It was hanging out. And then they asked Adolfina: 'Do you know him?'

'How am I going to know him if you bring him bathed in blood? You can't even see his face. I don't understand how you could believe that anyone could recognize this man.' That's what Adolfina told them. She shouted it instead of speaking it, always addressing the one she called Private Martínez.

And that's when I started having my doubts that I knew you. I don't know you and I don't want to know you. When I see your trousers, my head is filled with nightmares. I don't know you, I don't know you. From where do I get the idea that I don't know you? Who instructed me to deny you, or was it my hope that it really wasn't you? Who could have had that exact pair of trousers, even though they were barely recognizable with all the blood on them? And why were they looking for Adolfina and not for me? I could have identified you. What was the motive? Why that torture? Where does this evil come from among men who also have mothers, fathers, children, sisters? Who perverted them and watered down their blood? Theirs cannot be the blood of the race, nor of Christians, nor of poor people.

Adolfina's voice interrupts and tells me: 'Grandma, what is

happening to you?' And the voice of the authorities says: 'Perhaps you know him?'

My legs were then on the point of giving out. I felt the colour drain from my skin.

'Do you know this man?'

My body turns to ice. You have been transformed into a piece of meat bitten by dogs. I see your body through the rips in your clothes, looking as if they had grabbed you, and growling at you, pulled off chunks of flesh, sucking your blood. These vampires, sons of a hundred thousand whores.

Then I said No. It had to be a no without any quavering in my voice, without the least trace of hesitation. And at that moment your good eye opened, the one they had left you, which perhaps for that reason you had kept closed so as not to talk, so as not to be recognized. Your coffee-coloured eyes, the same ones I had seen for more than thirty years.

You are you, José, because that eye doesn't look like any other. You are you, I am sure of that, even if you hide from me. And God illuminated my mind, maybe, because I remembered you saying to me, 'If at any time you detect danger to yourself or our family, don't hesitate to deny me.' And you made me swear; I never believed it would come to this. 'Because, for us, we're always in danger. Remember Justino. Remember Helio, and remember all the others. We cannot afford to sacrifice blood needlessly.' That's what you told me.

I saw that there was no other way out. And that's why you were able to open your eye once I had denied you, because I had already done the most difficult thing. I took it as a greeting, as if you were saying, 'Thank you, Lupe' with the coffee-coloured eye that until that moment had remained shut.

I have not failed you, José. I understand that you were saying goodbye when you opened your eye, and that, besides greeting me, you were expressing your pride in me, seeing me standing with my arm around the shoulders of your granddaughter. I know that you are standing only because they're holding you up. You wouldn't have wanted to come back here and yet you still had the strength to say goodbye. As they say: Behave yourself, don't faint, stay with me because I had promised to sacrifice my blood for a just cause. In those moments I can see that you are keeping your word and you can see that I am keeping mine. I promise you, I will be true to you.

Private Martínez: 'Do you know him or don't you?'

I: 'No, I don't know who he could be.'

Private Martínez: 'We know that your granddaughter is going around getting mixed up in foolishness. You just saw how she misbehaved with me a while ago.'

I: 'I don't know what my granddaughter has been up to. I only know that she is a child who has ideas and ambitions that we old people don't have because we're half dead. We have allowed you to kill us slowly, but we've come to our senses while it's not too late. My granddaughter is alive and you are not going to kill her slowly. I know it, and it is what you don't like. She lives for all of us. She breathes for us. She is being born while we are in our death throes. It is also possible that she will save us.'

I don't know how I uttered these words. I had to close my eyes. I had to close my eyes to be able to speak. So as not to see you, José, so your inspiration could reach me better.

And I remember you, José, running behind the oxen along the road full of holes, the oxen that had escaped with the cart. I remember you running in your rubber boots. The cart was coming down on top of you—you eluded it—and still holding the stick in your hand you kept after the oxen. And we screaming in the cart.

That was when we had a cart.

When we weren't so poor.

We had two oxen and a cow, but then bad times came and we decided to sell them and to buy a sliver of land with the money. It's best to work on the land, even if one has to use one's own hands; that's what you used to tell me.

And we haven't done badly. We have food to eat and a spot to be buried in, at least. A few chickens that produce eggs for us and meat to sell. We have friends. Everyone likes us because we have never done any harm to anyone. We are honourable unto death. The neighbourhood knows that. Hard-working people. We live by the sweat of our brow. Everyone knows that. We have barely enough to get by, but we live. We don't wish anything bad to happen to anyone, not even now to Private Martínez.

The only thing we don't have is rights. And as we began to realize this, this place started filling up with the authorities with their automatics. From time to time they come to see how we are behaving, who has to be taken away, who has to be beaten to be taught a lesson.

They want to force us with machetes and at gunpoint into resignation to our miseries. There is a kind of poverty they understand, a poverty they think they can force on us with their guns. And because they can't, they invent their cruelties.

Why do they invent these cruelties? Why do they beat us? Because now we know where we're headed. And they know that we know where we're headed.

We don't brag about it. But we're marching on.

José Guardado accompanies us.

Translated from the Spanish by Bill Brow

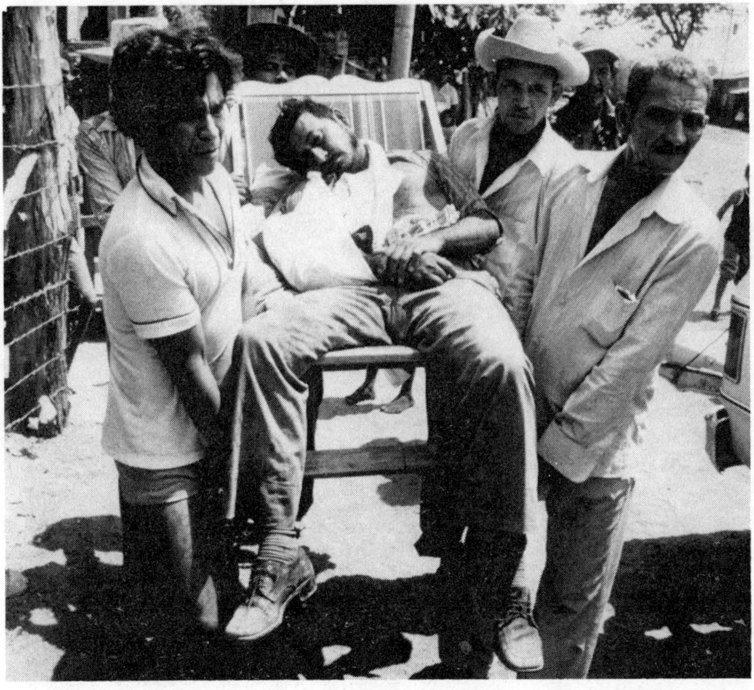

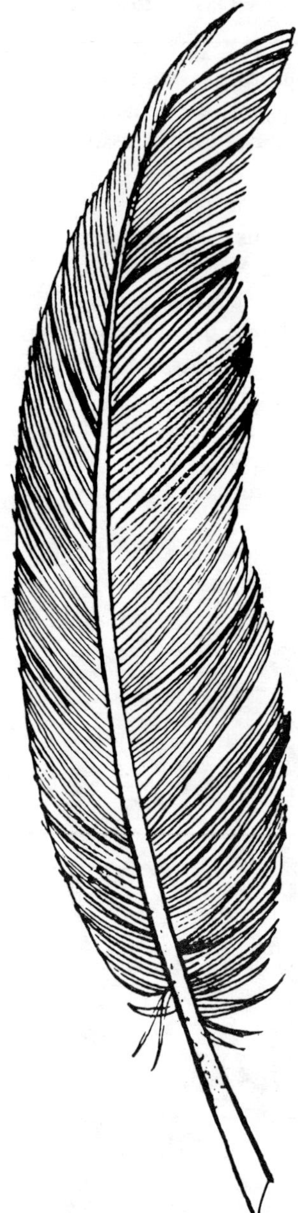

GRANTA

Joan Jara

September 11 1973

September 11, 1973

I wake early as usual. Victor is still asleep, so I get out of bed quietly and wake Manuela who has to get to school early. I go downstairs to put the kettle on and a few minutes later Monica appears, rubbing her eyes and yawning. Everything is normal, within the abnormality in which we are living. It is a cold, cheerless, overcast morning.

We have breakfast, Manuela and I, and set out for school. It isn't far by car, but difficult to reach by public transport even if there were any. Luckily we still have some petrol. We are obviously the only people stirring. Everyone else seems to have decided to stay in bed, except of course the maids, who get up early and go to queue for bread at the bakery on the corner. Monica had come back with the news that Allende's car has already raced down Avenida Colón accompanied by his usual escort, much earlier than usual. People in the bread queue and in the newspaper kiosk were saying that something is afoot.

Manuel de Salas is full of students. There is no sign of the strike here. Only a tiny percentage of families are not supporters of Popular Unity. On the way home I switch on the car radio and the news comes through that Valparaiso has been sealed off and that unusual troop movements are taking place. The trade unions are calling for all workers to assemble in their places of work because this is an emergency, a red alert.

I hurry home to tell Victor. He is already up when I arrive and is fiddling with the transistor radio trying to get Magallanes or one of the other radio stations that support Popular Unity. 'This seems to be it,' we say to each other, 'it has really started.'

Joan Jara was the wife of Victor Jara, the popular and influential Chilean singer of folk and political songs. She lived in Chile until 1973, when Salvador Allende was overthrown in a military coup led by General Pinochet. 'September 11 1973' will be included in her forthcoming book, *Victor,* to be published by Jonathan Cape.

Victor was due that morning to sing at the Technical University, at the opening of a special exhibition about the horrors of civil war and fascism where Allende was going to speak.

'Well, that won't happen,' I said.

'No, but I think I should go anyway. While you go and fetch Manuela from school—because it's better that you're all at home together—I'll make some phone calls to try to find out what is happening.'

As I drove out of the courtyard again, our neighbours were beginning to gather. They were talking loudly and excitedly, already beginning to celebrate. I passed them without glancing at them, but looking back in the mirror, I saw one of the 'ladies' squat down and give the most obscene gesture in Chilean sign-language to my receding back.

Back at the school, I found that instructions had been given for the younger students to go home, while the teachers and older students were to stay behind. I collected Manuela and on the way home, although the reception was bad, we heard Allende speaking on the radio. It was reassuring to hear his voice from the Moneda Palace—but it sounded almost like a speech of farewell.

I found Victor in the studio listening to the radio and together we heard the confusion as almost all the Popular Unity stations went off the air when their aerials were bombed or they were taken over by the military, and martial music replaced Allende's voice:

> This is the last time I shall be able to speak to you...I shall not resign...I will repay with my life the loyalty of the people...I say to you: I am certain that the seeds we have sown in the conscience of thousands and thousands of Chileans cannot be completely eradicated...neither crime nor force are strong enough to hold back the process of social change. History belongs to us, because it is made by the people.

It was the speech of a heroic man who knew he was about to die, but at that moment we heard it only in snatches. Victor was called to the phone in the middle—I could hardly bear to listen to it.

Victor had been waiting for me to come back in order to go out. He had decided that he had to go to his place of work, the Technical University, obeying the instructions of the CUT. Silently he poured out the last can of petrol, reserved for emergencies like this, into the car, and as he did so I saw one of our neighbours, a pilot of the National Airline, look over the balcony of his house and shout something mocking at Victor, who replied with a smile.

It was impossible to say good-bye properly. If we had done so I should have held on to him and never let him go, so we were casual.

'Mamita, I'll be back as soon as I can. You know I have to go. Just be calm.'

'Chao'—and when I looked again, Victor had gone.

Listening to the radio, between one military march and another, I heard the announcements. '*Bando Numero Uno ... Bando Numero Dos*': military orders announcing that Allende had been given an ultimatum to surrender by the commanders of the Armed Forces led by General Augusto Pinochet: that unless he surrendered by midday the Moneda Palace would be bombed.

Monica was preparing the lunch, and Amanda and Carola were playing in the garden, when suddenly there was the thunder and whine of a diving jet plane and then a tremendous explosion. It was like being in the war again. I rushed out to bring the children indoors, closed the wooden shutters and convinced them that it was all a game. But the jets kept on diving and it seemed that the rockets they were firing were falling on the people just above us towards the mountains. I think it was at this moment that any illusions that I may have had died in me: if this was what we were up against, what hope could there be?

Then came the helicopters, low over the treetops of the garden. From the balcony of our bedroom I saw them, hovering like sinister insects, raking Allende's house with machine-gun fire. High above, towards the cordillera, another plane circled. We could hear the high whine of its engine for hours on end—the control plane, perhaps?

Soon after, the telephone rings. I rush to answer it and hear Victor's voice. 'Mamita, how are you? I couldn't get to the phone before—I'm here in the Technical University. You know what's happening, don't you?'

I tell him about the dive bombers, but that we are all well. 'When are you coming home?'

'I'll ring you later on—the phone is needed now. Chao.'

Then there is nothing to do but to listen to the radio, to the military pronouncements between one march and another. The neighbours are outside on the patio, talking excitedly; some are standing on their balconies to get a better view of the attack on Allende's house; they are bringing out the drinks; one house has even put out a flag.

We listen to the news of the Moneda Palace being bombed and set on fire. We wonder if Allende has survived: there is no announcement about it. A curfew is being imposed. Quena rings to know how we are and I tell her that Victor isn't here, that he has gone to the university. 'Oh, my God!' she exclaims and rings off.

We have to assume now that all the telephones are tapped, but Victor rings about four-thirty. 'I have to stay here. It will be difficult to get back because of the curfew. I'll come home first thing in the morning when the curfew is lifted. Mamita, I love you.'

'I love you too...' but I choke as I say it and he has already hung up.

I did go to bed that night, but of course I couldn't sleep. All around the neighbourhood in the darkness you could hear sudden bursts of gunfire. I waited for morning wondering if Victor was cold, if he could sleep, wherever he was, wishing that he had taken at least a jacket with him, wondering if, as the curfew had been suddenly postponed until later in the evening, perhaps he had left the university and gone to someone's house nearby.

It was late next morning before the curfew was lifted and the maids trooped out to buy bread at the corner shop. But today the queue was controlled by soldiers who butted people with their guns and threatened them. I longed for Victor to come home, to hear the hum of the car as it drew up under the wistaria. I calculated how long it ought to take him to make the journey from the university.... As I waited, I realized that there was no money in the house, so I set out to walk the couple of blocks to the little shop belonging to Alberto, who had always co-operated with the JAP and might be able to change a cheque for me. On my way two trucks zoomed past me. They were packed with civilians armed with rifles and machine guns. I realized that they were our local fascists coming out of their holes into the light of day.

Alberto was very scared, and with reason. In the preceding weeks he had already had a couple of bombs exploding outside his shop. But he was good enough to change a cheque for me and asked after Victor. I hurried home, and on my way, bumped into a friend. By mutual consent she came home with me and didn't leave until several days later. She had been ill the previous day and had not gone to the government department where she worked. Now she was in agony, thinking about what might have happened there and how her colleagues had fared.

Together now we waited, but Victor didn't come. I sat glued to the television, although near to vomiting with what I saw, seeing the faces of the Generals talking about 'eradicating the cancer of Marxism' from the country; hearing the official announcement that Allende was dead; seeing the film of the ruins of the Moneda Palace and of Allende's home, endlessly repeated, with shots of his bedroom, his bathroom—or what remained of them—with an 'arsenal of weapons' which seemed pathetically small considering that his detectives had had to protect him against terrorist attacks. It was only late in the afternoon that I heard that the Technical University had been *reducida*—captured—that tanks had entered the university precincts that morning and that a large number of 'extremists' had been arrested.

My lifeline, although a dubious one because it had ears, was the telephone. I knew that Quena was trying to find out what had happened to Victor, and would be more able to make discreet inquiries than I. I was afraid to act, afraid of identifying Victor before the military authorities. I didn't want to draw attention to him—perhaps anyway he had managed to get out of the university before it was attacked: that was my hope.

Wednesday night passed, another cold night, bitterly cold for September. The bed was large and empty. I slept fitfully and dreamt of Victor's touch, his warm limbs entwined with mine. I woke to empty darkness. I remembered his nightmares.

Next morning, still no news. I tried to phone different people who might know what had happened in the Technical University. Nobody was sure about anything. Then Quena again—she had found out that the detainees from the Technical University had been taken to the Estadio Chile, the big boxing stadium where Victor had sung so often and where the Song Festivals had taken place. She wasn't sure if Victor had been among them; the women, most of them, had been released and had given her the news only they weren't absolutely sure that Victor had been arrested with the rest because they had been separated from the men.

In the afternoon the phone rang. Heart jumping, I ran to answer it. An unknown voice, very nervous, asked for Compañera Joan.

There was a message for me: 'Compañera, you don't know me, but I have a message for you from your husband. I've just been released from the Estadio Chile. Victor is there. He asked me to tell you that you should be calm and stay in the house with the children, that he left the car outside the Technical University in the car park. Maybe someone can fetch it for you. He doesn't think that he will be released from the stadium.'

'Thank you, compañero, for ringing me, but what did he mean by that?'

'That is what he told me to tell you. Good luck, compañera!' and he hung up.

When Quena rang a few minutes later I gave her the news. She began to do everything she could to find out more, to find out what would be the best way of trying to get Victor out. She even went to see Cardinal Silva Henriquez, asking him to intervene. What immobilized me was the fear of identifying Victor, if they had not already done so, his own instructions to me, which I assumed were for the best, and my blind faith in the power and organization of the Communist Party which would, I thought, know the best way of saving people like Victor.

Even now, at this stage, I had no real idea of the horrors that were taking place. We were deprived of news and information, although rumours were rife. A responsible political leader phoned me to tell me that General Prats was advancing from the north with an army—this must be the beginning of the civil war about which we had been warned. (Only later did we learn that General Prats had been imprisoned and that, during the night of 10 September, even before the *coup* really began, there had been a purge of all officers suspected of supporting Allende's government.)

During the short time the curfew was lifted on Friday I decided to make the journey across Santiago to fetch the car. I thought we ought to have it in case we had to leave home in a hurry. It was my first excursion outside our neighbourhood, and in the midday sun everything looked unnaturally normal: the buses were running again; there was food in the shops. The only abnormality was the number of soldiers in the streets, at every corner, but there were plenty of people about, walking hurriedly, their faces emptied of expression. As the bus made its slow way along the Alameda, we passed the Moneda Palace—or rather the shell of it, roped off from the square. Many people were passing up and down in front of it—I suppose with curiosity to see the results of the bombing and the fire—but no one showed any feelings at all, either of rage and sadness or of satisfaction.

Central Station and the stalls outside were as busy as ever. I got off the bus and hesitated on the corner of the side road leading to the Estadio Chile. I stood looking at the crowd of people outside, the guards with their machine guns at the ready. It was impossible to get near it, but anyway, what could I do? I walked the few blocks to the Technical University. The campus and the new modern building were strangely deserted.

And then I realize that the great plate-glass windows and doors are all broken, the façade of the building damaged and bullet-scarred. The car park in front, usually full to overflowing, is empty except for our solitary little car in the middle of it. There must be military guards about, but I don't notice them. I see only an old man sitting on a wall some distance away. I put one foot in front of the other until I reach the car, fumbling for my keys, and I find that I am stepping in a pool of blood which is seeping from under the car; that where there should be a window there is nothing; the car is full of broken glass. I think, 'This can't be ours,' and begin to try the keys to see if they fit. Then I see that the old man is walking towards me.

'Who are you?' he shouts at me.

'This is my car,' I stutter at him. 'This is my husband's car. He left it here.'

'That's all right then,' the old man says. 'I was looking after it for Don Victor. Look, I found his identity card on the ground. You'd better have it,' and he passes it to me.

'But where did all the blood come from, whose blood is it?' I ask.

'Oh, I expect someone knifed a thief who was trying to steal it. A lot of blood has been spilled around here lately. You'd better go as quickly as you can. It's not safe.' And he helps me clean the broken glass from the car seats so that I can drive it, and sees me on my way.

Tuesday, 18 September

About an hour after the curfew is lifted, I hear the noise of the gate being rattled, as though someone is trying to get in. It is still locked. I look out of the bathroom window and see a young man standing outside. He looks harmless, so I go down. He says to me very quietly, 'I am looking for the compañera of Victor Jara. Is this the house? Please trust me—I am a friend,' and he brings out his identity card to show me. 'May I come in for a minute? I need to talk to you.' He looks nervous and worried. He whispers, 'I am a member of the Communist Youth.'

I open the gate to let him in and we sit down in the living room opposite each other.

'I'm sorry, I had to come and find you. I'm afraid I have to tell you that Victor is dead; his body has been found in the morgue. He was recognized by one of the compañeros working there. Please, be brave, you must come with me to see if it is him—was he wearing dark-blue underpants? You must come, because his body has already been there almost forty-eight hours and unless it is claimed they will take him away and bury him in a common grave.'

Half an hour later I found myself driving like a zombie through the streets of Santiago, this unknown young man at my side. Hector, as he was called, had been working in the city morgue for the last week, trying to identify some of the anonymous bodies that were being brought in every day. He was a kind, sensitive young man and he was risking a great deal in coming to find me. As an employee he had a special identity card, and showing it he ushered me into a small side entrance of the morgue, an unprepossessing building just a few yards from the gates of the General Cemetery.

Even in a state of shock, my body continues to function. Perhaps from outside I look very normal and controlled—my eyes continue to see, my nose to smell, my legs to walk....

We go down a dark passageway and emerge into a large hall. My new friend puts his hand on my elbow to steady me as I look at rows and rows of naked bodies covering the floor, stacked up into heaps in the corners, most with gaping wounds, some with their hands still tied behind their backs. There are young and old—there are hundreds of bodies. Most of them look like working people. Hundreds of bodies, being sorted out, being dragged by the feet and put into one pile or another, by the people who work in the morgue—strange silent figures with masks across their faces to protect them from the smell of decay.

I stand in the centre of the room, looking and not wanting to look for Victor, and a great wave of rage assaults me. I know that incoherent noises of protest come from my mouth, but immediately Hector reacts. 'Ssh! You mustn't make any sign—otherwise we shall get into trouble. Just stay quiet a moment. I'll go and ask where we should go. I don't think this is the right place.'

We are directed upstairs. The morgue is so full that the bodies overflow to every part of the building, including the administrative offices. A long passage, rows of doors, and on the floor a long line of bodies, this time with clothes, and some of them looking more like students. Ten, twenty, thirty, forty, fifty...and there in the middle of the line I find Victor.

It was Victor, although he looked thin and gaunt. What have they done to you to make you waste away like that in one week? His eyes were open and they seemed still to look ahead with intensity and defiance—in spite of a wound on his head and terrible bruises on his cheek. His clothes were torn, trousers round his ankles, sweater rucked up under his armpits, his blue underpants hanging in tatters round his hips as though cut by a knife or bayonet—his chest riddled with holes, and a gaping wound in his abdomen. His hands seemed to be hanging from his arms at a strange angle as though his wrists were broken...but it was Victor, my husband, my lover.

Part of me died at that moment too. I felt a whole part of me die as I stood there. Immobile and silent, unable to move, speak.

GRANTA

José Donoso
The Country House

The Excursion

The grown-ups of the great Ventura family had said time and again how absolutely imperative it was to get an early start that morning, almost at sun-up, if they wanted to reach their destination at an hour that would justify making the trip. But the children just smiled and winked at this talk, without looking up from their bouts of chess or backgammon that seemed to drag on all summer long.

The night before the excursion which I propose to use as the crux of this fiction, Wenceslao left his mother snoring from the laudanum she took to help her sleep after the ferment of the preparations, and slipped from his bed to go snuggle in next to Melania. In a hushed voice, he bet her a crown that their parents, who always made things so complicated, would never get going before eleven the next morning if indeed they left at all, and that all the preliminary commotion would give way to that hollow rhetoric with which they habitually covered up their failures. Melania yanked his curls to punish him for this saucy prediction: in the intimacy of the bedsheets she would have liked to make him cry so she could dry the tears from his blue eyes with kisses, wipe his china-doll cheeks with her black braid.

But since he would neither take it back nor start crying, Melania refused to pay him so much as a single copper of the bet the next morning, when the little boy's prophecy proved true: it struck twelve before the grown-ups had finished locking the wrought-iron gate of the rail fence encircling the park, and fastening the grated windows in the market yard through which Casilda, Colomba and Uncle Hermógenes attended the naked natives balancing baskets of fruit on their heads, dangling strings of fowl, toting bundles of hammered gold or, strung from a pole between two shoulders, a deer or wild boar killed on the plain.

From inside the compound enclosed by the railing the children watched as Uncle Hermógenes, once satisfied that the bolts were secure, distributed the keys among his pockets. And after the mothers had cautioned their children for the last time, one finger in the air, to behave themselves and look after the little ones, the women, gathering the splendid folds of their travel skirts, and the men, flashing their polished boots, climbed into the carriages and set off, followed by wagons crammed with the army of boisterous servants in charge of the pillows and rugs to be spread under trees, the complex paraphernalia that the gentlefolk would need to help kill the time, and the provisions that the cooks had spent weeks preparing, sweating over their steaming pots fragrant with truffles and spices.

The thirty-three cousins of the Ventura family were left behind, locked inside the park. The older ones were perched in trees and hanging over balconies, waving farewell handkerchiefs, while the youngest stuck weeping faces through the wrought-iron bars, staring after the cavalcade as it disappeared from view among the grasses rippling over the flat landscape to the horizon.

'Good!' cried Wenceslao with a sigh, sliding off Melania's knee when the carriages had vanished in the distance.

'It's a good thing they promised to be back before dark,' she commented, trying to reassure herself that this promise would prove unbreakable, as she got up from the hammock on the balcony where she had been watching the departure.

Mauro stretched his legs in the same hammock, watching his cousin Melania comb Wenceslao's hair into ringlets *à l'anglaise.*

Intent on shattering the smug look with which Mauro sat, scratching the acne of his fuzzy new beard, Wenceslao asked, 'Didn't you think this whole goodbye had a suspiciously fictional air about it, like the final scene of an opera?'

'Everything about our life here,' Mauro replied, 'is like an opera. Why should this seem any stranger?'

'I'm convinced their idea is to go away and never come back.'

'No, I'm afraid I don't subscribe to your theories,' replied Mauro.'

But a shadow fell across his face as Wenceslao, submitting to his cousin's comb, proceeded in a voice of doom: 'No. I'm certain they won't be back. If their picnic site proves as enchanting as they hope, they won't come back today or tomorrow or ever. What's there to come back for? They've got cards and mandolins to amuse themselves, and butterfly-nets and fishing rods. And muslin kites with long pretty tails to fly if a good breeze comes up. After all, didn't they take every gun, every wagon, every last horse in the house? And all the servants, to keep a wall of comfort around them which they can't do without even for what they assure us will be just one afternoon's outing? No, my dear cousins: they won't be back. The truth, I must repeat, is that they ran away because they're afraid the cannibals will attack the country house.

'And, now that they've left,' Wenceslao continued, 'the cannibals probably will attack. Because as our parents are not coming back, we will soon start running out of provisions. The candles will all be used up and we won't know what to do.... Then the cannibals, with ladders they'll weave out of grass stalks, will storm the railing around the park and come howling into the house to eat us up....'

On the eve of the picnic, the existence of cannibals surrounding the country house—a nuisance the grown-ups had mentioned vaguely during other summers in Marulanda—had been revived thanks to Wenceslao's prophecies, becoming a bonfire that lit the whole place with its lurid flames. The smallest cousins—they could be seen below chasing the peacocks up and down the marble steps of the park—believed everything he said, and now, after the grown-ups' departure, they were undoubtedly running after those big peevish fowl with the innocent intention of laying in some meat in case the emergency Wenceslao foresaw should come to pass. At nightfall the implacable curfew bell inaugurated the terror: then, on the boundless plain that began on the other side of the lance railing, the restless sway of the tall grasses rubbing their stalks made a murmur so constant as to go almost unnoticed during the day, but which at night haunted the Venturas' sleep like the awesome rumble of the sea that tosses sailors in their bunks. This grassy monody stirred up nameless voices in the silence of the rooms where the children, eyes bulging under the silken canopies that guarded their sleep, lay sifting the whispers for threats of cannibals present or past, real or imagined.

The Venturas' picnic took place on a day shortly after the first half of summer, when as usual the spirits of the thirty-three cousins and their parents, stifled inside the great house and its parks, were beginning to flag under the monotony of croquet, naps in hammocks, magnificent sunsets and sumptuous feasts, with nothing new to do or say. It was the season when unwholesome rumours were bred spontaneously, as life breeds in stagnant waters gone foul. One particularly irksome rumour, from years back, reported that the natives who worked in the mines, up in the blue mountains along the horizon, were all falling victim to an epidemic which would cripple the entire population, and that as a result the production of gold—the foundation of our Venturas' opulence—might diminish if not cease altogether. But it was only an idle distortion: half a dozen natives were dead from black vomit in a village far from the mountains where the natives hammered the gold, beating it into the fine thin sheets which the family exported to gild the world's most sumptuous stages and altars. Adriano Gomara, father of our friend Wenceslao, would have paid them a visit because he was a doctor. But he was unable to do so, as he could not leave the tower in which the Ventura family now kept him.

That summer—the one we have imagined as a starting point for this fiction—the grown-ups had sensed as soon as they were settled in Marulanda, that their dearly beloved children were up to something. It struck them as particularly odd that the youngsters were not only making very little noise, but also that they were intruding on the adults' peace and quiet far less than in other years. Was it possible that at last they had learned to think of their parents' comfort? No. It was something else. They were obeying some kind of secret password. Their games seemed not only quieter but more distant, more incomprehensible than the games of summers gone by: the grown-ups, gathered on the south terrace, would suddenly realize that nearly the entire afternoon had gone by without seeing or hearing them, and recovering from their surprise, they sat straining their ears to catch the echoes that reached them from the garrets or from the confines of the park where a knot of children could be spied slinking under the elms. The grown-ups went on drinking their tea, embroidering, smoking, playing solitaire, leafing through the magazines. Occasionally someone ventured to call her child, who would appear immediately, perhaps *too* immediately, like a puppet popping from its box. This situation, defying all explanation, was becoming intolerable. But *what* about it was intolerable? Merely the children's silence? Or those faint smiles that embellished their acquiescence in everything? Or their waning eagerness to accept the privileges conceded to the older ones, such as coming down after dinner to the Blackamoor Chamber to pass around boxes of cigars and trays with demitasses of coffee and marzipan? Yes, details of this nature thickened the atmosphere, edging the Venturas toward the brink of terror. But terror, after all, of what? That was what the grown-ups asked themselves, drinking their nightly sip of water, waking with their throats choked by imaginary thistles, victims in a nightmare of slashed throats and stabbings. No. Absurd. Nightmares, everyone knows, are the product of overrich foods: better to stay up a little later and not trouble themselves over gluttony's bad dreams. Certainly there was nothing to fear from well-bred loving children.

Still, what better excuse to escape whatever it was that the children were plotting: merely fixing a date for the picnic meant they could all relax, for the details of this unwonted diversion would naturally have to be discussed at length, and the debate over the nature and proper significance of their fear was no longer of primary concern. This benign neglect enabled the established order—namely authority in its most venerable aspect—to emerge with its prestige still intact.

The rhythm of the house changed after that: fervent and gay, it pushed aside all thoughts of disagreeable matters because it was more urgent to organize the picnic. The children, meanwhile, were finding it harder and harder to fall asleep as the day of departure drew near, convinced as they were that the cannibals were hungry for human flesh, and that as soon as the grown-ups abandoned them to save their own skins, they would attack. As the bustle of preparation mounted, the children felt ever more certain that for them matters were pushing toward a total and inevitable end: the grown-ups alone were privileged to save themselves from the holocaust, belonging as they did to that class of people with the means to do so. While from the tower where his wicked relations kept him locked up, as if he too wished to partake in all the commotion. Adriano Gomara cried out for them to save him, to kill him, not to let him go on suffering. Until Froilán and Beltrán, his jailers, managed to stuff him back in the straitjacket and gag him so that he couldn't disrupt the Venturas' pastimes with his mad howling.

But Adriano Gomara had been screaming from his tower for so many years that the Venturas had learned to go about their lives without much regard for his insults and warnings.

It was only after the cavalcade had departed that Adriano Gomara's screams became especially important. It was only then that his jailers mysteriously disappeared and that he was, somehow, released. And it was only when released that Adriano discovered his real followers: not among the grown-ups, who had kept him locked up and out of the way for so long, but among the children and (perhaps most important) the Natives who lived on just the over side of the lance-fence which surrounded the Marulanda country house.

The Incursion

The first time the Venturas brought the newly-married Adriano Gomara to the country house and showed him around the emerald park, the doctor had noticed a crimson-clad lackey posted at the foot of one of the marble flights, apparently standing guard. Time and again he caught Adriano's eye, always standing stiffly in the same place, until finally Adriano decided to ask his new family what function that poor devil served, forever stationed at that particular spot.

'Don't you agree,' one of his new relatives replied, 'that a touch of red is needed just there, a complementary colour to focus the green composition, as in a Corot landscape?'

Adriano remained silent, not knowing whether to admire or despise these people who were capable of reducing human beings to decorative objects. The Venturas noticed his perplexity, whose meaning they readily guessed and counted against him. Nevertheless, this question of Adriano's, which my reader may well consider an insignificant detail scarcely worthy of mention, became a kind of parable within the family, repeated a thousand times as a typical example of the *faux pas* someone from a different class is apt to make, not apprehending that a servant's duty is to protect his masters even in such apparently insubstantial matters as these. His reaction was one of the first things that betrayed Adriano Gomara as a dangerous character. And every year during the instruction of the new servants this incident, which had assumed legendary proportions, was retold for their personal edification. At the same time it served to single out the new family member as the object of special treatment on the part of the staff, who without any outward sign were to keep a wary eye on this troublemaker.

Now, at last, the moment of conflict engendered by Adriano Gomara had arrived. In the flare of dawn, the line of carriages bristling with black gun barrels galloped over the plain, trampling the tall grass and shattering the silence with whoops and an occasional gunshot. The servants had long distrusted Adriano for 'not knowing how to command', since of course he hadn't been born to it, like the Venturas. But the night before, when the masters had revealed the influence which Adriano, in their absence, was exercising over both the children *and* the natives, and had therefore turned over their carriages and arms (not, it should be said, without some anxiety), they had also clearly defined the key to his dangerousness: namely, that in spite of his insanity, and not because of it—after all, it was for this very reason he had penetrated the family—Adriano was an agent of the cannibals, whose goal was the overthrow of traditional power; what's more, he was undoubtedly their ringleader; in any case, it was he who had whipped the savages' hatred to such a pitch that they would bring down the establishment, using as their instrument the innocent children whom they had corrupted for this purpose. It was necessary (the masters exhorted the servants) to leave the picnic and return to the country house, to wipe out, eradicate, demolish anything new that might have been constructed or organized, and to save whoever had escaped initiation into their abominable practices.

The Chef, the Head Groom and the Chief Gardener occupied the lead carriage, flying in the teeth of the wind. The Majordomo, ablaze with gold, sat alongside the coachman on the box, his rifle gripped firmly in his gloved hand, scanning the horizon with his amazing silken eyes, cleaving the air with his jaw and flinty lips. What were they to make of the children's behaviour? The Chef, dressed immaculately in white, with his high puffed hat, his ruddy cheeks and the tiny circumflex of his moustache jiggling over his fleshy lips, seemed to give voice to his leader's thoughts: 'How can it be that these people who have everything in the world, who in due time will become captains of the empire of hand-laminated gold and owners of mines and whole tribes, should suddenly turn anarchists and destroy their own things, jeopardizing, in short, their prospects for inheriting power?'

'The girls living as concubines to the natives...?' pondered the Head Groom.

'We can't be expected to believe that the natives would dare move into the mansion where we ourselves were rarely admitted,' observed the Chief Gardener.

'These must be hallucinations,' decided the Chef.

But the voice of Juan Pérez, who grasped the reins on the box next to the Majordomo, urging the horses with a recklessness that seemed out of place in so frail a figure, suddenly rang out: 'It's no hallucination!'

The Majordomo stared at him. Who was this fellow who dared to speak up so confidently? And Juan Pérez, to prove he was telling the truth, described what none of them had seen for himself: 'That's right, don't look so stupid, everyone knows the Ventura girls are all whores, daughters and granddaughters of whores. And it was true that the children were rotten to the bone. Yes, true that in Marulanda anarchy and mayhem reigned supreme. And true, above all, that at Adriano Gomara's instigation the cannibals had taken over the house, garden, mines, fields and furniture, implanting their savage way of life in the hopes of creating a new order. No. The cannibals were no invention: they were a clear and present danger, a stain that threatened to spread from Marulanda throughout the entire world. This was the moment when they, the servants—after all these years of waiting in decorative poses which at best served to focus the colour scheme of the park, contenting themselves with dreams of the heroic deed which alone could justify their submissive silence—were to defend at gunpoint the one, the true worthy cause.

Juan Pérez's speech roused the Majordomo—as well as the Chef, the Head Groom and the Chief gardener—and dispelled their doubts. The wind flew in their faces and they lapsed into silence, while the long grass sang beneath the horses' hooves and the flashing spokes whistled like whiplashes. Behind, in the winding cavalcade, the rest of the staff whooped wildly as if they too had heard Juan Pérez's harangue. Above the thunder of wagons racing across the plain rose loud bravos for the Majordomo, cries of loyalty to his person, curses for the cannibals and for Adriano Gomara, the ringleader without whose prodding the savages would never have awakened from their centuries-long sleep. The three captains rose to their feet in the open landau, waving their rifles, belligerent, impassioned, vociferous in their thirst for action, shouting that they would fight to the death at the Majordomo's side.

Juan Pérez remained silent at the reins. There was no time to lose.

My reader will appreciate that in the 'good old days' there was never so much as a stalk of thistlegrass to be seen inside the park of the great country house in Marulanda, even though an ocean began immediately outside the railing. This was because at the beginning of summer, while the Venturas and their progeny remained in the house opening wardrobes and trunks and plotting their summer strategies, squads of servants would fan through the park in a supremely efficient offensive, devoting the entire day to rooting out every last blade of the malignant weed which, after the autumn tempests had scattered the fluffy down in every direction, sought to worm its tender shoots into the bordered walks of the rose garden, across the lawn, into cracks in the marble steps and urns. At the end of this day's campaign not a single odious tuft remained in all the park. The next morning the staff donned their various uniforms and flung open the French windows for the masters to make their descent to the now weedless grounds, spared in this manner from any sight of the plebeian grass. But all summer long, in a silent and endless vigil, the keen-eyed gardeners patrolled the park, snatching out every sprig as soon as it reared its head.

It was a radically different aspect which the country house now presented. The railing around the park had been taken down—admitting all the elements it was once meant to keep out—and nothing remained but the fanciful gate chained and padlocked between two stone columns, as if adrift in the middle of the plain. The grass had succeeded in flooding its vast landscape over what had once been civilized grounds.It was sprouting wildly, fantastically, in the middle of walks and lawns, even from cracks in the eaves and gables of the deteriorated architecture, so that the mansion, formerly so majestic, now resembled one of those overgrown picturesque ruins to be found in paintings by Hubert Robert or Salvatore Rosa. But on closer inspection, an observer would have discovered that the grounds had been altered beyond recognition not only by that invasion, but by a series of ditches running from the *laghetto,* no longer a decorative pool but rather a source of irrigation for the garden plots that had replaced the once elegant flowerbeds. Groups of natives and children stood working with backs bent to the sun, raising a gate to flood one of the plots that needed water, or harvesting lettuce, raspberries and carrots.

Suddenly the labourers paused, raising their heads. What was that thunder they could hear on the horizon? Thunder in the air, shaking the earth, a whiff of danger that froze them warily in their tracks, listening, before dropping their garden tools and bolting for the south terrace, where from all corners the people were assembling, as had been agreed in case of emergency. Francis of Assisi, Adriano's greatest supporter among the natives, was passing out lances to those who came running up pell-mell, though nobody could as yet identify the menacing rumble. They nevertheless recognized it as danger, whatever it might be. During this year of communal labour, Adriano Gomara had impressed upon them that despite the internal threats of hunger and domestic strife, the real danger would come from outside, since at any moment they might be called on to defend the house with their lives against an attack from the grown-ups, determined to recover what they believed to be theirs. After a few minutes nobody doubted any longer that it was a thunder of hooves, shouts and gunshots.

Clustered on the terrace, children and natives stared at each other, certain that in another few moments they would no longer be the same, nor would things continue as before. Despite their pitiful assortment of arms the people were prepared: through the crowd of ashen faces and blue Ventura eyes bobbed the red crests of the warriors' helmets, advancing toward the outer edges of the terrace, ready to defend it with their lances and their lives. From the tiled tower boomed the voice of Adriano Gomara, who from that vantage could spy the headlong cavalcade, recognizing in its advance his own and everyone else's grim destiny:

> Those we have long been expecting are coming to destroy us! From here I see how they rush upon us with their horses, their coaches, their fury. We must not be afraid. We are strong because we have faith in our inalienable right and in our reason. They are attacking with gunpowder, we are defending with iron: no matter, because in the end, after the nightmare and the sacrifice in which I and many of you will surely perish, History shall pay us justice and Time will bring forth what we have sowed in her.

The clatter of galloping carriages, rounding the *laghetto*, drowned out Adriano's last words. The spoked wheels, the flashing hooves obliterated the paths, flattening cabbages and watermelons, devastating what remained of the beds of rhododendron and hydrangea, overturning wheelbarrows full of artichokes and spattering the freshly-watered earth as they flew up the gentle slope toward the rose garden, which they invaded, trampling it to mud underfoot. There were hundreds, possibly thousands of servants in the thundering coaches. The windows shivered into fragments, splinters flew from the towers and rooftops as the bullets found them. Something, curtains maybe, burst into flames inside the house, their smoke blinding the crowd huddled together on the south terrace. The smaller girls sobbed, still clutching their lances. Cordelia, one of the most beautiful of the children, ran forward with the intention of joining the warriors in the front rank, but Francis of Assisi, the native who was the father of the half-breed twins she carried slung on her back, turned her away with a kiss.

Lances in hand, the natives closed ranks behind the protection of the balustrade around the south terrace. The Majordomo gave the order to shoot to kill. The servants lowered their aim and sent a hail of bullets at the natives, who fell rank after riddled rank as they charged down the steps with their lances. Grooms and gardeners and scullery boys leaped in whooping hordes from their carriages, trampling corpses, despatching the wounded, mowing down those natives who, taking the places of the fallen, were valiantly trying to stop the enemy from seizing the south terrace. But resistance was hopeless with such paltry weapons. The defenders who could no longer fight were bludgeoned with pistol butts, whipped, handcuffed, reduced to helplessness. One by one the rebellious cousins were placed under guard in a corner of the terrace while squads of servants led the natives away to be executed, disappearing behind the piles of corpses and smouldering furniture.

And as the smoke began to clear, those children who had endured Adriano's rule but had secretly despised it, came trooping up onto the south terrace. They were accompanied by the Majordomo. Behind them marched the rest of the children. They paid no attention to their brothers and sisters, their cousins, who called them from the corner where the servants were holding them. They were returning home after a minor incident, but really, nothing at all had happened. Things would soon be put right, and once the troublemakers had been punished everything would go on as before. They would all calmly await the return of their parents from their one-day excursion. True, a few natives had suffered in the fray, but it was their own fault, they had asked for it themselves. Besides, any native was replaceable by any other, so in fact the whole affair had been quite trivial. And sentimentalism aside, surely those who suffered were not so numerous as the usual malcontents would soon be claiming.

The children so recently saved from the clutches of the cannibals were about to sink wearily into what remained of the charred and gutted armchairs. But before sitting down to map out a plan of reconstruction, while gunshots and screams still resounded through the house, it was necessary to carry out the most important business of all.

'Juan Pérez!' called the Majordomo.

'At your service, sir.'

'Do your duty at once.'

And trailed by thirty heroes armed with pistols and rifles, his chest criss-crossed by bandoliers full of cartridges and swollen with pride at his lofty mission, Juan Pérez marched to the tower to face the corruptor of the innocents who (till that fiend's intervention) had lived in peace, but who now (thanks to him) had been turned into cannibals.

The house shook from cellar to towers with the clatter of fleeing natives. Gunshots and screams rang out. The salons overflowed with prisoners being led off howling to the park from where the volleys of firing squads could be heard. Maddened with mystic rage against cannibalism, the servants were mowing down anyone, everyone not in a servant's uniform, under a hail of bullets. Smoke poured through the rooms, powder and blood stained the rugs where goats fled wounded by musketballs. But above the din rose the booming voice of the Majordomo.

'This chaos cannot go on!' he proclaimed, using his hands as a megaphone. 'Cannnibals trained to impose their savage customs at lance-point throughout the land! I'm warning the perpetrator of all this savagery, Don Adriano Gomara, to give himself up to us, the representatives of order and of the family to whom these lands belong!'

Juan Pérez and his men, fingers on their triggers, the image of the sinner printed as one target on every retina, marched up the marble staircase that wound gracefully along the wall of the oval vestibule. At that moment, whether or not his name would go down in history as saviour did not concern Juan Pérez: he knew that to posit things as an ideological confrontation was nothing but a clever ruse on the part of the Venturas to recover what they were afraid had been taken from them. This sham didn't matter. All that mattered was the throbbing heart of the white-bearded figure he had occasionally caught a glimpse of through the keyhole at his tower door, awaiting the bullet Juan Pérez could feel trying to escape from the barrel of his pistol and lodge in that breast—heart and bullet stopping each other dead.

Juan Pérez, from below, saw Adriano Gomara appear at the head of the staircase, flanked by his bodyguards. How to connect with that hapless figure in the apostolic white beard, the tattered white nightshirt, the wild warrior headdress flopping about his ears, the useless lance in his hand? With his platoon, Juan Pérez crept very slowly up the stairs, waiting, waiting, yet another moment so as to be closer and not miss, for it was his bullet, not some other, which must topple him. But the higher he climbed, and the closer he drew to Adriano Gomara and his men with outstretched lances, the more clearly could Juan Pérez discern on his enemy's face that terrible mystery of the man for whom humanity has meaning and a dream of a rational order. Adriano didn't see him. Consequently, he didn't exist. By ignoring him, Adriano Gomara loomed as the incarnation of moral judgement which, from the centre of whatever ideology, unmasked Juan Pérez, condemning and spurning his baseness.

Juan Pérez levelled his pistol at that lofty eminence and fired.

The news of Adriano Gomara's death spread like wildfire through the house. The screams of children and natives turned to sobs, but they did not end their resistance which, though hopeless, had swollen to practically suicidal proportions. Meanwhile the beatings, clubbings, whippings and shootings of anyone who dared to move or speak grew bloodier, as if the staff felt that, far from putting an end to the assault, Adriano Gomara's death drove them to defend their gains with even greater ferocity.

And then there were no more shots to be heard. Only one or two in the distance, at the edges of the park, aimed no doubt at a native fleeing for the blue mountains that dotted the horizon. In the grand hall, the shock that precedes full awareness of great disasters put an end to the wailing, and silence settled over the crowd. But only for a moment: a moan from Cordelia, who with her twins in her arms was standing behind the captains, was so wretched it seemed to exhaust her; she collapsed to the floor, stretching her hand between the Majordomo's open legs to stroke Uncle Adriano's gory beard. Only then, touched off by Cordelia's cry, did the general sobbing and shrieking burst out, to be cut short at once by a bellow from the Majordomo: 'Silence! Nothing has happened here!'

If what I am narrating were true, not invented, I might have added that several witnesses would later describe this first moment of shock as so solemn and at the same time so sinister that the children and natives who burst into sobs were joined by several of the weeping lackeys—the most ignorant, no doubt, or the youngest, who admired Adriano Gomara in secret, or those who were not very clear about the confrontation that was taking place in Marulanda.

In any event the Chef, his fat jowls crinkling with smiles, bent down, as soon as silence had been restored, to help Cordelia to her feet. As he was pulling her up, his dainty pink hands stroked her blond tresses and his beady eyes sought the little girl's wide green gaze.

'Let go of me, you disgusting pig!' shouted Cordelia, spitting in his face.

The Chef, wiping Cordelia's tubercular phlegm from his chin, drew back to strike her, but as he started to swing she ran and sought refuge in Francis of Assisi's arms. The Majordomo then joined the other household captains who were now surrounding Cordelia.

With a slight but prolonged nod of his head, as Ventura etiquette demanded, he addressed her as follows:

'I find myself obliged to beg Your Grace to observe a more decorous behaviour and to quit the embrace of this cannibal. After all, this man is a mere native—one of *them*—whereas Your Grace is the oldest daughter of Don Anselmo, who is a saint, and of Doña Eulalia, who is a lady of the loftiest qualities. You must understand that our intention is above all to liberate....'

And Cordelia spat in the Majordomo's face too.

At this the captains and servants crowding around Cordelia exploded into fury: 'Slut!' they shouted, 'Pervert! Consumptive! Defender of outlaws! Cannibal bitch who abandoned her babies which are floating dead this very moment with the rest of the bodies in the *laghetto*! Heartless mother who, like all the women under Adriano's depraved influence, has been turned into a whore, corrupted, rotten with God only knows what moral defects....'

'Juan Pérez!' the Majordomo called at last.

'At your service, sir!'

'Bring a guitar!' ordered the Majordomo.

Cordelia, trapped in the throbbing embrace of the Chef, recoiled, shrinking even further within herself as the Majordomo turned to her.

'All happy couples teach each other many things, wouldn't you agree, Miss Cordelia? If I remember correctly, you used to sing some very pretty songs which we, the servants, never had the privilege of hearing except from a distance. Surely you've taught at least one to Francis of Assisi, haven't you? Juan Pérez! Give this cannibal the guitar.'

Francis of Assisi took it, holding it tenderly by the waist, as if it were a body. No one in the crowd moved a muscle. No one breathed. Francis of Assisi stood in total silence, still holding the guitar around the middle.

'Juan Pérez, I command you to make him sing!'

Seizing the guitar, Juan Pérez marched him to the foot of the grand staircase. There he made him spread his open hands over the decorative bronze pineapple at the base of the spiral bannister.

'Are you going to sing?' asked Juan Pérez, his frog voice imitating the Majordomo's booming tones.

Francis of Assisi remained mute, haughty, the object of all eyes. He would not lower himself to answer. Juan Pérez felt the weight of his scorn. Then he hammered his pistol butt again and again on his fingers, again and again, until he heard the bone crunch—all the time shouting: 'Take that and that and that! Cannibal! Thief! Degenerate! Corrupter! Take that and that.... Even if I have to break every bone in your body you're going to play the guitar for us, the victors. Take that and that, for fondling Miss Cordelia's body.'

Francis of Assisi, whiter with horror than with pain, held every muscle in his body tense, like an imperial statue, steeling himself as best he could against the physical pain which for the moment drove out all other pains and protected him from them. But from the bottom of this pain he heard Cordelia's voice crying, 'Don't let them kill you!'

And the natives, and maybe the children too: 'Sing so they don't kill you!'

'We need you!'

The remnants of all his griefs rose up, and with what was left of his mangled hands he fumbled for the guitar. His lifeless fingers barely managed to strum a chord or two, but his voice rose strong, clear, certain, the manifestation of something which the servants would never understand but which, as they listened, struck them as more violent, more subversive than anything they'd ever heard before: the first sign of an unbreakable resistance which perhaps—they thought for a second in which they felt themselves wavering—neither they, nor the grown-ups nor anyone else could ever conquer:

Plaisirs d'amour
ne durent qu'un instant;
chagrins d'amour
durent toute la vie...

And at that instant one of the doors swung open. The guards had arrived, and at a wave of the Majordomo's hand, they dragged Francis of Assisi away to be executed.

And, breaking the stunned silence that followed, the Majordomo once again roared his decree, 'Nothing has happened here! Life will go on as before!'

My reader can readily gauge the absurdity of this statement if he will believe me that everything that had happened, with its triumphs and its inexcusable blunders, along with the pain and humiliation of the assault, had etched into every heart, native and child alike, a consciousness, an outrage that would never again allow anything to be as before.

Translated from the Spanish by
David Pritchard and Suzanne Jill Levine

The coup.

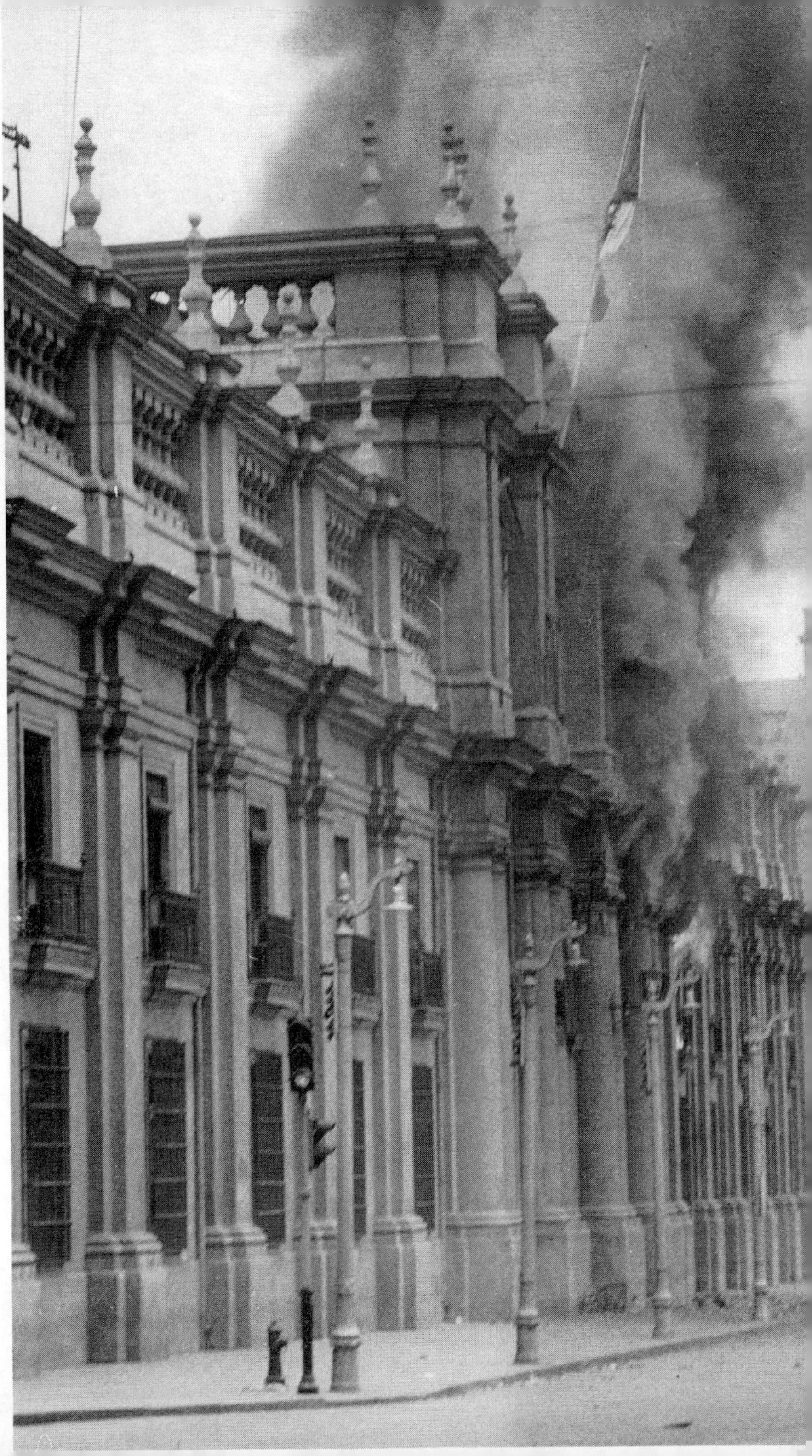

7,000 suspects in the national stadium (overleaf).

GRANTA

Sheila Rowbotham

Lance

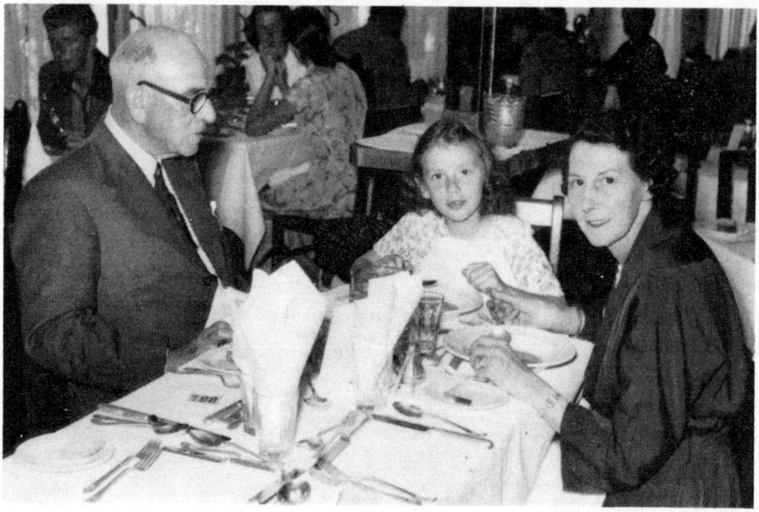

Sheila Rowbotham was born in 1943 in Yorkshire and studied history at St Hilda's College, Oxford. Apart from working on a number of socialist and feminist journals, she has written several books, including *Women, Resistance and Revolution, Hidden from History,* and *A New World for Women.* She is currently Visiting Professor in the Women's Studies Department of the University of Amsterdam, and is working in the Economic Policy Unit of the Greater London Council. 'Lance' is from *Fathers: Reflections by Daughters* which will be published by Virago Press on November 7 1983.

My father was in his fifties when I was born. We were separated in age by half a century and the gulf only seemed to grow wider. Our placings in the world and our relationship to where we found ourselves were contrary and apart.

Born in 1888, he was the seventh in a family of fourteen. The joke went that Grandmother Rowbotham was running out of names for the boys by the time he came along. From sober Charles and Tommy she began to branch out into Lancelot, Clifford and Randal. Combined with Rowbotham, these lofty names became somewhat absurd and Lancelot was reduced to 'our Lance'.

Grandfather Rowbotham had a small farm in a village called Aston, near Sheffield. He had worked in the mines, checking the wooden props and beams to make sure they were safe. The money he earned had been used to build up the farm. It was assumed that all the children would work on the farm; it was unthrifty to employ labour. Children worked for their keep.

My father remembered Grandfather as a harsh man who beat his children each day *in case* they had done something wrong which he had not found out about. Grandfather Rowbotham certainly assumed he had total rights over his children's lives. As he had so many to keep an eye on, he could not maintain complete control over his unruly brood. According to Auntie Glad, the daughters were locked in their rooms at night to prevent them going with their boyfriends, but they somehow found the means to escape.

My father went against his father. He sought a world beyond the farm and beyond the village. He won a scholarship to grammar school. Then he worked on the farm in the day and studied at evening classes in Sheffield to become an engineer. 'I walked both ways in all weathers,' he used to tell me. As an apprentice he began converting clocks so that they would run off electricity. While he was still in his early twenties, he got a good job as an electrical engineer in a colliery nearby. It was unusual to get a post like this so young. He was enterprising and rebellious, designing a safety lamp that was taken into use in the mines, reading the socialist paper *Clarion*, and exposing the council in the local newspaper. He had done well. But I always felt he retained a sense of hurt that his father put obstacles in the way of his studies and never acknowledged his accomplishments.

Despite these early successes, the rest of his life was to be full of ups and downs, partly because he was a rebellious individualist, partly because of what my mother described as his 'bulldog' sexual approach. He pursued too many women by the standards of the village, according to Auntie Glad. To everyone's surprise, he was quite successful in his philandering. As no one remembers him as either handsome or the life of the party, his attraction was assumed by his sisters to be based on craftiness, flattery and persistence. He possessed, more generally, tremendous will-power and a dogged determination to live and think as he pleased, which remained with him until the end of his days.

He met my mother, Jean Turner, when he was in his mid-thirties and already married. She was in her late teens, visiting a farm near Aston for her holidays.

Her family were (she thought) a cut above the Rowbothams. Her father owned a factory in Sheffield which made guns and ammunition. But the Rowbothams' version of themselves tended to prevail through sheer will and weight of numbers. They were as good as anybody and a great deal better than most.

When my mother returned to Sheffield, Lance continued his courtship. She portrayed him to me as a country bumpkin who drove off her other suitors with his rude manners and farm clothes and won her, by elimination, through perseverance. Once she stormed off and left him. He pursued her. She got on a tram. But he ran alongside it until the mirth of the other passengers forced her to get off.

My father maintained that the other suitors were shallow city slickers in spats. As a young girl, pondering these tales of the distant courtship in Sheffield just after the First World War, I was always a little disappointed in the other suitors' lack of grit, gump and heroism. It seemed to me that they at least could have challenged my father to a duel. I was somewhat hazy about what spats were; they were not to be seen on the streets of Leeds in the 1950s. Perhaps the spats had made combat impossible. Or perhaps my mother had misjudged the chivalrous suitors. Perhaps they were shallow city slickers after all and my mother was well rid of them.

She gave the impression that it was a matter of chance that she was telling me the story more than thirty years on. 'He swept me off my feet, your father did.' Once you were swept, apparently fate took its course.

After they both died, I was to learn that despite living together all those years they never married. My father's legal wife was a Catholic and regarded by the Rowbothams as socially inferior. Lance had married her in his teens in the face of his family's disapproval. Only his favourite sister, Glad, stood by him. By the time he met my mother, his wife had already left him for someone else, but because she was a Catholic she refused him a divorce.

When my mother died in the early 1960s, I found letters from Lance during this period which she had kept all those years. They revealed a man I did not recognize as my father. The atmosphere the letters evoked was reminiscent of that surrounding the characters who had fascinated me in H.G. Wells' novels: they conveyed the feel of a new century, a new rising man, coming up in the world through technical expertise and evening classes, impatient of upper-class privilege, determined to make his own way, blunt and passionate.

Lance and Jean left England for India in the early 1920s. He had been offered a job there and my mother said she was keen to get out of Sheffield and pushed him to go. Such a step was clearly pretty scandalous in those days. But in defying her family by going to India with Lance, she was from this point on totally dependent upon him materially, without any legal security. This, when I learned it, cast a new light on her insistence on my being educated so I could earn my own living, and on the fierceness of her love of freedom.

Lance worked as a mining engineer near Calcutta for twelve years under the British Raj, with the nationalist movement rumbling threateningly on the outskirts of their world of colonial privilege.

Stories of India in this period filled my childhood. My father would pontificate on the unappreciated virtues of Empire—everything having rashly been given away to the Indians by the Labour Party in their ignorance. Other stories came from my mother. They were long explorations of character and coincidence, embellished with observations and reflections. 'Tell me about the time...' I would say, longing for her to breathe life into all the household objects, imperial booty of elephants, embroidered paintings, Buddhas and carved screens which had found their way to

Harehills (in Leeds) by some quirk of history.

My father's Indias differed from my mother's. He did not talk of the details of his life and work there, perhaps partly because I was his daughter, not his son, but also because he never talked much about personal relationships. His India was transmitted either through opinion or had to be inferred. It must have felt a long way from South Yorkshire to Calcutta. And thirty years after he had left, Lance continued to see India through the eyes of a South Yorkshire man. He never shifted from a dogmatic and uncompromising stance. My mother had no more idea of the political complexities of imperialism and nationalism than he had, but she could see that there were other versions of India, not just the British one. It is possible to imagine that behind Lance's British identity there was considerable social discomfort among his 'betters' at the club, where he played bridge seriously and ponderously and joined the freemasons half-heartedly. He was too stubborn to be socially mobile, too proud not to smart before an upper-class accent. Years later, he kept his Kipling poems proudly amid Agatha Christie thrillers and adventure novels.

They stayed twelve years in India. They had to leave because Lance got the sack. This story he *did* tell me and I always felt very proud of him. His boss was away on leave in Britain. The next in command tried to lower the wages of the miners. Lance had to sign for the reduction to take effect. He refused, because he said the wages were below starvation level already and no human being could be expected to live on them. Amid the Tory paternalism there was a fierce sense of fair play which contradicted the small businessman's approach to the world of measured self-interest. Because he had worked in the mines, he appreciated the risks, discomfort, health hazards.

They returned to Britain during the Depression. Lance finally got work as an electrician in the mines: this was a come-down after India. He was in his forties and no longer used to manual work. Eventually Grandfather Turner relented and lent Lance the money to buy a car. He got a Morris and a sales job and went into partnership. Around the late 1930s they settled in lodgings with a family in Leeds. My mother loved this period, and her stories of it were all cheery. But Lance's partner ran off with the money.

My father never told me of his business failures and difficulties. He presented himself to me very much as the sagacious worldly-wise businessman. Treat the other chap fairly, but if he doesn't play square, knock him down. Neither a borrower nor a lender be. Never have an overdraft, as the bank makes money out of you....

In the 1940s my parents moved to a house in Harehills, Leeds. Lance got a job as a salesman for a firm in Keighley which made pit motors. He prospered with the expansion of the coal industry. He assured me it was by dint of his ability to judge character, read writing upside-down, hear several conversations at once and other entrepreneurial skills. My mother implied it was all hot air, luck and Grandfather Turner's loan.

By this time Lance was in his fifties and Jean in her early forties. But still their life together was full of upheavals. She became ill with breast cancer and had to have a breast removed. The operation left her weak and frail. I was born just after this, a 'mistake', in 1943. My brother, Peter, was seventeen.

Jean talked of sex with my father as an onerous chore. As long as I can remember they slept apart. She tried to buy quinine to abort me, but it had been withdrawn from the shops. She fell down stairs with me, but did not miscarry. She told me she had had a lot of miscarriages and I wondered as I grew older if some of them had been abortions.

My father never talked to me of his feelings about sexuality. But all the time I knew him he must have been sexually unhappy. I found it impossible to imagine this as a teenager. The idea that my father had sexual desires was unthinkable and merely ludicrous. My mother also communicated to me her sexual revulsion and the bitterness which she had accumulated in the course of his numerous sexual infidelities. With old age, he became very respectable, moralized sternly and watched the clock if I went out at night. 'The dirty old buggers are always the worst with their daughters. They know what you can get up to,' said Jean, who had no sympathy with hypocrisy.

Arguments were persistent between them. I would lie in bed hearing him upbraid her and the softer rhythm of her petulant defiance. He almost—but never quite—wore her spirit down. She would curse her misfortune that he worked at home and was always under her feet.

She chain-smoked and absent-mindedly put her lighted cigarettes on window sills while she did the housework. They burned brown scars into the wood. 'Jeannie, do you want to burn the house down?' he'd roar, filling the house with a male rage which still makes me wince and tremble, remembering the force of it. I suppose Jean Turner *did* want to burn the house down. But she had nowhere else to live and thus resorted to guerrilla warfare.

As I grew older, *I* became the cause of arguments. My beloved dog, Simon, urinated on bushes specially bought from a market garden for our new posh house in Roundhay. I began to drink coffee without putting cups on saucers. 'Nice people won't have you in their house,' he said. Simon and I were protected by an elaborate domestic underground which consisted of my mother and a series of home helps. My brother was an occasional member, but he worked with my father and it was implicitly recognized that, as a man, he was not to understand some things. The underground collected information, planned strategy, had a laugh and indefatigably worked out the best way to achieve objectives. My father, officially all-powerful in his home, had to resort to creeping up on the kitchen in his carpet slippers to gain access to information.

For years, passionate resentment against my father made it impossible for me to imagine how this affected him. To me, he was simply a tyrant to be resisted. The pattern was set by a childhood game my mother and I used to play. We were two waitresses, Rosie and Posie, who would get up to all kind of tricks until the boss came home. 'When the cat's away, the mice will play,' she would say. He controlled the material world, but she found freedom of the spirit in fantasy and imagination. My brother was old enough to see their conflict as tragic on both sides. I saw only how her life was constrained and thwarted, and I blamed Lance for his domineering ways.

Our moments of closeness were rare. Even when I was a small child, my father suffocated me with instructions. We battled over the formal politeness he thought children should show to adults, over my clothes, my table manners, my books. By the time I reached my early teens, I had moved from guerrilla resistance to frontal attack, and the area of struggle expanded to take in religion, Suez, the Queen, race, class, the Empire, my friends, the time I spent on the phone, the time I came in at night. Eventually all these found a name, 'socialism'.

Well, my father was not one for debate for the sake of it. The saying 'I'm not arguing, I'm telling tha'' was more like it. He simply *was* in the world. His views were how things were.

When he died in 1967 we were still unreconciled and locked in mutual incomprehension—though outsiders pointed out similarities between us. 'She takes after you, Lance,' they'd remark. After his death, I felt only a numbness and, behind that, a relief at being rid of the anger. No wild grief like the anguish of my mother's death. The sadness remained deeply buried; I had only an uneasy stirring at his memory over the years.

Then in 1976 a woman read my astrology chart. In the course of the reading, she looked at me and said with force, 'You were a terrible daughter.' She said I should try and sort out my feelings about him. I might have closed up on what she said and dismissed it, but I knew she was a feminist and the remark came from her commitment to women's freedom. Real freedom could not be based on evasion. I recognized in my heart the truth of what she said. For while it was true that he had been a dominating man, he had also loved me and was very proud of me. I had unfinished matters to explore with the spirit of my father. Death is not the end of such affairs.

I spent time on the moments of warmth and affection which had existed between us. They were rare, but I dredged them up. In the kitchen one night when I was in my teens, my mother interrupted him mischievously in the midst of a spate of moralizing: 'What about the woman with the fish-tail dress?' Out came the story. Travelling to India once, he had been playing bridge with a woman who, my mother said, was very haughty, dressed in a tight evening dress with frills in a kind of fish-tail. One night, when they were meant to be playing bridge, my father had contrived to take her up on deck. When they both eventually appeared again in the dance hall, she was rather flustered. The fish-tail frills were all standing on end and, try as she would, she could not flatten them—much to the amusement of my mother and the other passengers. Years later, the moralizer, caught in the act again, grinned boyishly and disarmingly and subsided.

When I got into a women's college at Oxford, my father was very chuffed. 'She'll get funny ideas, Lance, and won't want to get married,' warned his friend, Mr Kessler, who kept an electrical shop and believed in educating sons, not daughters. But my father let me go. He had dreams that I would dress in tweed suits, hobnob with the gentry, become a teacher, enter the Foreign Office. He gave a large sum of money to the college building fund. Believing that colliery managers and dons were basically the same breed of humanity, he took the view that just as presents to the managers secured orders, this was how you got your daughter a good reference for a job. I caught him by chance sneaking out of the college in a new hat he had bought in London. He had come to Oxford secretly, because he knew I would be cross at him giving money. There were many parents with more money. And how to explain that the upper-middle-class intelligentsia played the capitalist system with slightly different rules? However, taken by surprise, we both enjoyed meeting in this way and he took me and some friends out for a meal. It was one of the happiest times I remember with him.

When I was nineteen I went on an anti-nuclear march and a section of the march broke off to invade a regional seat of government, the whereabouts of which had been leaked. We tramped through the woods near Reading and hit the headlines. We were denounced in *Tribune* and Peggy Duff said we were anarchists. My father boasted to his National Coal Board friends that his daughter had done this. They were horrified, but he thought it showed grit and moral fibre, especially when he heard that the military police, whom he disliked, were there.

Always my staunch protector, Lance took his passport out when I went off with my boyfriend to build a library in Poland, organized by Progressive Tours. He wanted to be ready to come rescue me if I was captured behind the Iron Curtain. In vain, I explained that the Polish communists wanted students and young people to go on work camps. At the time it was infuriating, but in retrospect I can appreciate his concern for me and his readiness to stand by me in strange worlds, whether they were composed of women dons, the police or the Polish authorities.

I struggled through these memories to understand how a man like my father must have had love choked at the source, until its only expression became either possessing and controlling or protective.

I tried to find out more about him when he was young, before I was born, by talking to Auntie Glad, one of the few people he ever allowed close to him as an equal. My aunt described him as socially awkward, not joining in family games and dances in the evenings. He went his own way with his studying and his courting, as if he were somehow apart from the rest of them. After making his own break with the farm, he felt responsible for getting his younger brothers started as engineers.

I began to find certain recognitions across the gulf. Our lives were so different, yet there was a substance which he had imparted somehow to me. I saw his pride and stubborn determination in myself.

I joined a women's group and played there the tape I had made of the conversation with my aunt, and when we were discussing our families I talked about my father's influence on my life.

As I met more and more men who were prepared to talk about the experience of masculinity, it became easier to find openings through which I could enter my father's vision of the world. By realizing that to become a man was a social relationship, I could begin to connect his responses and his silences to those I could observe among men who were closer to me. This provided the tissue for speculation beyond my subjective reaction to him. I could begin to stretch my imagination towards him. There remain significant points where this just blanks out—for instance, as soon as I try to work out how he has marked my sexual feelings towards men. For a long time, I thought I simply fancied men who were not like him. As time passes, it is evident that this is far too simple. It is more that I fancy men who appear at first glance to be unlike him. At second glance, of course, there is more going on than immediately meets the eye. It is here I find my ability to observe and distinguish starts to blur.

Early in 1977, I had a son, Will. I was a parent and I had a different relation to another father—Will's father. This made my exploration more urgent: it was not only my own relationship to any father that mattered; there was also the possibility of someone being a different father from my father or my father's father. Or, put more generally, how can we develop relationships in which love can be expressed which does not seek to own and control?

No more *padre padrone.*

When Will was about one, some women who lived nearby formed a consciousness-raising group to explore collectively as feminists our relationships to our fathers. About half of us had children. Our backgrounds (donated by our fathers) ranged from working class to intellectual middle class. Our fathers were Londoners, Scots, Yorkshireman, a Polish Jew, a Viennese Jew. It would have been a bizarre social occasion if these fathers had met one another in the flesh.

There was considerable diversity in our tiny group. Some of the women had had fathers who were very obviously dominating men, who, like mine, had believed their word should be law. Others had mild-mannered fathers who went into retreat in the family. One woman had an exciting romantic father whom she adored, and who even taught her to poach. One had no father because he had died when she was a baby. She developed an idea of fatherhood by scrutinizing other people's fathers. Another had only met her father when she was eighteen because he had vanished when she was little.

One meeting was followed by another, and then another. They continued. There was a depth to the discussions, an openness to complexity and a trust of one another. The meetings became for me part of a quiet process of renewal, both of myself and of my political understanding of feminism. They clarified an uneasiness about an assumption which is often accepted without much examination by feminists and men who support feminism. Characteristics commonly associated in our culture with 'masculinity' are often just dismissed as bad, and the opposition to sexism is merely equated with negating them. Instead I think we should be looking at the potential that is thwarted by these characteristics, and we should be seeking to open out new possibilities.

Because we were not dealing with abstractions of a vaguely-defined 'patriarchy' but talking about actual men, with whom we were connected passionately and intimately, a complex picture began to emerge of 'manhood' and 'fatherhood' and our contradictory needs and images of both. We were exploring how versions of masculinity were taken on by real living men in the specific historical confines of their lives. They appeared not as helplessly moulded by an omnipresent unchanging sex-gender structure, but as individuals acting upon and shaped by the values and relationships within which they found themselves.

Our fathers surfaced, struggling and resistant, vulnerable, trapped, enraged, isolated, cut off. We wept at the gulf in communication which became acute in our adolescence. Suddenly it had seemed to dawn on them that they had given birth to girls and that we were not going to turn into boys. Our fathers sat stiffly in armchairs, clutching newspapers to protect themselves from female invasion. What was it they feared? What were they protecting? Why? Were they preordained, these patterns of non-communication? Or were they, like other relationships between people, subject to social transformation?

We did not find the answers in one small group. Men retained their perplexing mystery for us. But something moved as a result of these collective discussions. For me, the process effected certain significant shifts in my feelings about my father, which in turn altered my perception of the wider meaning of fatherhood.

In one meeting, we talked about our ideal fathers. Mine were thoughtful, sensitive, humane socialists with whom you could discuss ideas and relationships and with whom there was space for your inner being to move outwards. They were sea beings, red Neptunes who could be devoured by Saturn and be born again and were not afraid of the dark flow of the ocean.

But as I described these Neptunes, I became aware that I would have been a very different person with such a father. For whatever the scars of conflict, I had been partly formed by the kind of person my father was. An aspect of self-realization was thus bound up with recognizing him as both apart from and linked to my own sense of identity.

His life still echoes within me. The echoes are half-finished words, phrases which I cannot quite pick up with my everyday ears. I have to turn my ears inward to hear them, to be reminded of what I know through him. Then, it is as if I can almost remember the fragments of the social order from his village boyhood that he both reverenced and rebelled against. I carry scraps of an archaic countryman's world before the First World War, a smarting Wellsian class consciousness of the upwardly mobile 'little man', a peculiar mixture of the radical who read *Clarion* and the conservative who defended the Empire, the staunch Yorkshire patriot who thought nothing of buying on the black market in the Second World War. I know the awkward engineer in the British Raj, the paternalistic racialist white boss, the Tory who voted Labour in 1945 for a better deal for the unemployed, the affable salesman passing round cigarettes and overtipping waiters to show he had money, the skilled tradesman white with responsibility at news of a pit disaster. These were just parts of a man and the man my father.

But in the moment of touching his past and the past of the fathers which were also within him, it all dissolves in me:

Those are pearls that were his eyes.
Nothing of him that doth fade
But doth suffer a sea-change
Into something rich and strange.

I am not him, nor his father or father's father. Not only because I am a woman or because I was his child late in life, but because changes outside our immediate family have worked upon our lives. So the gulf and the lack of shared assumptions are not simply a matter of our being different sexes or being separated by half a century. I am a townswoman, educated at Oxford, part of the educated middle class, a Marxist, a feminist. This journey in one generation would have been inconceivable in an earlier epoch in our family history. The placings have gone all askew.

Reading Virginia Woolf's *A Room of One's Own,* I was struck by her assumption that feminists with the self-consciousness to seek an autonomous relation to culture and to the past would be the daughters of educated fathers. But the problems Virginia Woolf describes in our relationship as women to male-dominated culture are still very much there. Even the way we consider the extent of the problems is deeply tied up with those unfinished feelings I have towards my father. In my determination to open the wounds in which our love for one another congealed, I was seeking a means of coming to terms with more general timidities, fears of authority, my reliance on received ideas. I had to be able to feel him as a person hewing at his world and shaped by its confines. I could not make do with an emblem of political contest—'the enemy'—or a symbol—'the patriarchy'. These would mean that I would continue to see him only as the authority I had opposed. It would have left me for ever resisting aspects of male-defined culture while allowing men the power to intimidate me.

Lance Rowbotham—a man on the grand scale—had always been in the world, had travelled its length and breadth and could not be gainsaid. His knowledge came not from books, mere flibbertigibbet bits of paper, but from some source through which life itself was repeated, familiar as the earth and the sky but unknown since time began. This was what I wanted to encounter.

However, as I tried to glimpse him as he was to himself, rather than how he overwhelmed me, he became at once more complex and more vulnerable. And it was a terrible struggle to reach even this threshold. I cannot do more than glimpse him through chinks in the gate, never sure if the light is deceptive, a little fearful that as I gaze my eyes will harden like stones.

There is no absolute answer: how do you maintain your relationship with aspects of male-dominated culture that are needed by women and men, and how do you oppose those other aspects that thwart and destroy us? Anger and struggle against oppression and subordination are necessary, but not adequate alone, for we must develop resources to bring the new social order into being, not merely resist the old. This must involve not only the slogans of rebellion but, more profoundly, a changed relationship to the past, a lived cultural transformation. Creativity implies flowing into the process of metamorphosis, into something 'rich and strange'. It means the ability to emerge anew out of the moment of immersion. It is not just a redefinition of femininity. It means turning the understanding inside-out, so that what it is to be a man is no longer just 'there' in the world. It requires that the reason and imagination of women contribute partly to the cultural experience of being a man, just as men have appropriated and contributed to the social meaning of what it is to be a woman.

In searching for a different way of knowing my father's life, I am groping towards an understanding which brings freedom and I am groping towards the love behind the anger and resentment.

It is sad that he died when I was only able to deny him love. Bitter the death of a father I never really met.

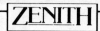

ZENITH

Behind God's Back

Negley Farson **£2.95**

As World War II was erupting Negley Farson drove across Africa. This record of his extraordinary journey provides vivid and indelible pictures of a vast continent, and a remarkable survey of colonialism at work.

A Small Yes and A Big No

George Grosz **£2.50**

A vivid autobiography of one of the most rebellious and explosive artists of the 1920's, whose life and work became a legend. He conjours up an exciting period and the central figures who were responsible for shaping it, including Thomas Mann, Lenin, Dali and von Sternberg.

The Pathway

Henry Williamson **£2.50**

Fourth in *The Flax of Dream* sequence is the moving story of a young man's haunting quest for love and peace as he feverishly sets his ideas down on paper.

Shining Scabbard

R C Hutchinson **£2.50**

The funny, touching story of a proud, doomed family. Renee Severin's stay at her husband's family home is disastrous as she waits for her husband, an army captain in Africa, to rescue her and their children.

Z Zenith Books are published by Hamlyn Paperbacks

GRANTA

RUSSELL HOBAN

PAN LIVES

Eelbrook Common, and evening coming on. Boys with a football in the blue-grey dusk in the empty paddling pond. Black ideographs on the dry grey concrete of the dry and winter paddling pond. A scrawl of boys, a scribble on the dry grey concrete, black against the blue-grey dusk. The dusk purpling a little behind the black trees. The trees on Eelbrook Common are not the same as loose trees, random trees. The trees on Eelbrook Common enclose, enfold, embrace the time, the light, the space, the airs of morning, winds of evening, cries of night on Eelbrook Common. Golden headlamps of the District Line approach with gleams of sliding gold along the curving rails from Parson's Green. The flanged iron wheels rumble on the rails. Steel they may be, but iron is before steel, iron is elemental. There is the idea of iron in the train wheels, the rails of the District Line snaking round the curve speak themselves in iron. There is a rosy blur of westering light behind the darkening silhouettes, behind the blocks of dusk and buildings. Red lights, green lights, a cluster of white and yellowish lamps on the Parson's Green station platform. Stains of yellowish light down corrugated iron, down various wooden slants and angles by the station. Stains of light like rust stains down the sides of iron freighters long at sea. The richness of the deep blue-grey above the westering pink, a blue-grey seen in old picture books, a blue-grey by Edmund Dulac. Wings of night and golden domes in that blue-grey; safe good nights and wooden stairs to bed. The white sparks flashing as the flanged wheels with their carriages recede towards Parson's Green. The blue-grey deepens more and more towards night. The golden windows of the District Line rumble townwards, rumble homewards through the deepening dark. The buildings mass themselves against the night, stand up in solid black behind the black trees on the common. Behind those blacks the dusk commits itself with deepening blue to night as all at once the white lights of the football pitch come on. Overhead an airplane slants droning evenwards to Heathrow. And still the layers of the last blue daylight can be seen between the blocks of dark like mortar in the bricks of night. To those passing on foot or in the carriages of the District Line this window where I sit is one of evening's golden windows. Here behind that golden window six-and-a-half-year-old Jake dances to the music of Ravi Shankar. From the gramophone the sitar, the tabla, the tanpura thump and drone and buzz and jangle. Jake laughs as he dances like a little Shiva. The music makes him dance, he says; he can't help it.

I've just described the coming of evening to Eelbrook Common as seen from my window. I used language to do it. It seems to me, however, that what I was describing was itself language, all of it, from the blackness of the trees to my son's dancing. I was using our little language of words to describe the big language of nightfall. To me it seems that everything that happens is language, everything that goes on is saying something.

Well, you might say, what difference does it make, really, if someone chooses to call everything language? It's only a manner of speaking. It's only words. Only words, you might say. Because although we recognize words as our only official language we don't attach too much importance to them. Words are only words. In my description of nightfall on Eelbrook Common the events are familiar ones: our part of the earth is turning away from the sun; the trains of the District Line are taking people home; boys are playing football in the empty paddling pond and so on. It's pretty much what happens every evening between five-thirty and six. We all know pretty well where we are with it and we don't really need to bother about what to call it. The words don't matter all that much.

And yet, you see, there's more to it. Keep in mind what St John says: 'In the Beginning was the Word, and the Word was with God, and the Word was God.' I think that idea is in us independently of Christianity; I think it's simply in us and inexplicable. Keep in mind St John and keep in mind the scrawl, the scribble, the graffito of boys in the dry and winter paddling pond. At the same time move with me to another picture in my mind: a school yard full of small boys on a cold grey January afternoon. Jake had forgotten his swimming trunks and I had brought them for him. I came through a narrow passage into a brick-walled space of concrete sudden with boys like migrant warblers blown against a lighthouse. O, the sadness of childhood! Not that the boys were being sad. They were running, scuffling, fighting, or standing about as if they had been caught in a wild state and herded into that enclosure. Jake was being some kind of large slow bird, a stork or a crane perhaps. He was flapping slowly and peacefully singing to himself as he circled the yard. But ah, the sadness of childhood in all those little boys!

Returning to the Gospel of St John: 1.1. 'The Word was with God, and the Word was God.' 1.14. 'And the Word was made flesh.' The Word here is the Greek *Logos. Logos* means both word and reason, and in the Gospel of St John the *Logos* is nothing less than God. Can God and word and reason be thought of separately? Obviously not. (When I talk of God here I don't mean any particularized denominational God, I mean the primal force and mover of the cosmos, I mean the universal mind, I mean whatever it is that pervades the universe and requires us to take notice of it.) If God is the origin of all things then word and reason along with everything else must come from God. That being so, any thinking about language will necessarily be religious thinking. Any thinking about *anything* will necessarily be religious thinking, but it's language that we're concentrating on now, language and the sadness of childhood and the Word made flesh.

What is this language that I'm insisting on? The sky grows dark, the trains rumble towards Wimbledon, towards Upminster, boys play football in an empty paddling pond and I call that language. Why? Because there is a continual telling and asking going on, a continuous conversation that is trying to happen between everything around us and us. All of it is without words, much of it is silent. Listen, look, let it come to you—the turning of the earth away from Father Sun to Mother Night, the rolling of our cloud-wreathed planet in the vasty deeps of space. Enormities of space and gathered night all round and yet the trees are saying the blackness of themselves, the purple of the sky all round them. You can hear it in your throat if you look attentively. That rumbling of the trains, that mumbling of the iron wheels on the iron rails—if you were to invent a rolling-through-darkness sound it would be that sound, wouldn't it, the sound of tunnelling humankind rolling home through the dark, rolling on iron wheels under the earth, willing to endure a double darkness, willing to exchange the light of the dusk for the speed of the tunnel. Through the rock and through the dark with lighted windows swaying, faces entranced, speaking mysteries of silence. For God's sake, for the sake of the Word that is God, hear it say itself, hear the murmurous silence of the daily Word made flesh. Hear the earth say itself, say itself ponderous with evening, turning to the night while little Words of flesh kick a football in the empty paddling pond. All of it needs to be taken in not as event but as language, as the allness of everything saying itself to us because we are what it talks to.

What has the sadness of childhood to do with language? Can we agree that there *is* a sadness in childhood? Can we agree that sometimes in a quiet moment when you look at a child in the grey light from a window you will feel a pang in your heart? Is it the thought of how small the child is and how big everything else is that lies beyond the window? Yes, I think that's in it. But I think it's mostly something else that gives the sadness, something on this side of the window, something with all of us right now: time. Time that will one day take away even this little child who is now so very young and new and not at all tired. This child must, like all children, grow old and die and that gives us the heart pang, that makes us sad. That's the heart of the matter, isn't it? Out of the silence for a little time and back into it again for ever.

The child by the window is not thinking of the brevity of life, the child has as yet no idea of it. Time! The child has all the time in the world, time to look at everything without hurrying, time to be intimately concerned with string and the space behind the sofa and the traffic of ants and beetles. There is a sadness in that too, in the child's not knowing how little time there is. Or is the sadness in our not knowing how *much* there is? Do we miss our grip on the moments of our life, do we lose time that we could find? Is our language of words reductive?

For example: my five-year-old son Ben comes to my desk, climbs on to my lap, and shows me a fountain brush he's borrowed from me. It's a Japanese-style brush with a hollow handle in which there's a reservoir of ink. 'Look,' says Ben. He finds a bit of paper with a clear space on it, draws something abstract with the brush and colours it in. 'Look,' says Ben. 'With a pen you get a little little thin line but with this one it just goes *blup!* So fast it comes out and you can colour in a whole lot all at once. Why is that?' I say, 'It's because of the way the ink flows off the brush. Brushes are made so that ink or paint will flow off them like that.' 'Yes,' says Ben. 'That's what it is: it flows.' He is strongly satisfied at putting the word *flow* to the action he has just described. The one word takes in all of the phenomena involved when ink comes off a brush on to a sheet of paper. It comes to my mind while saying that that I have read in one of Lafcadio Hearn's translations from the Japanese of a god of ink, or at least a spirit of ink—some personification, at any rate, of ink, some being responsive to prayer, flattery, or propitiation; something in the ink that makes it come on to the paper dull or clever, beautiful or ugly. Certainly those of us who use ink and paper daily would pray to such a god if we knew its name.

This is what always happens as soon as you pause even for a moment to look at anything at all: you suddenly have many, many things to ponder. And while I write this, the evening, another evening, again says itself, speaks itself, tells itself on Eelbrook Common. Along the District Line the red lights and the green, the yellow and the white arrange themselves as the trees go dark. The violet evening seems to sit in perfect stillness, as if entranced with itself, before the mirror of the sky.

I worry a little—and yet why should I worry?—about Ben's now having the word *flow* in his mind instead of what was there before. The ignorance that was there before was in its way a *religious* ignorance—the person was in a respectful relationship to something not fully understood, the person was respectfully offering the mind to the thing, was holding the mind open to all of the thing. Now he doesn't know any more than he did before but he has a word to call it by. Will he think less about what the word refers to now? I look at my child in the grey light from the window and I think: Can there come a time when he will perceive only those things there are words for? No, not Ben. Not my Ben. And yet everybody was somebody's somebody as a child, and as a child must have lived in religious ignorance like Ben.

The people who run the world now were children once. What went wrong? What is it that with such dismal regularity goes wrong? Why do perfectly good children become rotten grownups? If I say there's a language failure somewhere does that make any sense? Keep in mind my claim that everything is language. Am I saying then that there's an everything failure? Yes, because nothing has a chance of working right when people won't listen to what it says and with the proper action say the right things back. Go from the big to the little for a moment. Go in your mind from the world to your own body.

Can there by now be anyone who doubts that the body is continually talking to us? You say to your head, 'We're going to that party tonight and we're going to smile and talk to all those people we don't want to smile at and talk to.' Your head says, 'Ache ache ache.' You say to your gall bladder, 'I'm so bitter, life is so hard!' Your gall bladder says, 'If you feel that way about it I'll commemorate it with a stone.' Your heart says, 'I am heavy. I have no ease. You are doing things with only half of me. You are not doing what is close to me. You are following a path without me. I am not in good self. I have no self for what you're doing. You have not gone to the me of the matter. I feel attacked. Maybe I'll attack you.' When your heart says that of course you'll listen, because by then you're probably getting pains down your left arm and let's hope your local emergency ward isn't on strike. Language! Twenty-four hours a day, fourteen hundred and forty minutes daily, eighty-six thousand, four hundred seconds from dawn to dawn our bodies are talking to us. Now go from the little to the big, from the body we live in to the world we live in: trees and buildings, mountains and cinemas and supermarkets and oceans—all of it, complete with sky and weather. All of it, I insist, is talking to us. How could it be otherwise? Ugliness shrieks and gabbles; beauty sings, growls, whispers; the everyness of days bellows like a dying bull; the dead leaves rattle, the madness of nations crouches in its newsprint and chatters its teeth. The stones cry out to be spoken to and we must find a language base from which to respond.

Language base, I said. The idea of a language base has been in my mind for nearly half a year now and I know it's important. I don't understand it fully but I know it's not just an idea—it's something real and it's something that matters. I'll tell you how this idea came to me. It happened in September 1978 on the Greek island of Paxos, which was of course the proper place for it to happen, and I'll tell you why.

Robert B. Palmer, in his introduction to his translation of Walter F. Otto's book *Dionysus, Myth and Cult,* discusses the history in literature of Pan. He quotes Elizabeth Barrett Browning and Plutarch. The Elizabeth Barrett Browning lines are from 'The Dead Pan'—lines which she herself says were partly 'Excited by Schiller's *Götter Griechenlands,* and partly founded on a well-known tradition mentioned in a treatise of Plutarch according to which, at the hour of the Saviour's agony, a cry of "Great Pan is dead!" swept across the waves in the hearing of certain mariners—and the oracles ceased.' Mrs Browning went on to write a poem that gloats over the passing of Pan and the old gods. She says, in Stanza XXXIV:

Earth outgrows the mythic fancies
Sung beside her in her youth:
And those debonaire romances
Sound but dull beside the truth.
Phoebus' chariot-course is run.
Look up, poets, to the sun!
Pan, Pan is dead.

Palmer's introduction starts with the opening stanza of Mrs Browning's poem:

Gods of Hellas, gods of Hellas,
Can ye listen in your silence?
Can your mystic voices tell us
Where ye hide? In floating islands,
With a wind that evermore
Keeps you out of sight of shore?
Pan, Pan is dead.

Palmer continues: 'When Elizabeth Barrett Browning wrote these lines which sound so pessimistic and so limited to any lover of the beauty and truth of Greek mythology, she had in mind a famous passage out of Plutarch's *De Oraculorum Defectu* in which it was reported on good authority that Pan had died.'

Palmer then lets Philip tell the story:

> As for death among such beings [the deities], I have heard the words of a man who was not a fool nor an impostor. The father of Aemilianus the orator, to whom some of you have listened, was Epitherses, who lived in our town and was my teacher in grammar. He said that once upon a time, in making a voyage to Italy, he embarked on a ship carrying freight and many passengers. It was already evening when, near the Echinades Islands, the wind dropped, and the ship drifted near Paxi. Almost everybody was awake, and a good many had not finished their after-

> dinner wine. Suddenly from the island of Paxi was heard the voice of someone loudly calling Thamus, so that all were amazed. Thamus was an Egyptian pilot, not known by name even to many on board. Twice he was called and made no reply, but the third time he answered; and the caller, raising his voice, said, 'When you come opposite to Palodes, announce that Great Pan is dead.' On hearing this, all, said Epitherses, were astonished and reasoned among themselves whether it was better to carry out the order or to refuse to meddle and let the matter go. Under the circumstances Thamus made up his mind that if there should be a breeze, he would sail past and keep quiet, but with no wind and a smooth sea about the place, he would announce what he had heard. So, when he came opposite Palodes, and there was neither wind nor wave, Thamus, from the stern, looking toward the land, said the words as he had heard them: 'Great Pan is dead.' Even before he had finished, there was a great cry of lamentation, not of one person, but of many, mingled with exclamations of amazement.

This event occurred supposedly in the first century AD, during the reign of Tiberius, in a Roman world in which the rationalistic and evolutionistic approach to religion had already done much to bring death not only to Pan but to many of the other greater and lesser gods of the Greek pantheon. Later, however, Christian legend was to suggest that Pan had died on the very day when Christ had mounted the cross. It is this later tradition which leads to the hymn of triumph with which Mrs Browning's poem ends. Now Mrs Browning's last stanza:

> Oh brave poets, keep back nothing,
> Nor mix falsehood with the whole!
> Look up Godward, speak the truth in
> Worthy song from earnest soul;
> Hold, in high poetic duty,
> Truest Truth the fairest Beauty!
> Pan, Pan is dead.'

There I shall leave Palmer's introduction so that I can move on to the subject of the language base. I must pause, however, to offer the last stanza of Schiller's lament for the passing of the old gods, the poem to which Mrs Browning's poem was a reply:

Yes, they did go home, and everything beautiful,
Everything high they took away with them,
All colours, all sounds of life,
And for us remained only the de-souled Word.
Torn out of the time-flood, they float
Saved on the heights of Pindus;
What undying in song shall live
Must in life go under.

On the island of Paxos they just throw the garbage down the hillsides. I don't know what they did before Pan died but that's what they do now. Over the terrace, *blup!* Beautiful Ionian island in the sparkling blue sea and it's got plastic mineral-water bottles all over it. There was a yellow plastic meat-grinder blooming by the roadside—we used to pass it every day—it was slowly working its way into the town. Thrown-away cookers rusting in the olive groves. Black donkeys braying, hee-hawing in mysterious green-lit olive groves. Goats. Goats and donkeys, they're not big, they don't have to be big, they are the familiars of the really big things. Look at a goat's eyes, listen to a donkey bray. Magic. Cocks crowing among the rusting iron in the olive groves. Magic. Stones. Stones walling the terraces, stones islanding the olive trees, dry stones holding the earth to the hillsides. Stones. Broken stones and bits of stone. Some are tawny, some are grey, some are white. Some look like curtains of stone, some look like broken monuments. Very good for writing on or drawing on—the ink goes on to the stone as if it were prehistoric. Mostly I drew on the road stones and wrote on the beach stones. The beach stones are all kinds of rounded shapes and some of them fit together in strange ways. The olive trees, of course, they produce olives. You can see the olives like black dots in a vase painting, black against the blue sky. But it isn't just olives growing on the trees, there's the light. Light lives in those olive trees: it flashes and glimmers like a shoal of fish turning where the sun slants through the green sea. Light sings and twitters in the silvery-green leaves like birds. O yes, there's more to olive trees than olives. The blue sky through the green, through the silver leaves, the green light in the groves, the whispering, the twittering of the sunlight in the leaves. Whispering, conversing, beckoning. Very, very old, some of those olive trees. Old and hollow, gnarled and twisted, holding themselves open like magical garments, showing the ancient hollow darkness in them. They look as if they might have nymphs, dryads, gods or demons inside them. Twisting their roots into the ground, holding open their hollow darkness for someone, something, to go in, come out. Olive trees producing light effects, breeze effects. Black donkeys get tied to the olive trees. Perhaps the donkeys are the familiars of the spirit indwelling in the olive tree. Perhaps each olive grove has its genius who has a black donkey for its familiar and the black donkey has an oracle-eyed goat for his communicant who in turn listens to the crowing of a cock in the middle of the night, before dawn, at dawn, at midday, at dreamy noon when Pan sleeps. Because Pan isn't dead, don't think that for a moment. There are no dead gods. Bel, Marduk, Tiamat, they're all with us still: every god that was ever named and worshipped, not one of them is dead. No god is ever supplanted, no god ever becomes obsolete. Pan lives, he makes his music on the hills and in the groves he stamps his cloven hooves and dances.

The house we stayed in on Paxos looked as if it had been stained long ago with the juice of red and purple berries. It had a red-tiled roof. It had a flagged courtyard. There was a table under a grape arbour. There were orange trees and a pomegranate tree.

Water for the house came from a cistern that was the same colour as the house: it was a little square building with steps going up to the low flat roof of it. There was a long pipe from the roof gutters of the house to the cistern. When it rained the water ran through the pipe into the cistern. There was a pump on the cistern. Whenever a tap was turned on or the toilet was flushed the pump would gasp and pant as it pumped water into the pipes of the house. It whined and howled and panted like an animal by day, a beast of work. At night it was like a dark brother howling in the courtyard while mopeds traced a line of putter up the hill past a little chapel.

It came to me while listening to that pump one night that it was foolish to make too many distinctions between the animate and the inanimate; everything was talking, the world was full of constant language. What did all the language mean? It meant itself, that's all, and itself was something I knew. I didn't know it the way you know something to tell about it but the knowing was in me. There is no sound, no silence, no pattern of sound and silence that will not correspond to something in your head. Try it some time: find the farthest-out record of the most avant-garde electronic music or whatever is the most alien and chaotic sound for you. Listen to it a few times; very quickly the blips and bleeps become orderly and familiar, become the voice and language of something that was in you waiting for that music. However random the composer tries to be, it's impossible to compose sound that has no pattern: anything you hear is a pattern of sound waves and every pattern refers to all other patterns; everything is some kind of information. The universe is continually communicating itself to us in a cosmic eucharist of waves and particles.

So there I was in what you might call a state of aroused language response. I sensed that I was in a better place with language than I'd been before. I was writing a letter to a daughter thousands of miles away. I could feel that even before a word was said I was further out into the world than words had ever taken me before. The communion with the donkeys, the stones, the goats, the olive trees had given me a language base more advanced than I had had before.

How to explain it? What is the language fabric of olive trees and cisterns, pumps and donkeys, stones in the road, plastic mineral-water bottles, sunlight in the leaves, water rushing through the pipes? It is that continual transmutation I have described; it is everything for ever in the process of becoming everything. In that process the language base is both a place and a relationship; it is where you are to everything that isn't you—stones and olive trees and donkeys, everything: Pan. Pan, a god not much revered, not always taken seriously in the books, a lewd and rustic god. His name means *all, everything.* From his name comes the word *panic,* the panic of the all-terror, the everything-terror. Half-human, half-animal is Pan—horned man, goat below the waist, potent with animality, standing his ground with animal hooves. A shepherd's god, he is the Old Word of the groves and hills, and the legend has him dead when the New Word, Christ, rises on the cross. One source equates him with demons, another with the Christ who supplants him and all the high gods of Olympus. With the reed that was the body of the nymph Syrinx, the object of his unsatisfied lust, he makes music. A humble god, an intimate, a *Thou* who whispers in the wind in the leaves, howls with the pump on the cistern. Why cannot he die? Why cannot any god die? Because gods do not replace one another. Let prophets and kings do what they will: gods are a cumulative projection of everything in us. I'm not trying to reduce this to psychiatry—I mean that we worship the gods projected by the god-force that projects us as well on the screen of its mind. Gods and no-gods are a cumulative projection, and, as we well know, the most monstrous of the gods are alive and present in us equally with the most gentle of them: the new and the old jostle for place in a continually shifting balance. If there is conservation of energy and conservation of matter how could there not be conservation of God?

Pan, the *all,* the *everything* half-human, half-animal god, is there to be a *Thou* for us to talk to. Because that's what the language base is. It's a place where the *Thou* of things is perceived and the silence speaks. The best that words can do is to make a space in which the silence can speak, in which the language of the everything can be heard. Humankind is naturally and properly religious, and I suggest that one definition of religion is that it is a mode of being and perception in which everything is *Thou* and nothing is *It.* Certainly we've tried the other way; we've tried making both things and people *It,* and we've seen the results.

Is it possible that the sadness we sense in childhood is the sadness of the *Thou* perceiver who knows that the world will come between them and the *Thou* of things, will stop its mouth and their ears? Is it the sadness of the listener who will not be allowed to hear the silence speak? Or is the sadness something else? Is it that whatever looks out through the child's eyes knows that it must destroy the child to make the adult, must close the garden of the child to the grownup just as Adam and Eve closed Eden to themselves? Is the sadness of the child the knowledge that it is doomed to repeat the original sin, deny its knowledge of the *Thou,* kill humble Pan and crucify the Word?

I look at the back of Ben's neck as he kneels on the floor cutting out something with quite a large pair of scissors. He's very good with scissors; he can cut string with a razor blade without cutting himself;

he uses a hammer and a bolster well. He's very patient about all the heavy tools and delicate equipment he's not yet allowed to use. And yet I can't know what might be in him waiting to rise up towering like a giant mushroom-shaped cloud. The Japanese called the bomb that fell on Hiroshima *Gensu Makkadan,* 'the Original Child Bomb'. Well, it's a chance you take when you decide to have children and keep the human race going. There was a toy sold a few years back, a box with an on-off switch. When you switched it on a little hand came out of the box and switched it off.

A cold noonday on Eelbrook Common. A train recedes to Parson's Green, the tracks are empty. The sky is bleak, a cold wind flattens last year's dead leaves against the wire netting of the football pitch. The dry paddling pond is empty of boys. The wind stirs the bare March branches. But I know that under Eelbrook Common runs a secret Eelbrook with its olive groves. Soon I shall hear the tawny owl at night, and in his London voice will be another voice, that far Ionian pump, dark brother to the cistern.

GRANTA

Graham Swift

A Short History of Coronation Ale

About the Fens

Which are a low-lying region of eastern England, over 12,000 square miles in area, bounded to the west by the limestone hills of the Midlands, to the south and east by the chalk hills of Cambridgeshire, Suffolk and Norfolk. To the north, the Fens advance, on a twelve-mile front, to meet the North Sea at the Wash. Or perhaps it is more apt to say that the Wash summons the forces of the North Sea to its aid in a constant bid to recapture its former territory. For the chief fact about the Fens, children, is that they are reclaimed land, land that was once water, and which, even today, is not quite solid.

So forget, indeed, your revolutions, your turning-points, your grand metamorphoses of history. Consider, instead, the slow and arduous process, the interminable and ambiguous process—the process of human siltation—of land reclamation.

Is it desirable, in the first place, that land should be reclaimed? Not to those who exist by water; not to those who have no need of firm ground beneath their feet. Not to the fishermen, fowlers and reed-cutters who made their sodden homes in those stubborn swamps, took to stilts in time of flood and lived like water-rats. Not to the men who broke down the medieval embankments and if caught were buried alive in the very breach they had made. Not to the men who cut the throats of King Charles's Dutch drainers and threw their bodies into the water they were hired to expel.

The Dutch came, under their engineer Cornelius Vermuyden, hired first by King Charles, then by His Lordship, Francis, Earl of Bedford. Honouring their employer's name, they cut the Bedford River and then the New Bedford River alongside it, to divert the main strength of the Ouse from its recalcitrant and sluggish course by Ely, into a straight channel to the sea. They built the Denver Sluice at the junction of the northern end of the new river with the old Ouse, and the Hermitage Sluice at the southern junction. They dug subsidiary cuts, drains, lodes, dykes, eaus and ditches, and converted 95,000 acres into summer, if not winter, grazing. Practical and forward-looking people, the Dutch. And my father's forebears opposed them; and two of them were hanged for it.

Vermuyden left (he should have been rich but the Dutch Wars robbed him of his English fortune) in 1655. And nature, more effectively than my ancestors, began to sabotage his work. In the 1690s the Bedford River burst a sixty-foot gap in its banks. In 1713 the Denver Sluice gave way and so great was the silting below it that the water from the Bedford River was forced landwards, upstream, up the old Ouse to Ely, instead of discharging into the sea. Thousands of acres of farmland were submerged. Cottagers waded to their beds.

And at some time in all this, strangely enough, my paternal ancestors threw in their lot with the drainers and land-reclaimers.

They ceased to be water people and became land people; they ceased to fish and fowl and became plumbers of the land. They joined in the destiny of the Fens, which was to strive not for but against water. For a century and a half they dug, drained and pumped the land between the Bedford River and the Great Ouse, boots perpetually mud-caked, ignorant of how their efforts were, little by little, changing the map of England.

One of them is called Atkinson. He is not a Fenman. He is a prosperous Norfolk farmer and maltster from the hills where the Leem rises and flows westwards to the Ouse. But, in the 1780s, for reasons both self-interested and public-spirited, he forms the plan of opening up for navigation the River Leem, as a means of transport for his produce between Norfolk and the expanding market of the Fens. He hires surveyors, drainage and dredging experts. A confident and far-seeing man, a man of hearty and sanguine, rather than phlegmatic, temperament, he offers work and a future to a whole region.

Before Vermuyden came to the Fens and encountered the obstinacy of the Fen-dwellers, an Atkinson forefather, in his shepherd's hut, conceived the idea of becoming a bailiff; and his son, a bailiff born, conceived the idea of becoming a farmer of substance; and one of the fourth, fifth or sixth generation of idea-conceiving Atkinsons, while land was being enclosed and the wool trade fluctuating, sold most of his sheep, hired ploughmen and sowed barley, which grew tall and fruitful in the chalky soil and which he sent to the maltster to be transformed into beer.

Those acres of land he ploughed must have been special, and Josiah Atkinson must have known a thing or two, because word got around that the malt made from his barley was not only exceptional but there was magic in it.

The good—and exceedingly good-humoured—villagers of west Norfolk drank their ale with relish and, having nothing to compare it with, took for granted its excellence as only what true ale should be. But the brewers of the nearby towns, eager men with a flair, even then, for market research, sampled the village produce on foraging excursions and inquired whence came the malt. The maltster in his turn, a simple fellow, could not refrain while praise was being heaped on his malt from declaring the source of his barley. Thus it came about that in the year 1751 Josiah Atkinson, farmer of Wexingham, Norfolk and George Jarvis, maltster of Sheverton, entered a contract, initiated by the former but to the advantage—so it appeared—of the latter, whereby they agreed to share the cost of purchase or hirage of wagons, wagoners and teams of horses to convey their mutual product, for their mutual profit, to the brewers of Swaffham and Thetford.

This partnership of Jarvis and Atkinson thrived. But Josiah, who had already conceived another idea, did not deny himself in this agreement the right to send his barley, if he so wished, to be malted elsewhere. Atkinson foresight told him that in his son's or his grandson's lifetime, if not in his own, the brewers in their market towns would find it expedient to operate their own malting houses, close to hand, and that Jarvis, who for the present believed Atkinson to be tied by their joint commitment to the brewers, would suffer.

So he did—or, rather, so did his successors. While across the Atlantic the first warning shots were being fired in what is known to you, children, as The War of American Independence, William Atkinson, Josiah's son, began sending his barley direct to the brewers. Old George's son, John, perplexed, enraged but powerless, could only fall back on local trade. His malting business declined. In 1779, with the boldness of a man only pursuing an inevitable logic, William Atkinson offered to buy him out. Jarvis, humbled, broken, agreed. From that day the Jarvises became overseers of the Atkinson malting house.

William, nothing compunctious, had only to complete the well-laid stratagem of his father.

William's wagons lumbered from Sheverton to Swaffham and from Sheverton to Thetford with their sacks of malt. In time, brewers from Fakenham and Norwich, who had tied up no capital in maltings of their own, found it worth their while to send to Sheverton for their malt.

But William, who was growing old and already transferring many of his affairs to his son, Thomas, knew that success could not continue unthreatened. Other Norfolk barley-growers, showing the farming enterprise he and his father had shown, must compete for the brewers' favours. Besides, Will Atkinson was still having ideas. He dreamed that the Atkinsons would one day follow the wondrous barley-seed from its beginning to its end without its passing through the hand of a third party. That the former shepherds who now farmed and malted would one day brew, and in a style far surpassing the tin-pot brewers of Thetford and Swaffham.

Looking down from his hilltop in an expansive and prophetic manner (which perhaps explains how, when I tried to visualize that God whom Dad said had such a clear view, I would sometimes see a ruddy, apple-cheeked face, beneath a three-cornered hat, with snowy hair tied back in the eighteenth-century fashion)—looking down from his Norfolk hills, William clasped his son's shoulder and said perhaps some such words as these: 'We must help these poor besodden Fenlanders. They need a little cheer in their wretched swamps. They cannot survive on water.'

Picture another scene, in the parlour of the red-brick farmhouse that Josiah built in 1760 (still standing in all its Georgian solidity on the outskirts of Wexingham) in which Will unfurls a map specially purchased from a Cambridge map-seller and points with a nut-brown index finger to the region of the Leem. He takes as a centre the little town of Gildsey near the confluence of the Leem and Ouse. He compares the distance, by way of the Leem, from their own farmland to Gildsey, with that by way of the Cam and Ouse from the barleyland of the south. He draws his son's attention, for which no map is necessary, to the hamlet of Kessling, but a few miles west of Wexingham—a run-down cluster of dwellings amidst rough heathland and pasture where the young Leem, after its journey from the hills, begins to slow and gather itself—from which most of the inhabitants have already departed to become Atkinson labourers. He taps the map with his pipe-stem: 'The man who builds a malting-house at Kessling and has the keys of the river will bring wealth to a wasteland. And himself.'

Thomas looks at the map and at his father. The keys of the river? He sees no river; only a series of meres, marshes and floodlands through which perhaps a watery artery is vaguely traceable. Whereupon William, pipe-stem back in the corner of his mouth, utters a word which falls strangely and perplexingly on the ears of a man who lives on top of a chalk hill: 'Drainage.'

By the year of Trafalgar, Thomas had drained 12,000 acres along the margins of the Leem; dykes had been dug by the score; some sixty or so wind-pumps were in operation; and tenant farmers were paying the lucrative rents and drainage levies that went with equally lucrative soil. From Kessling, where by now almost every villager received Atkinson wages, to Apton—a distance, by water, of nine miles—the river had been embanked and sluices and staunches built to control the flow.

And though no boat has yet made the auspicious journey between Kessling and Gildsey, numerous craft are already plying their way with materials and waste between Kessling and Apton, Apton and Gildsey, and overtures have been made to the boat-builders in Ely and Lynn regarding the construction of a permanent fleet of lighters.

In 1813, while Napoleon, whose army once advanced so proudly in the opposite direction, retreats from Leipzig to the Rhine, Thomas Atkinson begins building the maltings at Kessling. He is now in his fifty-ninth year.

In his fifty-ninth year he is still a hale and hearty—and a merry—man; a man who would claim no affinity with the vainglorious Emperor of the French. With his young wife (who now affects the loose gowns and coal-scuttle bonnets made familiar to us through pictures of Lady Hamilton and the mistresses of Byron), he strolls round the barge-pool at Kessling and inspects progress on the works. Is it merely coincidence that it is in the year 1815 that the large and lofty building is completed, and christened, by inevitable choice, the Waterloo Maltings? Is it merely coincidence that at the outset of that year his father-in-law, the brewer of Gildsey, falls ill and is declared by his doctor to be not long for the world? Is it coincidence alone that the dignitaries of Gildsey, amid the flush of national rejoicing, decide to forget their differences with this Norfolk upstart and to welcome him instead as one of their own, the bringer of prosperity to their town and a living emblem of the spirit of Albion? Is it any more of a coincidence that, on a September day in 1815, amid cheering and the fluttering of red, white and blue bunting, a little gang of four newly-built lighters manoeuvres by means of sail and quant-pole across the Ouse, then, linked to a beribboned draught-horse, enters the Leem from Gildsey and passes through the newly-completed Atkinson Lock? And is it no more than a sop to the times—or a sign of personal exultation, or a mark of willingness to be turned into a symbol—that the foremost of this gang—the flagship, as it were—should bear on its bows, beside the bright red stem-post and the device, soon to be familiar, of two crossed yellow barley-ears above a double wavy blue line, the name *Annus Mirabilis*?

Something is happening to Thomas, now a still robust sixty-three. He is becoming a monument. Man of Enterprise, Man of Good Works, Man of Civic Honour. The portrait painted of him in this same year shows a countenance of undoubted character, but it does not have the twinkle of his father's eye or the soft creases of his father's mouth—nor will his two sons, George and Alfred, revive these features of their grandfather. Thomas is becoming aloof. He can no longer stand by one of his new drains and clap the shoulder of the man who has helped to dig it. The labourers who once worked beside him—the Cricks perhaps among them—now touch forelocks, venerate him, regard him as a sort of god. And when, with the express purpose of showing he is not aloof, he enters the tap-room of The Swan or The Bargeman and orders a pint for every man, a silence descends on these haunts of mirth, like the hush inside a church.

He does not wish it—he cannot help it—but he feels himself measured up and fitted out for the stiff and cumbersome garments of legend. How he made the River Leem from a swamp. How he brought Norfolk beer to the Fens. How he fed the hungry by the barge pool, became a pillar of.... And, deep inside, he thinks, perhaps, how better and brighter things were that day in the old house at Wexingham, when the summer breezes blew through the window the sound of whispering barley and his father uttered the curious password: Drainage.

But even this he could bear, even this would be all right—for, God knows, Thomas Atkinson never believed in heaven on earth—if it were not for the matter of his wife. In 1819 she is thirty-seven. The playful, girlish looks which once won his fancy (and suited his business ends) have been transformed by the years into something richer and mellower. Mrs Atkinson is beautiful; with a beauty which is apt to remind Mr Atkinson of the beauty of an actress—as if his wife occupies some strongly-lit stage and he, for all his public eminence, watches from a lowly distance. It seems to him that he has worked hard and achieved much and yet failed to give due attention to this wonderful creature with whom, once, he bounced so casually through the rituals of procreation.

In short, Sarah Atkinson is in her prime; and her husband is growing old and doting—and jealous.

In his sixty-fifth year attacks of gout confine Thomas within doors and disturb his usually even temper. He cannot accompany his wife on their accustomed walks, drives and visits. From the window of the house in Market Street, he watches her step into waiting carriages and be whisked away, and the constant paperwork before him, which concerns plans for the modernization and further enlargement of the brewery, the extension of the Ouse wharves and the conveyance of Atkinson Ale by river or road to ever more numerous points of consumption, cannot stop his thoughts, while she is gone, returning repeatedly to her.

Several men fall under his suspicion. His own brewery manager; a King's Lynn corn merchant; the younger members of the Drainage Commission; the very doctor who calls to treat his gout. And none of them can explain, for fear of imputing to the Great Man of Gildsey a slander which he has not openly voiced, that Mrs Atkinson is innocent, innocent, and has nothing but loyalty and devotion for her husband, whom everyone knows she adores.

One night in January 1820, an incident occurs for which no first-hand account exists yet which is indelibly recorded in innumerable versions in the annals of Gildsey. That January night Sarah returned from an evening spent, so it happened, in the irreproachable company of the rector of St Gunnhilda's, his good wife and assembled guests, to a Thomas more than usually plagued by the pains of gout. It is not known exactly what passed between them, only that—according to what was unavoidably overheard by the servants and what Atkinson himself later gave out as confession—Thomas was gruff, grew surly, angry, and while giving vent to the most unwarranted accusations and abuse, rose up from his chair and struck his wife hard on the face.

Doubtless, even if this action had not had the terrible consequences it did, it would have been regretted infinitely. Yet Thomas had indeed cause for infinite regret. For, having been struck, Sarah not only fell but in falling knocked her head against the corner of a walnut writing-table with such violence that though, after several hours, she recovered consciousness, she never again recovered her wits.

Whether it was the knock against the writing-table or the original blow which caused the dreadful damage, whether it was neither of these things but the moral shock of this sudden fury of her husband's, whether, as some have claimed, the knock against the writing-table was only an invention to hide the true extent of Thomas's violence—is immaterial. In a distraction of remorse over the motionless body, Thomas calls his sons and in a voice heard by the whole house announces: 'I have killed my wife! I have killed my darling Sarah!' Horror. Confusion. Running along passageways. The sons, inclined at first, at what they see, to believe their father's bald summary of the case, send for the doctor—the self-same doctor whose innocent attentions have contributed to this terrible scene—who is obliged not only to tend the stricken wife but to administer copious draughts of laudanum to the husband.

On that night in 1820 Thomas Atkinson is supposed to have lost completely all the symptoms of gout. At least, he no longer took heed of them. For far worse torments awaited him. All through the next day and on into the next night he must watch by the bedside, praying for those sublime eyes to open and those exquisite lips to move. He must experience the rushing relief and joy of seeing, indeed, the lips part, the mouth flutter, only to suffer the redoubled agony of knowing that though the eyes open they do not see him, or if they do, do not recognize him. And though those lips move they will never again utter to Thomas Atkinson a single word.

Sarah Atkinson is thirty-seven. Fate has decreed that, knocks on the head or no, she will live a long life. She will not go to her rest till her ninety-third year. For fifty-four years she will sit on a blue velvet chair before the window in an upper room (not the room once shared by her husband but a room to be known simply as Mistress Sarah's room), staring now straight before her down the cluttered thoroughfare of Water Street to the Ouse, now to her left over the rooftops to where, in 1849, the tall chimney of the New Brewery, on its site by the Ouse wharves, will rise.

For two, three, four years, Thomas will look closely into his wife's eyes. For four years he will continue to sit with her in the upper room, wringing her hand and his own heart. And then in December 1825—story has it that it was in this self-same upper room, in his wife's presence, that death occurred, and that the two were discovered, the one stone dead, the other not batting an eyelid—this once vigorous and hearty man, who a decade ago, though sixty then, would have been credited with another twenty or thirty years, worn out with remorse, is released from his misery.

He is buried with due dignity, ceremony and appreciation of his Works, but with what seems also a certain haste, in St Gunnhilda's churchyard, a little distance from the south transept, in a grave capped by a massive marble monument, its corners carved in high relief in the form of Ionic columns. An inscription on the south face gives Thomas's dates and a record in Latin of his deeds (*qui flumen Leemem navigabile fecit...*) but not his misdeed; and the whole is surmounted by an enormous, fluted, krateriform marble urn, half covered by a shroud of marble drapery on which, where it extends on to the flat surface of the monument, lie (an incongruous touch on such a classical edifice, but no visitor fails to be caught by it or to note the extraordinarily life-like rendering) two sorrily strewn ears of barley. In his last will and testament Thomas leaves it to God, Time and the people of Gildsey, but, before all these, to Sarah herself—'whom Providence restore swiftly to that wholeness of mind so to pass judgement but long to await its execution'—to determine whether his dear wife shall one day, again, lie beside him.

To Thomas's sons, George and Alfred, mere striplings of twenty-five and twenty-three, yet already fashioned by regrettable circumstance into brisk and earnest young men of business, it seems that the air is cleared, purified. Their debt of shame has been paid and now with renewed righteousness, with renewed purpose, they can start once more. For has not the shrewdness of old William been borne out? No Fenland brewer, dependent on barley from the south, can compete with Atkinson barley malted at the Atkinson maltings and brought down the Leem in Atkinson lighters without a single toll charge. Soon not only the people of Gildsey but the people of March, Wisbech, Ely and Lynn will appreciate the fine quality and fine price of Atkinson Ale. And if Atkinson lighters can carry Atkinson Ale to all these places, and beyond, why should they not carry other things? Why should the Atkinsons not avail themselves of their favourable position at the junction of Ouse and Leem, and of the general improvement of the waterways, to turn Gildsey into an *entrepôt* of the eastern Fens? The Atkinson Water Transport Company along with the New Brewery is perhaps already a living creature in the minds of young George and Alfred as they drive away from their father's burial.

And what creature stirs in the mind of Sarah Atkinson? If anything stirs in the mind of Sarah Atkinson. Popular opinion will not entertain the possibility that Sarah Atkinson is stark mad. (Was it not her husband who was the mad one when he struck his wife for no cause at all?) Popular opinion learns scarcely anything of Sarah Atkinson, though it knows that she sits constantly in that upper room, surveying the town like a goddess. And it begins to tell stories. It tells, for example, how although Sarah Atkinson never uttered a word to her husband after that fatal day, nor ever gave him a single glance of recognition, such was not the case with her two sons. That to them indeed she imparted, perhaps in plain words, perhaps by some other, mystical process of communication, wisdom and exhortation. That it was from her, and not from their father, that they got their zeal and their peculiar sense of mission. Not only this, but the successes that came to the Atkinson brothers came to them not from their own sterling efforts but from this wronged Martyr.

In short, children, that that blow on the head had bestowed on Sarah that gift which is so desired and feared—the gift to see and shape the future.

Thus it was she who so uncannily predicted the exact timing of the repeal of the Corn Laws; it was she who devised a cunning strategy to outface the Challenge of the Railways; it was she who divined, and even caused to be, the boom years of the mid-century and who envisaged, even as they stood by their father's grave, her George and Alfred, masters respectively of the Brewery and the Transport Company and jointly of the Leem Navigation and the Atkinson Agricultural Estates, as kings in their own country.

Yet some imaginative Gildsey souls went much further than this. For when that portrait of Sarah in her old age, in her black satin dress and diamonds, was painted, and donated by the brothers, in a gesture both poignant and magnanimous, to the town, to be hung in the lobby of the Town Hall, it became the object of no small local pilgrimage. And it was not long before someone asked: did not the gaunt yet angelic features of Sarah bear a striking resemblance to those of St Gunnhilda, in the precious Gunnhilda triptych (then still in the church of her name)—to St Gunnhilda who looked out over the devil-ridden Fens and saw visions?

Whether any of this contains a grain of truth; whether the brothers themselves regarded their mother as oracle, priestess, protectress, or merely allowed these rumours to circulate as a means of securing the favour of the town, no one can tell.

But a further story—which supports the stark-mad theory—which has been handed down and repeated too often to be lightly dismissed, relates that, whatever the bonds between Sarah and her sons and whatever the true description—serene, dumb, inscrutable—of her long and stationary vigil in the upper room, she would be seized every so often by a singular form of animation.

It began with a trembling and twitching of her nostrils; then a wrinkling of her nose and an energetic and urgent sniffing. This would be followed by a darting of her eyes hither and thither in an alert fashion and a claw-like tightening of her hands. Then her lips would rub furiously at themselves and while her face contorted and her body wriggled and bounced so violently in her chair that its oak legs sometimes lifted from the floor, she would utter the only words specifically attributed to her in all the years following her husband's dreadful fit of rage. Namely: 'Smoke!', 'Fire!', 'Burning!', in infinite variations of repetition and permutation.

In 1830—when in Paris the barricades go up again, the mob once more invade the Tuileries and the air is full not only of smoke and revolution but of the heady scent of *déjà vu*—George Atkinson marries Catherine Anne Goodchild, daughter of the leading banker of Gildsey. A marriage in every way predictable, laudable and satisfactory. In 1832—for the brothers conducted their lives to a pattern and in almost all things Alfred, being two years the junior, did what his brother did, only two years later—Alfred married Eliza Harriet Bell, the daughter of a farmer who owned land on both banks of the Leem to the west of Apton, once drained and sold to him by Thomas. A marriage less predictable and laudable, for though everyone can see how Alfred is consolidating the navigation interest, this is not a prosperous time for farmers of the likes of James Bell.

Was this Sarah's work? Was it she who saw what a handsome profit James Bell's wheat would fetch in the post-Repeal era of the '50s and '60s? And was it she who saw how the Norwich, Gildsey and Peterborough Railway, which in 1832 was but a tentative pencil-mark in some planner's rough-book, must one day pass through James Bell's land, either north or south of the river? When the time came, James Bell would be readily persuaded to hold out for two years to the railway company—not just so that, when he finally sold, it would be at double the price, but so that Eliza's husband and brother-in-law could complete in the interval the replacement of draught-horses, quant-poles and sails by steam-barges and narrow steam-tugs on the Leem, thus ensuring that steam would compete (favourably) with steam.

Sarah's work perhaps. Sarah hears, in her room, the sounds of work in progress. There comes a time when above the crooked house-tops on the northern side of Water Street appear scaffolding, the tops of cranes and hoists, then the iron skeleton of the roof itself, over which workmen crawl and strut, as if on some giant flying-machine.

Then the chimney, phallically rising to abash the Fenland sky. Does she notice? Does she care? Is she pleased, proud? No record notes that she is present among the guests of honour on that day in June 1849, outdoing for splendour even that former day of triumph in 1815, when a band played once more, when no less than two Lords were in attendance, when speeches rang out first from a flag-bedecked rostrum and again at the Grand Reception in the Town Hall; when the Atkinson bargees raised their caps and sounded the horns of their steam-barges, when the crowd hurrahed and the first, ceremonial shovelfuls of malt-grist were loaded into the mashing tuns. But was she there in spirit? Was she cheering with the rest of them? Or was she still, in her upper room, keeping her watch over Nothing?

When can we fix the zenith of the Atkinsons? When can we date the high summer of their success? Was it on that June day in 1849? Or was it later, in 1851, when among the products privileged to be represented at the Great Exhibition was a bottled ale from the Fens, known appropriately as Grand '51, which, in the face of strong competition, won a silver medal for excellence, outdoing even the noble brewers of Burton-on-Trent? Was it before that, in 1846, when, having served his six years as alderman of the town, George Atkinson was unanimously elected mayor? Or was it in 1848 (two years later) when his brother Alfred succeeded to the same office, and the tacit principle became established that whoever, thereafter, would be nominal and official mayor, the true mayoralty of the town would belong always to its brewers?

Was it in 1862? When George and Alfred, stout men now with greying whiskers, as old as the ageing century, decided that their labours had earned them the right to stylish seclusion, to a rural retreat to complement the bustle of the town; and so had built at Kessling, though not near the maltings and their father's former residence but a good mile or more to the south, an opulently ugly country mansion, Kessling Hall, complete with gargoyles and turrets, happily concealed by thick woods. Where at weekends or for longer sojourns George and Catherine would occupy one wing and Alfred and Eliza another, but would meet together in the Long Room or the Dining Room to entertain visiting men of rank and their families. And where the cousins, Dora and Louisa, young ladies in their mid-twenties—but not so young that they did not give cause for recurrent concern—would suffer and deter, on the terrace, or the croquet lawn, suitor after suitor. For they preferred, above all suitors, their darling papas, and to the company of young men that of each other, and perhaps a volume of moody verse.

Or was the pinnacle not yet reached even in the luxury of Kessling Hall? Is there no end to the advance of commerce? But should we speak only of the advance of commerce, and not of the advance of Ideas—those Ideas which the Atkinsons cannot help conceiving? For though the Atkinsons would be the first, if need be, to point with rigid fingers to facts—to figures of Profit and Sale, to sacks of malt, barrels of ale, chaldrons of coal—they are apt also, when the mood takes them, which it does more and more, to make light of these material burdens, and to assert in almost self-renouncing tones that what moves them is indeed none other than that noble and impersonal Idea of Progress.

Have they not brought Improvement to a whole region, and do they not continue to bring it? Do they not travail long and indefatigably in the council chamber as well as in the board-room, for the welfare of the populace? Have they not established, out of their own munificence, an orphanage, a town newspaper, a public meeting-hall, a boys' school, a bath-house and a fire-station? And are not all these works, and others, proof of that great Idea that sways them; proof too that all private interest is subsumed by the National Interest and all private empires do but pay tribute to the Empire of Great Britain?

What is happening to our little Fenland outpost, once but a mud hump with a wattle chapel, once so removed from the wide world?

How many times does the Union Jack flutter above the arched and motto-inscribed entrance to the New Brewery to mark some occasion of patriotic pride? How often does the *Gildsey Examiner* (founded with Atkinson money and an organ for Disraeli-ite Toryism) refer in its columns, in the same breath and the same tone, to the March of Industry and the Might of Albion? How many times do George and Alfred and Arthur pause in their board-room addresses, hands on lapels, to allude to some new instance of imperial prowess? And how often do those barrels and bottles of Atkinson Ale find new wonders to celebrate? 'The Grand '51'; 'The Empress of India'; 'The Golden Jubilee'; 'The Diamond Jubilee'...?

Children, why this seeking for omens? Why this superstition? Why must the zenith never be fixed? Why has the spread of merriment been transformed into the Idea of Progress? And why has land reclamation in the eastern Fens become confused with the Empire of Great Britain? Because to fix the zenith is to fix the point at which decline begins. Because merriment never made history. Because if you construct a stage then you must put on a show. Because there must always be—do not deny that there must always be—a future.

And yet when, in 1874, Arthur Atkinson is elected Member of Parliament for Gildsey and concludes his maiden speech with the much-applauded phrase, 'For we are not masters of the present, but servants of the future', does he know what he means? Does he mean what he says? Is he merely masking behind that gesture towards duty and sacrifice the smug knowledge that he is, indeed, master of the present, and is that why his words receive, from his Tory-democratical compeers, such loud and self-congratulatory 'hear-hears'? Does he see the future as only a perpetuation of the present? Does he see what the future will bring? Does he see that the fate of the future (my father's and my own, early twentieth-century present, when there were still plenty of copper pennies bearing the rubbed-away profile of Victoria) will be only to lament and wearily explain the loss of his confident sentiments?

Which way do we go? Forwards to go backwards? Backwards to go forwards? What's Progress?

Does Sarah know, who in 1874 has seen ninety-two years and yet, since that bang on her head, has forgotten the date of her birthday and has perhaps been oblivious of the passage of time? Does Sarah know, who now, so old yet so vigilant in her eyrie above Water Street, is required to add to her various guises—Guardian Angel, Holy Mother, St Gunnhilda-come-again—yet another? To take in her left hand a trident and in her right a shield, to submit her wrinkled scalp and thin white locks to a plumed helmet, to allow her blue velvet chair to be transformed into a sea-girt rock and to evoke an intrepid Britannia, staring, staring—to where?

Yet does Sarah Atkinson still sit in that blue velvet chair? For some say that she no longer occupies that upper room. She is really locked away in an asylum—put there, despite all their filial piety, by her two sons and her grandson. Some say that Sarah Atkinson is, indeed, quite raving... And others say—the Atkinson servants say it to deter further inquiry—that she is dying.

And then, in the autumn of 1874, Sarah Atkinson does die.

It is announced, in a black-bordered column, in the *Gildsey Examiner*. All Gildsey is hushed. There are those who regard her death with loyal and poignant remembrance. There are those, a majority perhaps, who regard her death as, when all is said, a merciful release. And there are those—the ones who believed it was always Sarah and never George, Alfred or Arthur who fostered the fortunes of the town—who regard her death with anxiety and foreboding.

But everyone wants to know one simple thing. Will all be reconciled, will all be resolved in good old story-book fashion—in a fairy-tale ending to make the heart melt? Will the brothers bury Sarah beside old Tom?

Then it is given out: Mrs Atkinson will be buried in St Gunnhilda's churchyard in the plot (which no other parishioner has dared claim) adjoining the grave of her husband. God rest both their souls. In honour of one so beloved and lamented not just by her children and grandchildren but by the whole town, the brewery will be closed on the day of interment and public houses and shops are requested to suspend business. The hearse will pass down Water Street, along the Ousebank, past the brewery gates and thence to St Gunnhilda's. The funeral service will be at eleven.

The town is overjoyed—if overjoyed a town can be at a funeral. Because there is nothing like a good ending to turn mourning into smiles, and stop the asking of a thousand questions. Moreover, there is another distraction from gossip-mongering. For on the morning of the funeral it is raining. Not heavily, not torrentially, but with a steadiness, a determination, that Fenlanders have come to know cannot be ignored. All over the country of the Ouse and the Leem that morning they are watching water-levels, fuelling auxiliary pumps, tending sluices and flood-gates. The Cricks—my father's grandfather and his brethren—are spitting into the mud and saying to themselves there is work to be done. And the rain increases. Moreover, if it was raining that day, in the Fens, it was raining also over those upland regions to the south and west whence the rivers descend for which the Fens are a basin; and it was raining with particular intensity, with particular intentness, some will assert later, over Kessling, Kessling Hall and those Norfolk hills where the Leem has its source.

The brothers, who, since the decision to bury Sarah by her husband, have been elevated from the status of stern businessmen to that of sentimental heroes, do not mind the rain. Rain is good for a funeral: it masks human tears and suggests heavenly ones. Furthermore, rain is peculiarly reassuring when old Sarah had ranted so much about fire. The cortège proceeds down Water Street, and the mourners feel that the rapid ruination of so much black crape, black horses' plumes and black funeral outfits can only add to the impression of authentic and unself-regarding sorrow. Likewise, among the shopkeepers and artisans who dutifully line the streets, bareheaded, while water trickles down their necks, those who hold that the rain is a good sign (compare the unbefitting sunshine of old Tom's funeral day) far outnumber those who hold it is bad.

But the rain doesn't stop. It doesn't stop for two days and two nights. For two days watery palls unfurl themselves over the Fens. And thoughts of divine weeping and so forth are soon put to one side as the flood takes hold. The folk of Gildsey know from long observation that however brown, swirling and threatful their old Ouse becomes, they have little to fear from a flood confined to that river alone. A few traders near the banks will receive a wetting and be bailed out literally and, if they are lucky, financially, by their drier neighbours. Nothing worse. But if the Leem floods simultaneously with the Ouse then the effect of the torrents discharged by the former into the latter will be like a liquid dam causing the Ouse to flow back on itself and spill out in every direction. All of which could make the position of Gildsey, so near the junction of the rivers, a disastrous one on which to build a town—were it not for the fact that Gildsey rests upon a hill, the one-time mud-isle of St Gunnhilda—a mere bump to a non-Fenlander, but enough to keep the community from drowning.

The waters rise. At first with a steady increase, and then with a sudden rush which signals that the Leem has indeed thrown in its forces. The watermen along the Ouse embankment haul in their boats and punts; the eel fishermen bring ashore their nets. Wagons carry shop-wares, livestock and household furniture to the safe vicinity of the church and the market-place. The waters rise. They creep up the slopes of Water Street. The lower buildings are, as everyone expected, inundated, and here and there a forlorn if defiant figure—in many cases not unused to the situation—squats immovably on a roof.

It is soon abundantly clear that the River Leem, navigable water-course and traffic-lane of the Atkinson malt barges, is temporarily no more. The rain has indeed been heavy—malignly heavy—over the westernmost hills of Norfolk. It has caused the Leem to show such contempt for its confines that an aerial panorama would reveal its raised embankments, over long stretches, only as dark parallel lines against a watery sheen, like scratches on a mirror. The Hockwell Lode has overflowed into Wash Fen. The bridge is threatened at Apton. At the Atkinson Lock the lock-gates have been wrenched loose and the iron sluice-gate, so accustomed to restraining water, has been torn bodily from its supports and flipped like a slate into the current, watched by the lock-keeper and his family who are forced to pass four days in their attic. While at Kessling, the barge pool has vanished: water flows through the front doorway of Thomas Atkinson's one-time home, and despite the heroic efforts of the pool manager, refugees from the flood, already astonished enough, encounter to their amazement for miles around Kessling, empty lighters, broken free of their moorings, their red stemposts and painted insignia plain to see, drifting at random over former fields of wheat and potatoes.

But what is the greater cause for astonishment that hangs over Kessling? What is the greater cause for alarm that presses, amid all this destruction and confusion, on Kessling Hall, where on the second morning of the rain, while the roads are still passable—on the morning after Sarah's funeral—the Atkinson family, with the exception of Arthur and his wife, have come in what must be considered, despite the natural desire of the bereaved for privacy and seclusion, a certain fugitive haste?

Rumour is unleashed with the floodwaters. Rumour has it that on the night of the twenty-fifth of October the figure of a woman dressed in the style of fifty years ago is seen on the rain-soaked terrace of Kessling Hall, among the dripping urns and stone pineapples, tapping on the French windows for admittance. Dora Atkinson—for she is the witness—is roundly scolded for this fanciful vision. It is the product of reading too much Tennyson. And, in any case, how could Dora, who had not even been born at the time a certain fateful blow was struck on a certain head, be sure that what she had seen was the younger image of her grandmother? Her grandmother who was *buried yesterday*.

Yet that Dora is shaken—by something—is plain. For the female servant who unloosed this rumour on to the world (though she did not do it till years afterwards, till old George and Alfred were both safely dead) found cause to loose another on its heels. Namely, that when Dora went to bed that night it was not to her own room but to that of her cousin, Louisa; it being a well-known fact that these two confirmed spinsters would occasionally, in times of stress—thunderstorms, floods, the like—curl up in the same bed together, just like little children.

Rumour is but rumour. But several rumours, of similar vein, from different sources, cannot be ignored. On the same night of the twenty-fifth, Jane Casburn, the wife of the Sexton of St Gunnhilda's, sees in the churchyard the form of a woman, in outmoded dress, bending imploringly over the grave of Sarah. She sees it—she is sure that she sees it—but she does not tell her husband till some time later, because the Ouse is in flood and the good man is helping with emergency arrangements.

Back at Kessling, by the barge-pool and the maltings, more than one mystified if not frightened witness will later claim to have seen during these confused times a female shape, moving about the hithes and moorings in the manner of someone searching; seeming to glide, some say, over the rising water; seen in the maltings and seen again, more than once, outside the evacuated manager's residence—at the door where Thomas Atkinson brought his young bride—seeming to implore entrance. Which was soon granted—if not to her, then to the swollen waters of the Leem.

And at Gildsey, in the house overlooking Water Street (which is earning its name), in the room where—?

But nobody knows what spectral visitations, if any, have occurred in the house which at present Arthur and Maud are occupying. The only rumour to emerge from that quarter—but it is a precise and corroborated one—is that in the early morning of the twenty-seventh the Atkinson doctor arrives, with some urgency.

Two things, for ever connected with those floods of '74, are less in dispute. One is that numerous patrons of The Swan and The Pike and Eel and even of The Jolly Bargeman, who do not let a mere flood or even a cellarful of mud keep them from their tankards, notice a subtle change in their pints of ale. The beer is weak. It is watery. Is this a mental illusion brought about by so much rain and inundation? Or is it really the case that the floods have somehow infiltrated the Atkinson barrels, invaded the bowels of the brewery, and what they are drinking is—God forbid—part river-water? The brewers affirm that no such shameful dilutions have occurred, that the ale in question is none other than the good old fortifying ale, made in the good old Atkinson manner. Yet the beer does not improve; and a large body of Gildsey opinion will rigidly maintain that—river-water and bad barrels apart—the beer brewed by the Atkinsons after those floods, after poor Sarah's funeral, never was the same as the beer brewed before; that after 1874—until a certain memorable time in the next century—Atkinson Ale, which for over fifty years had been the pride of Gildsey, was an inferior stuff. And whether this is true or not, the profits of Atkinson beers in the last quarter of the nineteenth century and the first decade of the twentieth show a gradual yet distinct decline.

And the second thing concerns that doctor's visit in the early morning. What has brought him in such haste? Has something terrible taken place within? No—or, that is, no and perhaps yes too. For Mrs Arthur Atkinson, three weeks before her expected time, is being delivered of a son.

What has induced this premature birth? Some sudden shock, at something seen, perhaps, in that upper room where Sarah, we are given to believe, breathed her last? The stress and agitation—which, who knows, might have betokened guilt as well as grief—attendant upon that rain-drenched funeral? Or was it that the swelling waters of the Fens, the bursting dykes, the rising river—already, through the window, visibly lapping at the foot of Water Street—awoke a mysterious affinity in Mrs Atkinson's system and caused her own waters to break in sympathy? No one knows. But certain it is that on the twenty-seventh of October 1874, Maud Atkinson is delivered of a baby son. And the baby lives and is healthy....

And that, children, is how, amid floods and flying rumour, my grandfather, Ernest Atkinson, future owner of the Atkinson Brewery and the Atkinson Water Transport Company, came into the world.

Meanwhile, the rain continues. It transforms the lands around the Ouse and Leem into an aqueous battlefield, it turns them back into the old swamp they once were.

Drainage. Begin again. The Cricks get to work.

And down the swirling, swelling, slowly relenting Leem come willow branches, alder branches, fencing posts, bottles....

About my Grandfather

Could he be blamed, my grandfather, Ernest Richard Atkinson, for being a renegade, a rebel? Could he be blamed for showing but scant interest in his future prospects as head of the Atkinson Brewery and the Atkinson Water Transport Company? Could he be blamed—having been sent by his father, Arthur Atkinson MP, to Emmanuel College, Cambridge, to receive the finest education any Atkinson had so far received—for squandering the time in undergraduate whims, for flirting with ideas (European socialism, Fabianism, the writings of Marx) directly aimed at his father's Tory principles; for spending large parts of his vacations in nefarious sojourns in London, where he was called upon by the police to explain his presence at a rally of the unemployed (he was there 'out of curiosity') and whence he brought back to Kessling Hall in the year 1895 the woman, Rachel Williams, daughter of an ill-paid journalist, to whom, he brazenly declared (omitting to mention other ladies with whom he had toyed), he had already engaged himself?

Born in those memorable floods of '74, born amid whispering and aspersion, born, moreover, at a time when the sales of (a suspiciously weak) Atkinson Ale were showing signs of decline, was it entirely his fault that he was disposed to be wayward and obstinate? And was it entirely surprising that when, in 1904, at the still youthful if mellowed age of thirty, the father by now of an eight-year-old daughter, Helen, he became director of both the Brewery and the Water Transport Company, he should accept his inescapable fate with misgiving, with reluctance and a good deal of hard thinking?

For Ernest Richard, my grandfather, was the first of the brewing Atkinsons to assume his legacy without the assurance of its inevitable expansion, without the incentive of Progress, without the knowledge that in his latter days he would be a richer and more influential man than in his youth. The profits of Atkinson beer were not the only thing to decline after that flood year of 1874. For that last quarter of the nineteenth century, which, children, we could analyse at length if it happened to be our 'A' level special subject and which is apt to be seen as a culminatory period leading to that mythical long hot Edwardian summer so dear to the collective memory of the English, was, if the truth be known, a period of economic deterioration from which we have never recovered. A period in which the owner of a Water Transport Company, when water transport and inland navigation were falling nationally into neglect and losing, indeed, their fight against the ever-spreading railways, could scarcely view the future with confidence.

How did Arthur Atkinson, who was not a master of the present but a servant of the future, endure, in his later years, these implacable trends? By applying himself more and more to his political activities (five times re-elected for Gildsey), by being a staunch advocate of forward imperial policies (for here, after all, expansion was still possible), by reminding his Fenland constituents of the wide world and their national destiny; by becoming a caricature statesman—by alienating his son.

And how did Ernest Atkinson confront the same writing on the wall? By remembering, after an errant and experimental youth, his origins.

In 1904, while Balfour and Loubet were raising the Kaiser's hackles by signing the Anglo-French Entente, Ernest Atkinson saw as no Atkinson had clearly seen for four generations the essential desolation of the Fens. Affected perhaps by the watery circumstances of his birth, he wished that he might return to the former days of the untamed swamps, when all was yet to be done, when something was still to be made from nothing; and there was revived in him the spirit of his great-great-grandfather, William Atkinson, standing amid the barley-corn. Since a brewer he must be, albeit a brewer of fading fortunes, what else could he do but serve faithfully his trade and brew better beer? What finer cause could there be to labour in than the supplying of this harsh world with a means of merriment?

But does merriment belong to him who gives it? Testimonies from those times—amply confirmed by his last years, and by the photographs which I still possess of my maternal grandfather (brooding brows, deep-set, glowering eyes)—suggest that even in his restless youth Ernest Atkinson was a melancholy, a moody man. That the flightiness of those early years was merely pursued—as is so often the case—to combat inner gravity; that his dabbling with socialist doctrines was not done solely to spite his father but out of an inclination (true to his name) to take the world in earnest; that he dedicated himself to the manufacture of merriment because despondency urged him, and because—but this is mere speculation, mere history teacher's conjecture—he had learned such dark things (what death-bed confessions preceded old Arthur to the grave in 1904?) about his far-reaching progenitors that he wished for nothing more than to be an honest and unambitious purveyor of barrels of happiness.

In 1905 Ernest Atkinson proceeded to sell off most of the Water Transport Company's stock and the larger part of the Gildsey Dock (snapped up by the Gas and Coke Company as the site of a future works), while retaining the barges and lighters for the malt carriage from Kessling and pooling his remaining water-borne interests in the Gildsey Pleasure Boat Company: three steam-launches, the *St Gunnhilda*, the *St Guthlac* and the *Fen Queen.* Trips to Ely, Cambridge and King's Lynn. For pleasure, mind you.

At the same time he entered into lengthy consultations with his under-brewers, experimented, with a research chemist's finesse, with different hops, yeasts and sugars, with temperatures and proportions, and produced in 1906 a New Ale which the lip-smacking die-hards of The Swan and The Bargeman, or those of them whose memories stretched that far, declared to be the equal—no, the superior—of the Atkinson Ales of the middle of the old century.

But the Gildsey folk at large did not approve of Ernest's retrenching policies, which seemed to bring dishonour on their once flourishing town. They did not approve of an Atkinson who, be he a brewer in name, actually rolled up his sleeves and committed the indignity of conducting trial mashings and fermentations. For such was Ernest's style; and it was even said that, in out-buildings specially converted for the purpose at Kessling Hall, he concocted brews of a much more powerful character than any that issued from the Gildsey brewery. Not only this, but drank large quantities of the stuff himself. They resented his attempt—unpatriotic shirking they called it in this time of arms-racing and gunboat-sending—to shun the political sphere in which his father had so distinguished himself. But reserved the right to spread the rumour nonetheless that Ernest was a socialist sympathizer. They drank Ernest's New Ale, but they seemed to have lost the simple faith that the spirit of festivity could be poured at any time from a brown bottle and was not the prerogative, as it had been for the last time in Gildsey on Mafeking night, of occasions of national celebration.

Added to my grandfather's (conjectural) inward sorrowfulness was the knowledge that even when they are offered merriment, people do not necessarily want it.

Added to my grandfather's inward sorrowfulness was the continuing fall in the Brewery profits.

Added to my grandather's (surely no longer conjectural) inward sorrowfulness was the succumbing of his wife, Rachel, my grandmother, to a severe asthmatic complaint for which the damp atmosphere of the Fens may have been partly to blame and her subsequent early death in April 1908.

Ah, what stocks of merriment we need, what deep draughts of it are required to counter the griefs life has in store....

People who drew simple-minded comparisons and conclusions, people whose sense of history was crude, who believed that the past is always tugging at the sleeve of the present, people of the sort who claimed they had seen Sarah Atkinson when Sarah Atkinson was dead—began to speak again of a curse upon the Atkinsons....

And Ernest Atkinson, in mourning at Kessling Hall, mixing, for consolation, the wort of a still unperfected but potent beer and assisted by a twelve-year-old daughter, began to speak of his 'Special'.

In November 1909, at a public meeting held in Gildsey Town Hall, my bereaved grandfather announced the return of his family to the political arena by declaring his intention to stand as Liberal candidate during the general election then considered imminent. Outlining his creed, he inveighed against the Conservative tradition which for so long had gripped his home town. Without disclaiming his one-time socialist propensities, he approved the recent Liberal reforms and championed Lloyd George's 'enlightened and level-headed policies'. He did not shrink from accusing his own father (muttered protests); from berating him as one of those who had fed the people with dreams of inflated and no longer tenable grandeur, who had intoxicated them with visions of Empire (which ought to have been clouded for ever by the disgraces of the South African War), thus diverting their minds from matters nearer home. While he, the son of the father, advocated restraint, realism, the restoration of simplicity and sufficiency, and, alluding to his station in life as the proprietor of a brewery—a joke which fell on stony ground—a return from pompous solemnity to honest jollity.

He described—I have in my possession a verbatim copy of this brave and doomed speech—how it was conscience alone and no love of taking public stances (heckles from rear) that had spurred him into the political field. How fear for the future had already soured his pleasure-giving role of brewer. How he foresaw in the years ahead catastrophic consequences unless the present mood of jingoism was curbed and the military poker-playing of the nations halted. How civilization (had Ernest inherited the prophetic gifts of Sarah? Or was he, as many suspected and attested with nudges to their neighbours, just plain drunk?) faced the greatest crisis of its history. How if no one took steps... an inferno....

Further and louder heckling, mingled with smiles from the more knowing representatives of conservatism who see that in one stroke and at the very outset Ernest has ruined his electoral chances. A speaker from the floor rises to be heard: 'If your father, sir, intoxicated our minds with imperialism, what are you doing with that stuff that comes out of your brewery?' Laughter, applause. Another speaker, with apophthegmatic brevity: 'Mr Chairman, drunkenness ill befits a brewer!' More laughter, intenser applause. 'Or abusing his own father!' (from another). 'Or his country!' (another still).

Howling, jeering; hammering of the Chairman's hammer ('I must ask that gentleman in the audience to withdraw his—').

My grandfather (amid uproar): 'I warn you...if you will not listen...I foresee a...if...I foresee....'

But as he returns to the uncanny quiet of Cable House, knowing his reputation to have been cast away, as he clasps his daughter Helen, now thirteen years old, with an intensity—if anyone had been there to witness it—suggesting a man clutching his only comfort, he reflects perhaps on that cuttingly invoked word: drunkenness.

Drunkenness. Not merriment—drunkenness.

And, retiring to the leaden seclusion of Kessling Hall, and dictating to his daughter who diligently enters in a notebook figures, quantities and even the names of certain additional ingredients which have remained and always will remain secrets, he perfects his 'Special'.

About Coronation Ale

He retreats to Kessling Hall, a brewer by trade, a politician by erroneous aspiration. A brewer: a fermenter.

In the election of January 1910 my grandfather polls only eleven hundred votes and, notwithstanding his name and his being Gildsey-born, is passed over in favour of an outsider, John Sikes, a Yorkshireman, quickly bustled in to snap up an easy seat, and duly returned as Conservative member, albeit under a Liberal government. My grandfather accepts defeat, having expected, perhaps, nothing more; having already resigned himself to the role of a political Cassandra and the loss of his candidate's deposit.

But though he accepts defeat he does not accept inaction. He waits for the moment to give the people what they want.

And finds it, in the summer of 1911.

In the summer of 1911, as you will surely know if you have learned by heart your Monarchs of Great Britain and their Dates, good old gadabout King Edward was dead and diligent family-man—but still King and Emperor—George V had acceded. And when a king accedes he must be crowned, in order to give his people an occasion for rejoicing and for the expression of their loyal fervour.

And how convenient, how fitting that such an occasion should exist at such a time. When the Dreadnought programme, even under a Liberal government, had been doubled; when the Kaiser—monster of presumption—was committing indiscretions all over Europe; as Britons entered this second, momentous decade of the twentieth century.

In June 1911, during the preparations in Gildsey for celebrating the coronation of George V, amid the hanging of flags, the building of bonfires, the arranging of floral mottoes and planning of banquets, my grandfather, the morose and unpopular brewer of the town, proposed to make his own contribution to the festivities by producing a commemorative bottled ale, to be called, appropriately enough, Coronation Ale; the first thousand bottles to be issued free, but no drop to pass any man's lips till the king was indeed crowned. Though it had already passed, in a form known simply as 'Special', my grandfather's lips. And perhaps too the budding lips of Helen Atkinson, my mother.

Warmed by patriotic zeal and softened by a mood of reconciliation (so, when it comes to it, the peevish brewer can say his God Save the King like any man), the townspeople chose to forget for a moment their differences with Ernest Atkinson. The jubilant day drew near. They cast their minds back to other times when they had been licensed to swill beer in a noble cause; to the Diamond and Golden Jubilee Ales, even to the Grand '51, and so to those halcyon days when the fortunes of the town had bloomed. Were those days gone for ever? Could this National Occasion—so Ernest Atkinson ventured, addressing the Celebrations Committee, with no hint of politics but with a curious glint in his eye—not include a local one? For was it not, he pointed out, the glint becoming curiouser, almost exactly one hundred years ago that Thomas Atkinson received, to the great grudgingness (uneasy laughter among the committee members) of certain Gildsey factions, the Leem Navigation, thus inaugurating the process by which this once obscure Fenland town gained its place in the Nation—if not, indeed, the World?

What was in this Coronation Ale, offered in a dark brown bottle of a shape narrower and more elongated than the beer bottle of later days, with 'Atkinson-Gildsey' embossed upon it and a label bearing a large crown, centre, and a continuous border of alternating smaller crowns and union jacks? Nectar? Poison? Merriment? Madness? The bottled-up manias of His Majesty's subjects?

Rest assured, it was no ordinary ale that they drank by the Ouse while in Westminster crowds thronged, guns fired, and the Abbey bells pealed. For when the men of Gildsey jostled into The Pike and Eel and The Jolly Bargeman to be among the privileged first one thousand to receive their bottle gratis and to raise their glasses in decent good cheer to toast the King, they discovered that this patriotic liquor hurled them with astonishing rapidity through the normally gradual and containable stages of intoxication: pleasure, satisfaction, well-being, elation, light-headedness, hot-headedness, befuddlement, distraction, delirium, irascibility, pugnaciousness, imbalance, incapacity—all in the gamut of a single bottle. And if a second bottle was broached—

Precise accounts of the events of that day are hard to track down. Partly because it was a day that Gildsey wished to forget: partly for the more pertinent reason that many of those who might have acted as reliable witnesses were, at the time, hopelessly drunk.

With alarming frequency the women of the town were called upon to restrain displays of intemperance in their menfolk, only to succumb themselves to the temptation of tasting this brew which had such a remarkable effect. The landlords of the town's twenty-three public houses began to fear for the respectability and physical safety of their establishments. A parade of schoolchildren down Water Street demonstrating their innocent, flag-waving allegiance to the new Monarch, was marred by the raucous—and possibly obscene—choruses emanating from The Swan and The Pike and Eel. Sky-rockets and Roman candles intended for a dazzling evening display were let off in broad daylight and along alarming trajectories. A horrific incidence of shipwreck and drowning almost occurred when the *St Guthlac,* whose steersman had quaffed his bottle, as had a good many of his passengers, took a zig-zagging career across the river, pennants aflutter and steam-horn braying, and was almost run down by the *Fen Queen*, under a similar state of captaincy.

Drunkenness. While the bells of St Gunnhilda's ring in the new reign. Drunkenness in many sudden and wonderful forms.

A deputation of the two senior police officers of the town addressed themselves, in the canvas structure known as the

'Coronation Pavilion', to Ernest Atkinson, to express their urgent view that in the name of law and order the public houses of the town should be closed, and to ask, in the meantime, what on earth was in those bottles, and was there no antidote? To which Ernest is said to have replied, with a detectable mimicking of his election speech style, that it would be a most deplorable action, to suppress, on this day of all days, a gesture intended only to do honour to King and Country; that though he was responsible for the beer, he could hardly be held responsible for those (these were his words) who did not drink it wisely. And to illustrate this latter point, he proceeded, before the eyes of the police chiefs, to drain in one draught a bottle of the ale in question (of which several crates had penetrated the Coronation Pavilion) without the slightest visible effect, thus putting to the lie the slanders made at that same election speech and proving the adage that it takes more than his own beer to get a brewer drunk. The officers were cordially invited to try for themselves. Being in their best ceremonial uniforms, they declined.

To these same senior officers it had soon regrettably to be reported that a number of their constables had yielded to the general intoxication and tasted the extraordinary potion. A young reveller had attempted to climb a flag-pole and broken a leg. The Processions and Events were falling into disarray. And numerous participating citizens who even on this day should have maintained a necessary degree of sobriety, had failed to do so, including the members of the Gildsey Free Trade Brass Band, whose much rehearsed programme suffered from wild improvizations and whose rendering of Elgar's Cockaigne Overture broke down irredeemably.

It was now a question of some difficulty, for those still able to judge the matter, whether prohibiting the supply of this by now clamoured-for beer might not lead to even greater uproar than that caused by its consumption.

During the course of this riotous afternoon several of those invited to attend the Coronation Banquet (at eight, in the Great Chamber of the Town Hall) began to wonder how (given that they too had drunk) they might conceivably excuse themselves from such a dignified gathering. But no Coronation Banquet was to occur. For the worst of this outrageous day was yet to come.

No one knows how it started. Whether the alarm was first given by individuals (and was ignored as one of innumerable hoaxes and hallucinations) or whether the whole town as a body was suddenly aware of the palpable fact. But as twilight descended on this more than festive day it became evident that the brewery, the New Atkinson Brewery, built in 1849 by George and Alfred Atkinson, was on fire. Palls of thickening smoke were rapidly followed by leaping flames, then by the loud crackings and burstings that signal an advanced conflagration.

A crowd rushed and swarmed. The Coronation Banquet, in the face of such a dire emergency, was summarily cancelled. The Gildsey Fire Brigade (founder, Alfred Atkinson) was called out in full complement. But whether this stalwart body, with its three engines and two auxiliary tenders, was of any use on this disastrous night is to be doubted. For not only had the Fire Station throughout the day been improvidently undermanned (one of the engines having been decked out with ribbons and flags as part of the celebratory procession) but almost every fireman, struggling now just as much to sober himself as to get into his cumbersome fireman's garb, had drunk his share of the Ale; with the result that when the engines at last arrived, in ragged order, with much clanging of bells, and in one case still festooned with patriotic rosettes, the brewery was already past saving. And it was claimed by several eye-witnesses that the gallant crews devoted much more of their energy to a variety of insubordinate antics (such as playing their hoses upon the watching crowd) than they ever did to the fire.

So the fire burned. Subsuming all bonfires and all other pyrotechnic displays arranged for this joyous evening. The crowd, indeed, eyes glazed as much by their intake of ale as by the glare of the flames, watched as if this were not their town brewery being burned to the ground but some elaborate spectacle expressly arranged for their delight and contemplation. And perhaps it was. The ineptitudes of the Fire Brigade were cheered and encouraged. Few accounts speak of dismay, of panic, even of apprehended danger. When the fire performed particularly impressive stunts (a row of upper windows bursting all at once like a ship's broadside) it did so amid hearty applause; and when, at twelve midnight (for that was the last hour ever to be registered on its lofty clock-face) the brewery chimney trembled, tottered and, with its Italianate friezes and paralyzed iron clock-hands, sank swiftly, vertically, into the blazing shell of the brewery, it was to the accompaniment of a resounding ovation, notwithstanding the fact that if the chimney had chosen to adopt a different angle of collapse it might have crushed several score of the spectators.

An unearthly glare lit all that night the clustered rooftops of Gildsey. On the oily-black surface of the Ouse fiery necklaces scattered and rethreaded themselves. In the deserted, garlanded market-place the paving stones throbbed, and in the Town Hall where the places were laid for a banquet that was never to be, the shadows of the tall municipal window frames quivered on the walls. For miles around, across the flat unimpeded outlook of the Fens, the fire could be seen, like some meteoric visitation—a gift to Fenland superstition; and on the morning of the 23rd of June, in place of the familiar chimney, a great cloud of smoke, lingering for days.

Was it the case—for no sooner had the blaze gone out than the talk began to be fanned—that this Coronation Ale, which so fired internally those who drank it, had found a means to manifest its power externally and in a process of spontaneous combustion engulfed in flames its own source? Had this phenomenal ale, intended to regale the people on a day of national festivity, only exposed the inflammatory folly of their jingoistic ardour and revealed to them that they preferred destruction to rejoicing? And was that the meaning of Ernest's cryptic and bitter remark when in the autumn of 1914 he left Gildsey for ever: 'You have enjoyed one conflagration, you will see another'? Had the brewery fire been started—as was widely credited—by drunken revellers who, bursting into the buildings in search of further supplies of the ale and, accidentally or otherwise, starting a fire, had discovered a new and more consuming thirst? Or was the counter-theory true, that the fire was started by the town authorities as a desperate means both of preventing a night of wholesale lawlessness and of destroying at one go all stocks of the offending brew? For indeed, after the razing of the brewery, no more Coronation Ale was ever seen (or drunk) again (with one exception). And the secret of its concoction remained a secret.

Did the burning of the brewery give final and positive proof to the notion that a curse lay on the Atkinson family? Yet if it did, how did this accord with that other theory that sprang up quietly at first but with greater boldness in the ensuing years when Ernest, having made no plans to rebuild, sold his remaining business assets and retired—all too guiltily it seemed—to Kessling Hall? That Ernest himself, under cover of getting the whole town drunk, had set fire to the brewery. Because he wished to get his hands on the massive insurance sums.

And because, children (allow your history teacher his fanciful but not ill-researched surmise), far from being the victim of a curse he was glad to be its instrument. Because he saw no future for this firm of Atkinson and its one-time empire, let alone for these people who courted disaster. Because he wanted nothing better than to see this brewery utterly destroyed and finished with. To wipe the slate clean.

For where, indeed, was Ernest Atkinson while his brewery was ablaze? Not in evidence. Though everyone assumed he must be there, among the gaggle of astonished and agitated dignitaries, many in their banqueting regalia, toasting themselves in an unanticipated fashion before the fire, no one, afterwards, could distinctly remember having seen him. Though he was there in the Coronation Pavilion and popped up again (quelling certain fears) in the morning to view the still red-hot ruins, no one could quite account for him in the interval. A most implicating absence.

And yet while Ernest had been making himself scarce, another and not unrelated presence had apparently stood in. For, dismiss it if you will as yet another hallucination brought on by the mixture of flames and ale, yet more than one member of that crowd of fire-watchers recalled encountering a woman—a woman who put them suddenly in mind of a preposterous old story. And when, indeed, at about eleven-thirty, when, Ernest being looked for and not being found, two police constables (whether sober, we do not know) were despatched to Cable House, it was to find a solitary maid, Jane Shaw (all the other servants having departed to watch the blaze), in a highly wrought condition; who swore blind, first that she had touched none of that dreadful beer and, second, that she had gone up to the top room in order to see the fire, because she feared for her safety in the streets, and she had seen—she had *seen*—Sarah Atkinson. Because she knew her from that portrait hanging in the Town Hall, not to mention other pictures in the house. Because she'd heard all those silly old tales, and now she knew they were true. Sarah was standing before the window, where the leaping flames could be seen and the top of the chimney, which was soon to disappear, and she was saying with a grin on her face and a pertinence that had eluded, long ago, her husband and two devoted sons: 'Fire! Smoke! Burning!'

GRANTA

T. Coraghessan Boyle

Greasy Lake

It's about a mile down on the dark side of Route 88.
Bruce Springsteen

There was a time when courtesy and winning ways went out of style, when it was good to be bad, when you cultivated decadence like a taste. We were all dangerous characters then. We wore torn-up leather jackets, slouched around with toothpicks in our mouths, sniffed glue and ether and what somebody claimed was cocaine. When we wheeled our parents' whining station wagons out into the street, we left a patch of rubber half a block long. We drank gin and grape juice, Tango, Thunderbird and Bali Hai. We were nineteen. We were bad. We read André Gide and struck elaborate poses to show that we didn't give a shit about anything. At night, we went up to Greasy Lake.

Through the centre of town, up the strip, past the housing developments and shopping malls, streetlights giving way to the thin streaming illumination of the headlights, trees crowding the asphalt in a black unbroken wall: that was the way out to Greasy Lake. The Indians had called it Wakan, a reference to the clarity of its waters. Now it was fetid and murky, the mud banks glittering with broken glass and strewn beer cans and the charred remains of bonfires. There was a single ravaged island a hundred yards from shore, so stripped of vegetation it looked as if the Air Force had strafed it. We went up to the lake because everyone went there, because we wanted to snuff the rich scent of possibility on the breeze, watch a girl take off her clothes and plunge into the festering murk, drink beer, smoke pot, howl at the stars, savour the incongruous full-throated roar of rock and roll against the primeval susurrus of frogs and crickets. This was nature.

I was there one night, late, in the company of two dangerous characters. Digby wore a gold star in his right ear and allowed his father to pay his tuition at Cornell; Jeff was thinking of quitting school to become a painter/musician/head-shop proprietor. They were both expert in the social graces, quick with a sneer, able to manage a Ford with lousy shocks over a rutted and gutted blacktop road at eighty-five while rolling a joint as compact as a tootsie-pop stick. They could lounge against a bank of booming speakers and trade 'man's' with the best of them or roll out across the dance floor as if their joints worked on bearings. They were slick and quick and they wore their mirror shades at breakfast and dinner, in the shower, in closets and caves. In short, they were bad.

I drove. Digby pounded the dashboard and shouted along with Toots & the Maytals while Jeff hung his head out the window and streaked the side of my mother's Bel Air with vomit. It was early June, the air soft as a hand on your cheek, the third night of summer vacation. The first two nights we'd been out till dawn, looking for something we never found. On this, the third night, we'd cruised the strip sixty-seven times, been in and out of every bar and club we could think of in a twenty-mile radius, stopped twice for bucket chicken and forty-cent hamburgers, debated going to a party at the house of a girl Jeff's sister knew, and chucked two dozen raw eggs at mailboxes and hitch-hikers. It was two a.m., the bars were closing. There was nothing to do but take a bottle of lemon-flavoured gin up to Greasy Lake.

The tail-lights of a single car winked at us as we swung into the dirt lot with its tufts of weed and washboard corrugations: '57 Chevy, mint, metallic blue. On the far side of the lot, like the exoskeleton of some gaunt chrome insect, a chopper leaned against its kickstand. And that was it for excitement: some junkie half-wit biker and a car freak pumping his girlfriend. Whatever it was we were looking for, we weren't about to find it at Greasy Lake. Not that night.

But then all of a sudden Digby was fighting for the wheel. 'Hey, that's Tony Lovett's car! Hey!' he shouted, while I stabbed at the brake pedal and the Bel Air nosed up to the gleaming bumper of the parked Chevy. Digby leaned on the horn, laughing, and instructed me to put my brights on. I flicked on the brights. This was hilarious. A joke. Tony would experience premature withdrawal and expect to be confronted by grim-looking state troopers with flashlights. We hit the horn, strobed the lights and then jumped out of the car to press our witty faces to Tony's windows: for all we knew we might even catch a glimpse of some little fox's tit, and then we could slap backs with red-faced Tony, rough-house a little, and go on to new heights of adventure and daring.

The first mistake, the one that opened the whole floodgate, was losing my grip on the keys. In the excitement, leaping from the car with the gin in one hand and a roach clip in the other, I spilled them in the grass—in the dark, dank, mysterious night-time grass of Greasy Lake. This was a tactical error, as damaging and irreversible in its way as Westmoreland's decision to dig in at Khe Sanh. I felt it like a jab of intuition, and I stopped there by the open door, peering vaguely into the night that puddled up round my feet.

The second mistake—and this was inextricably bound up with the first—was in identifying the car as Tony Lovett's. Even before the very bad character in greasy jeans and engineer boots ripped out of the driver's door, I began to realize that this chrome blue was much lighter than the robin's egg of Tony's car and that Tony's car didn't have rear-mounted speakers. Judging from their expressions, Digby and Jeff were privately groping towards the same inevitable and unsettling conclusion that I was.

In any case, there was no reasoning with this bad greasy character—clearly he was a man of action. The first lusty Rockettes' kick of his steel-toed boot caught me under the chin, chipped my favourite tooth and left me sprawled in the dirt. Like a fool, I'd gone down on one knee to comb the stiff hacked grass for the keys, my mind making connections in the most dragged-out, testudinal way, knowing that things had gone wrong, that I was in a lot of trouble, and that the lost ignition key was my grail and my salvation. The three or four succeeding blows were mainly absorbed by my right buttock and the tough piece of bone at the base of my spine.

Meanwhile, Digby vaulted the kissing bumpers and delivered a savage kung fu blow to the greasy character's collarbone. Digby had just finished a course in martial arts for phys. ed. credit and had spent the better part of the past two nights telling us apocryphal tales of Bruce Lee types and of the raw power invested in lightning blows shot from coiled wrists, ankles and elbows. The greasy character was unimpressed. He merely backed off a step, his face like a Toltec mask, and laid Digby out with a single whistling roundhouse blow...but by now Jeff had got into the act, and I was beginning to extricate myself from the dirt, a tinny compound of shock, rage and impotence wadded in my throat.

Jeff was on the guy's back, biting at his ear. Digby was on the ground, cursing. I went for the tyre iron I kept under the driver's seat. I kept it there because bad characters always keep tyre irons under the driver's seat, for just such an occasion as this. Never mind that I hadn't been involved in a fight since sixth grade when a kid with a sleepy eye and two streams of mucus depending from his nostrils hit me in the knee with a baseball bat, never mind that I'd touched the tyre iron exactly twice before, to change tyres: it was there. And I went for it.

I was terrified. Blood was beating in my ears, my hands were shaking, my heart turning over like a dirt-bike in the wrong gear. My antagonist was shirtless, and a single cord of muscle flashed across his chest as he bent forward to peel Jeff from his back like a wet overcoat. 'Motherfucker,' he spat, over and over, and I was aware in that instant that all four of us—Digby, Jeff and myself included—were chanting 'motherfucker, motherfucker,' as if it were a battle cry. (What happened next? the detective asks the murderer from beneath the turned-down brim of his porkpie hat. I don't know, the murderer says, something came over me. Exactly.)

Digby poked the flat of his hand in the bad character's face and I came at him like a kamikaze, mindless, raging, stung with humiliation—the whole thing, from the initial boot in the chin to this murderous primal instant involving no more than sixty hyperventilating, gland-flooding seconds—I came at him and brought the tyre iron down across his ear. The effect was instantaneous, astonishing. He was a stunt man and this was Hollywood; he was a big grimacing toothy balloon and I was a man with a straight pin. He collapsed. Wet his pants. Went loose in his boots.

A single second, big as a zeppelin, floated by. We were standing over him in a circle, gritting our teeth, jerking our necks, our limbs and hands and feet twitching with glandular discharges. No one said anything. We just stared down at the guy, the car freak, the lover, the bad greasy character laid low. Digby looked at me, then Jeff. I was still holding the tyre iron, a tuft of hair clinging to the crook like dandelion fluff, like down. Rattled, I dropped it in the dirt, already envisioning the headlines, the pitted faces of the police inquisitors, the gleam of handcuffs, clank of bars, the big black shadows rising from the back of the cell...when suddenly a raw torn shriek cut through me like all the juice in all the electric chairs in the country.

It was the fox. She was short, barefoot, dressed in panties and a man's shirt. 'Animals!' she screamed, running at us with her fists clenched and wisps of blow-dried hair in her face. There was a silver chain round her ankle, and her toenails flashed in the glare of the headlights. I think it was the toenails that did it. Sure, the gin and the cannabis and even the Kentucky Fried may have had a hand in it, but it was the sight of those flaming toes that set us off—the toad emerging from the loaf in *Virgin Spring,* lipstick smeared on a child: she was already tainted. We were on her like Bergman's deranged brothers—see no evil, hear none, speak none—panting, wheezing, tearing at her clothes, grabbing for flesh. We were bad characters, and we were scared and hot and three steps over the line—anything could have happened.

It didn't.

Before we could pin her to the hood of the car, our eyes masked with lust and greed and purest primal badness, a pair of headlights swung into the lot. There we were, dirty, bloody, guilty, dissociated from humanity and civilization, the first of the Ur-crimes behind us, the second in progress, shreds of nylon panty and spandex brassière dangling from our fingers, our flies open, lips licked—there we were, caught in the spot-light. Nailed.

We bolted. First for the car, and then, realizing we had no way of starting it, for the woods. I thought nothing. I thought escape. The headlights came at me like accusing fingers. I was gone.

Ram-bam-bam, across the parking lot, past the chopper and into the feculent undergrowth at the lake's edge, insects flying up in my face, weeds whipping, frogs and snakes and red-eyed turtles splashing off into the night: I was already ankle-deep in muck and tepid water and still going strong. Behind me, the girl's screams rose in intensity, disconsolate, incriminating, the screams of the Sabine women, the Christian martyrs, Anne Frank dragged from the garret. I kept going, pursued by those cries, imagining cops and bloodhounds. The water was up to my knees when I realized what I was doing: I was going to swim for it. Swim the breadth of Greasy Lake and hide myself in the thick clot of woods on the far side. They'd never find me there.

I was breathing in sobs, in gasps. The water lapped at my waist as I looked out over the moon-burnished ripples, the mats of algae that clung to the surface like scabs. Digby and Jeff had vanished. I paused. Listened. The girl was quieter now, screams tapering to sobs, but there were male voices, angry, excited, and the high-pitched ticking of the second car's engine. I waded deeper, stealthy, hunted, the ooze sucking at my sneakers. As I was about to take the plunge—at the very instant I dropped my shoulder for the first slashing stroke—I blundered into something. Something unspeakable, obscene, something soft, wet, moss-grown. A patch of weed? A log? When I reached out to touch it, it gave like a rubber duck, it gave like flesh.

In one of those nasty little epiphanies for which we are prepared by films and TV and childhood visits to the funeral home to ponder the shrunken painted forms of dead grandparents, I understood what it was that bobbed there so inadmissibly in the dark. Understood, and stumbled back in horror and revulsion, my mind yanked in six different directions (I was nineteen, a mere child, an infant, and here in the space of five minutes I'd struck down one greasy character and blundered into the waterlogged carcass of a second), thinking the keys, the keys, why did I have to go and lose the keys? I stumbled back, but the muck took hold of my feet—a sneaker snagged, balance lost—and suddenly I was pitching face forward into the buoyant black mass, throwing out my hands in desperation while simultaneously conjuring the image of reeking frogs and muskrats revolving in slicks of their own deliquescing juices.

AAAAArrrgh! I shot from the water like a torpedo, the dead man rotating to expose a mossy beard and eyes cold as the moon. I must have shouted out, thrashing around in the weeds, because the voices behind me suddenly became animated.

'What was that?'

'It's them, it's them: they tried to, tried to...*rape* me!' Sobs.

A man's voice, flat midwestern accent. 'You sons a bitches, we'll kill you!'

Frogs, crickets.

Then another voice, harsh, r-less, lower East Side: 'Motherfucker!' I recognized the verbal virtuosity of the bad greasy character in the engineer boots. Tooth chipped, sneakers gone, coated in mud and slime and worse, crouching breathless in the weeds waiting to have my ass thoroughly and definitively kicked and fresh from the hideous stinking embrace of a three-days-dead corpse, I suddenly felt a rush of joy and vindication: the son of a bitch was alive! Just as quickly, my bowels turned to ice. 'Come on out of there you pansy motherfuckers!' the bad greasy character was screaming. He shouted curses till he was out of breath.

The crickets started up again, then the frogs. I held my breath. All at once there was a sound in the reeds, a swishing, a splash: thunk-a-thunk. They were throwing rocks. The frogs fell silent. I cradled my head. Swish, swish, thunk-a-thunk. A wedge of feldspar the size of a cue ball glanced off my knee. I bit my finger.

It was then that they turned to the car. I heard a door slam, a curse, and then the sound of the headlights shattering—almost a good-natured sound, celebratory, like corks popping from the necks of bottles. This was succeeded by the dull booming of the fenders, metal on metal, and then the icy crash of the windshield. I inched forward, elbows and knees, my belly pressed to the muck, thinking of guerrillas and commandos and *The Naked and the Dead.* I parted the weeds and squinted the length of the parking lot.

The second car—it was a Trans-Am—was still running, its high beams washing the scene in a lurid stagey light. Tyre iron flailing, the greasy bad character was laying into the side of my mother's Bel Air like an avenging demon, his shadow riding up the trunks of the trees. Whomp. Whomp. Whomp-whomp. The other two guys—blond types, in fraternity jackets—were helping out with tree branches and skull-sized boulders. One of them was gathering up bottles, rocks, muck, candy wrappers, used condoms, poptops and other refuse and pitching it through the window on the driver's side. I could see the fox, a white bulb behind the windshield of the '57 Chevy. 'Bobbie,' she whined over the thumping, 'come *on.*' The greasy character paused a moment, took one good swipe at the left tail-light and then heaved the tyre iron halfway across the lake. Then he fired up the '57 and was gone.

Blond head nodded at blond head. One said something to the other, too low for me to catch. They were no doubt thinking that in helping to annihilate my mother's car they'd committed a fairly rash act, and thinking too that there were three bad characters connected with that very car watching them from the woods. Perhaps other possibilities occurred to them as well—police, jail cells, justices of the peace, reparations, lawyers, irate parents, fraternal censure.

Whatever they were thinking, they suddenly dropped branches, bottles and rocks and sprang for their car in unison, as if they'd choreographed it. Five seconds. That's all it took. The engine shrieked, the tyres squealed, a cloud of dust rose from the rutted lot and then settled back on darkness.

I don't know how long I lay there, the bad breath of decay all around me, my jacket heavy as a bear, the primordial ooze subtly reconstituting itself to accommodate my upper thighs and testicles. My jaw ached, my knee throbbed, my coccyx was on fire. I contemplated suicide, wondered if I'd need bridgework, scraped the recesses of my brain for some sort of excuse to give my parents—a tree had fallen on the car, I was blindsided by a bread truck, hit and run, vandals had got to it while we were playing chess at Digby's. Then I thought of the dead man. He was probably the only person on the planet worse off than I was. I thought about him, fog on the lake, insects chirring eerily, and felt the tug of fear, felt the darkness opening up inside me like a set of jaws. Who was he, I wondered, this victim of time and circumstance bobbing sorrowfully in the lake at my back. The owner of the chopper, no doubt, a bad older character come to this. Shot during a murky drug deal, drowned while drunkenly frolicking in the lake. Another headline. My car was wrecked, he was dead.

When the eastern half of the sky went from black to cobalt and the trees began to separate themselves from the shadows, I pushed myself up from the mud and stepped out into the open. By now the birds had begun to take over from the crickets, and dew lay slick on the leaves. There was a smell in the air, raw and sweet at the same time, the smell of the sun firing buds and opening blossoms. I contemplated the car. It lay there like a wreck along the highway, like a steel sculpture left over from a vanished civilization. Everything was still. This was nature.

I was circling the car, as dazed and bedraggled as the sole survivor of an air blitz, when Digby and Jeff emerged from the trees behind me. Digby's face was crosshatched with smears of dirt, Jeff's jacket was gone and his shirt was torn across the shoulder. They slouched across the lot, looking sheepish, and silently came up beside me to gape at the ravaged automobile. No one said a word. After a while

Jeff swung open the driver's door and began to scoop the broken glass and garbage off the seat. I looked at Digby. He shrugged. 'At least they didn't slash the tyres,' he said.

It was true; the tyres were intact. There was no windshield, the headlights were staved in and the body looked as if it had been sledge-hammered for a quarter a shot at the county fair, but the tyres were inflated to regulation pressure. The car was driveable. In silence, all three of us bent to scrape the mud and shattered glass from the interior. I said nothing about the biker. When we were finished, I reached in my pocket for the keys, experienced a nasty stab of recollection, cursed myself, and turned to search the grass. I spotted them almost immediately, no more than five feet from the open door, glinting like jewels in the first tapering shaft of sunlight. There was no reason to get philosophical about it: I eased into the seat and turned the engine over.

It was at that precise moment that the silver Mustang with the flame decals rumbled into the lot. All three of us froze, then Digby and Jeff slid into the car and slammed the door. We watched as the Mustang rocked and bobbed across the ruts and finally jerked to a halt beside the forlorn chopper at the far end of the lot. 'Let's go,' Digby said. I hesitated, the Bel Air wheezing beneath me.

Two girls emerged from the Mustang. Tight jeans, stiletto heels, hair like frozen fur. They bent over the motocycle, paced back and forth aimlessly, glanced once or twice at us and then ambled over to where the reeds sprang up in a green fence round the perimeter of the lake. One of them cupped her hands to her mouth. 'Al,' she called. 'Hey, Al!'

'Come on,' Digby hissed. 'Let's get out of here.'

But it was too late. The second girl was picking her way across the lot, unsteady on her heels, looking up at us and then away. She was older—twenty-five or six—and as she came closer we could see there was something wrong with her—she was stoned or drunk, lurching now and waving her arms for balance. I gripped the steering wheel as if it were the ejection lever of a flaming jet, and Digby spat out my name, twice, terse and impatient.

'Hi,' the girl said.

We looked at her like zombies, like war veterans, like deaf and dumb pencil peddlers.

She smiled, her lips cracked and dry. 'Listen,' she said, bending from the waist to look in the window, 'you guys seen Al?' Her pupils were pinpoints, her eyes glass. She jerked her neck. 'That's his bike over there—Al's. You seen him?'

Al. I didn't know what to say. I wanted to get out of the car and retch, I wanted to go home to my parents' house and crawl into bed. Digby poked me in the ribs. 'We haven't seen anybody,' I said.

The girl seemed to consider this, reaching out a slim veiny arm to brace herself against the car. 'No matter,' she said, slurring the t's, 'he'll turn up.' And then, as if she'd just taken stock of the whole scene—the ravaged car and our battered faces, the desolation of the place—she said: 'Hey, you guys look like some pretty bad characters—been fightin', huh?' We stared straight ahead, rigid as catatonics. She was fumbling in her pocket and muttering something. Finally she held out a handful of tablets in glassine wrappers: 'Hey, you want to party, you want to do some of these with me and Sarah?'

I just looked at her. I thought I was going to cry. Digby broke the silence. 'No thanks,' he said, leaning over me. 'Some other time.'

I put the car in gear and it inched forward with a groan, shaking off pellets of glass like an old dog shedding water after a bath, heaving over the ruts on its worn springs, creeping towards the highway. There was a sheen of sun on the lake. I looked back. The girl was still standing there, watching us, her shoulders slumped, hand outstretched.

GRANTA

DAVID HARSENT

PEFKOS

'Shall we go to the taverna today? Do you want to?'

He turned and looked at her as she levered herself up on one elbow and shaded her eyes with her free hand. Tiny patches of sand, stuck there by sweat, blotched her breasts and flanks; there were crumbs of sand in the strip of pubic hair and a dusting of it in the damson-coloured crease where her buttocks began.

'I don't mind.' He tried to anticipate her. 'We've got the bottle of water. I'm not really hungry.'

'It's such a hike, all across that vineyard.' She watched the others who had come on the boat getting ready to leave the beach, the girls pulling T-shirts and bikini-bottoms on, the men getting into shorts. Manos was rounding them up and herding them towards the inland path, his cigarette-holder jutting from the side of his mouth and twitching up and down as he spoke round it to give instructions. 'We mus' be here once more by 3 o'clock,' he said. 'The sea is perhaps not soft then.'

'It's just a fiddle.' She rested her chin on the backs of her hands and watched them waiting in a group, before being led off. 'That repulsive man has some sort of deal with the taverna-owner; we don't have to eat; we've paid for the boat.'

Manos came over to where they lay, stamping through the sand, clapping his hands. 'You are coming for food?' She turned her head to the side and closed her eyes.

'I don't think so.' He looked up at the gigantic paunch swathed in blond fur, the half-hidden trunks tight over the bundle of genitals; then he sat up to confront the man more directly. 'No. Not today.'

Manos looked sulky. 'Good food. Fish come from here,' he gestured out to sea, 'today. Salad. Feta cheese. You like it all.'

'I think we'll just hang on here, okay?'

'Okay.' He turned round and waved the others off. 'At three o'clock we leave. All mus' be on this beach.'

'At three? That's earlier than usual.'

'Today a wind will come. It is difficult for boating.'

'Repulsive,' she said, after he'd set off across the beach. 'He must be every day of forty-five...that ludicrous teddy-boy haircut.'

They usually travelled to the beach with a different captain on a smaller boat. That morning, though, it had been Manos's turn to take the Pefkos trip. He'd lowered a bucket on a rope from the jetty and made the passengers wash their feet before going aboard: that was the first indignity. Then, when they'd reached the near-deserted beach, he had anchored in deep water, worried about going aground. She had jumped off and swum round to the prow, then lowered her feet. 'I can just touch bottom here,' she'd yelled. 'If you jump over me—beyond me—you'll be in your depth.'

'Are you sure?' He'd stood on the very edge, holding on to a rope. 'What if there's a hollow or something?'

'I don't know. Just jump for Christ's sake.'

'You can bloody swim.' There was panic in his voice. One or two of the other swimmers had glanced at him.

She'd moved her arms, treading water, and squinted up into the sun. 'For God's sake!'

'Stupid bitch.' He'd gritted his teeth in fear and leaped out over her head, trying to come down with his legs beneath him, gone under, emerged, found his feet and quickly waded off so that the water-level fell to his lower chest.

'I'm sorry,' she'd said later. 'I knew you'd be okay.'

'You can swim.' He'd rubbed oil on, not asking for help, and opened his book.

At half-past two, the others returned. A couple of the men looked across at her as they passed to the stretch of beach they'd staked out earlier. She was lying on her back, her thighs slightly parted so that they didn't glue with sweat.

'I should imagine,' he told her, 'that they can see the roof of your mouth when you lie like that.'

'Fine.' She didn't open her eyes.

'You don't mind people peering straight up your snatch?'

'It's a bloody delight being on holiday with you.' She rolled over and wriggled a new declivity in the sand.

'I dreamed about my father last night.' He put the book down, letting the pages flap over in the breeze. 'Something about the war. There were guns firing. You know the acropolis above the village ...he was up there; I can't get the rest of it. I woke up with some sort of memory of something that had to be done urgently.' She didn't reply. 'It was very vivid. There was some sort of death-fear involved. I mean, *I* was frightened of dying, but he was in the battle....'

'You're always frightened of dying.'

'What the hell does that mean? I was simply telling you...'

'The dog,' she said. 'It was so ridiculous.'

The dog plagued him. They had a room with a Greek couple high above the sea. Between the house and the first lane into the village was a patch of scrub; donkeys grazed there and the boy who tended them had a dog. He'd marked it on the first day as they'd carried their bags up to the house; she'd seen his wary glance and had known what it would mean. Trips down to the beach and back again after the sun had lost its heat, had been like running a gauntlet. The dog would bark at them and make little feinting runs down the slope towards the path. Each time, he strode yards ahead of her, arms rigid, his shoulders hunched.

'Dogs make me nervous,' he'd told her. 'Dogs in foreign countries. Even if it hasn't got rabies—all right, it hasn't—you still have to go through the six-inch needles in the stomach routine. It takes a year to incubate, you know that, do you?'

That morning, the dog had come at him, snapping and jumping. He'd swung the bag holding the water-bottle and books at it, yelling with fright, scrambling sideways down the hill until the boy had called it off. They still hadn't resolved the row they'd had about changing their room for one in the village.

He dug a shell out of the sand and lobbed it at the surf. 'I'm sorry you find me ridiculous.'

'It's only a puppy. You *are* ridiculous.'

'Jesus.' He stood up. 'What is that Greek asshole doing?'

Manos had cast off the ropes that ran from the prow to the beach; the boat had swung sideways, wallowing slightly in the rising swell, tethered by its stern anchor only. They could see the fat figure standing on deck, yelling and beckoning. 'What the hell is he up to?'

The other passengers trooped past and began to get into the water. Manos lowered a rope-ladder. The boat was well offshore. Less than half-way there, those nearest had begun to swim.

'I don't fucking believe it.' He jabbed her with his foot and she sat up. 'The stupid bastard. Look. I can't get out there. Look.'

She stood up and gazed towards the boat. After a few seconds, she began to put her bikini on. 'I'll go and tell him,' she said. He stood at the sea's edge while she waded in; as she began to swim, he looked along the beach and saw that it was empty of people. He walked into the sea until his bathing trunks were covered and stood there while she gained the boat and hung on to the lower rungs of the ladder. Manos leaned over to speak to her, his elbows resting on the rail, his forearms spreading and rising as he emphasized whatever it was he was telling her. The sea was distinctly choppy. Every now and then, she'd be clouted by a wave and her hand would go up to wipe her face or push hair away from her eyes. Then she kicked off from the side of the boat and swam back.

'Well?'

'The sea's got up. He cast off because he wants to get going. He seems to think it's dangerous. He's anxious to go.'

'Terrific. That's wonderful.'

'The thing is—I think I ought to go back. All our stuff's on the boat: passports, money, travellers' cheques... everything. There's some arrangement with the taverna man. You have to walk back there and he'll drive you to the village. Don't you think that's best? Tell him what happened. Manos has got a deal with him; it's happened before. We could meet by the jetty. I mean, you're bound to be back before me.'

'All right.' He turned and waded back to the beach. 'Go on then.' He flapped a hand at her.

'Will you be okay?'

'You'd better go.' He sat down and shook the sand out of his plimsolls.

'Okay?' she asked again. She continued to look at him for a moment, then went deeper. He heard the splash as she started to swim.

It took him fifteen minutes to walk to the taverna. There were trestle tables set on a concrete verandah. They were still cluttered with the remnants of lunch, but no one was clearing them. The doors were locked. He knocked for a while, then walked round the place tapping at windows until he found the empty garage. Without looking further, he backtracked to the verandah, took a half-full bottle of retsina from one of the tables and went out to the track that led to the village. They'd talked about walking to Pefkos earlier in the week; it was three miles, or so the locals said. The heat of the sun made his shoulders and back tingle. He took a swig from the bottle and started to walk. No one was there to see him or make him feel vulnerable in his trunks and plimsolls. A strange pleasure came on him, indivisible from malice. She would be back first, waiting at the jetty, wondering about him, knowing that she'd better stay put, but having no notion of what had happened or where he was.

He drank off the wine and tossed the bottle against a rock. Everything was still and silent. The dirt road, white with dust, lay between a steep, rocky hillside and sparse vineyards. A prickly, green stubble sprouted here and there between boulders. The landscape was bleached and bare: no trees, no hedges, no gentle curves, nothing to stop the eye but the brusque contours of the ground itself. He walked, looking from side to side at first, then he let his head drop and fell into thought. The landscape suited him; it was the kind of place he'd always thought of as sympathetic in his imaginings. He pictured his father, jolting along the road in a camouflaged truck towing the thirteen-pounder. He was as in the photographs: young, handsome, wearing a slightly-too-large beret, his sleeves rolled up to where the chevron-point of sergeant's stripes married with the straight crease in the khaki cotton. He began to describe it, working at the construction; then he caught a movement at the corner of his vision and turned to see the dog coming down the steep hillside, an awkward, spraddle-legged descent, its forepaws splayed to keep a balance, until it reached the road fifteen or twenty feet behind him, trotted forward and then stopped. It looked directly at him, ears back.

He didn't move; the dog advanced in a crouch and stopped again. 'Go on!' He stamped a foot. 'Go on! Out of it!' The dog snaked towards him a foot or so. He turned his back and began to walk off and it was alongside, snapping, its teeth startlingly white against the black muzzle. 'Out of it!' He screamed the words, backing off. The dog paused, then ran at him again. Picking up a rock from the road, he pitched it at the creature's front legs, making it scramble and retreat. Slowly, holding its stare, he crouched down and packed rocks into the crook of his left arm; when it rushed him again, he started to throw.

He missed with the first. The second rock hit the dog square on its face, between the ears. There was a crack, distinct and loud, like the sound made when a wishbone is pulled, and the dog stumbled and dropped a shoulder as its left leg folded; its muzzle scraped the dust; the entire forequarters seemed to tangle and slump. He threw again, taking it on the back directly over the spine. A triangle of skin tore off, making a dark, jagged smudge. The dog screamed and whipped round to nose the place, but couldn't keep its balance and fell on to its side, still screwed into a circle. Then he threw rock after rock, advancing, thumping them into the black fur, into the snarling, half-lifted head. When he ran out of stones, he gathered more: running to the verge and returning, aiming for the head and ribs. A sudden dark volley of blood squirted from the dog's nostrils. Bone was glistening on its brow where the fur had gone and its body was scabbed with wounds. It snarled and snatched at him but couldn't get up to attack. Finally, he straddled it and hurled the rocks straight down. Its hind legs bunched and flexed violently all the time as if it were trying to rise or run, and it gargled through its screams. When it voided its bowels, he stood back and threw from a few paces away, but it was as good as dead. He used up his stones, then left it and walked on.

After a mile, he began to shake. In order to keep going, he had to reach down and hold his left knee to give it strength. He thought that the sun must have burned his bare back and neck because his teeth were chattering and he felt light-headed. He took ten minutes to rest, sitting in the shade of an olive tree just off the road. A tethered donkey was standing nearby, shaking its head ceaselessly to ward off flies. More than anything, he wanted a drink and a cigarette and to be in the village among people. When he began to walk again, he was picturing himself sitting beside her in their usual bar, drinking a cold beer and smoking a cigarette.

She was waiting on the jetty. As he approached, she got up and came to meet him. He could see that she was more worried than angry.

'What happened. I've...'

'You've been back for ages. Yes.' He put an edge of irritation into his tone. 'Taverna-owner, he gone. Car gone. Place deserted.'

'You walked?'

'I walked.'

'Oh, Christ. Oh, look, the guy said...that bloody idiot!'

'Yes. Have you got the bags?'

She retrieved them from the jetty and dug out his T-shirt. 'I could use a drink.'

They walked past the telegraph office and the tiny shops selling lace and painted plates and past the restaurant with the crenellated walls where they ate most evenings. The bar was in the last street before the lane that led up to their room.

'It was terrible,' she said. 'The bastard can't sail, to begin with. Add to that, his fucking boat hasn't got a keel. We were all over the fucking ocean. One guy almost fell over the side; a woman lost her camera: that went full fathom five. Then one of the girls—the blonde one, freckles—she was sick and when she asked for water, bloody Manos claimed not to have any. Then he stood at the wheel swigging Evian from a plastic bottle. The killer was, he made me pay for your trip back. I just paid up. I was imagining you waiting for me and wondering why we'd taken so long. Twenty-five drachs. He simply can't sail; he's hopeless. He stood there spinning the wheel, bloody cowboy, with his belly and his tortoise-shell cigarette-holder.'

'Manos drinks in here,' he said, as they climbed the six steps into the bar. 'I'll find him later.' They sat down at a table on the verandah and lit cigarettes. 'Can you get the drinks?' he asked. 'I'd like two bottles of beer.'

'Yes, all right.' She pushed her chair back and stood up, then hung on to the rail for a second or two and closed her eyes. 'God,' she said. 'I can still feel the deck under my feet.'

GRANTA

NOTES FROM ABROAD

New York
James Wolcott

So cliquish is the New York media cartel that novels by its members are often assumed to have an intimate cast of characters. 'Who's in it?' the brusque and formidable Philip Rahv would ask when a fiction manuscript landed on his desk at the *Partisan Review.* (Rahv himself was left smarting when Mary McCarthy had a satirical go at him in *The Oasis,* and McCarthy in turn was impaled on the devil's trident of Randall Jarrell's wit in his ramble through academe, *Pictures from an Institution.*) Although time and death have dispersed most of the *Partisan Review*'s original quarrelling family, the question 'Who's in it?' has lingered and taken on a special piquancy in 1983. A number of novels newly published in New York are notable only for those rumoured to be in them, smuggled in under aliases and false whiskers. Ellen Schwamm's *How he Saved Her* features a man of diabolical flamboyance based—it is said—on the novelist Harold Brodkey, who has for years now been trying to carve his greatness on the rock-face of the age. (Like Truman Capote's *Answered Prayers,* Brodkey's magnum opus, *A Feast of Animals,* has been so long promised and is so long overdue that a few cynics wonder if it will ever truly surface or will instead remain a submerged legend.) Faye Levine's *Splendor and Misery* is a self-caressing look at Levine's days at Harvard, giving us indiscreet glimpses of class-mates who have since come to occupy positions of prominence at publications like *The New Yorker* and *The New Republic*; and Mary Breasted's *I Shouldn't be Telling You This* picks its way through the miry intrigue of *The New York Times,* where Breasted was once allowed to run around loose. But by far the most talked-about wad of mischief and gossip in the spring was Nora Ephron's first novel, *Heartburn,* which drew flak the moment it landed on desks of editors in Manhattan familiar with Ephron's comings and goings. These editors didn't need to ask, 'Who's in it?' They knew.

Nora Ephron is a gifted commentator and reporter who won her reputation making humorous forays into the foibles and excesses of life after feminism. Pornography, consciousness-raising, feminine hygiene, the uneasy eminence of Betty Friedan—Ephron handled these topics in a manner that was deft, sensible, chattily straightforward. She was also a briskly-discerning media critic, skilfully capturing the snobbery and malice lurking beneath the gentlemanly aplomb of Brendan Gill's *Here at the New Yorker* and making wonderful fun of Theodore H. White's dinosaur chronicles of presidential campaigns. (Ephron's articles found their way into three highly-praised collections: *Crazy Salad, Wallflower at the Orgy,* and *Scribble Scribble.*) As a journalist, Ephron was never one to turn bashful and pull down the shade. She was a disarmingly personal writer, confiding to the reader her chagrin over having teeny breasts, her dashed hopes on being this era's Dorothy Parker. Ephron was once married to Dan Greenberg, a writer who specialized in fictional and true-life memoirs of being an urban Jewish schnook, subsisting on a diet of guilt and bagels. After their divorce, Ephron jumped off the dock (as they say in P.G. Wodehouse) with celebrity-reporter Carl Bernstein of Woodward-and-Bernstein Watergate fame; pregnant with their second child, Ephron discovered that Bernstein was chasing around with Another Woman, and she rang up a gossip columnist and had her run an item declaring the marriage kaput. With only the flimsiest of camouflage, Ephron has put the break-up of her second marriage on public display in *Heartburn,* determined to get a few vengeful licks in on her philandering ex.

Shiny and bright and compact, *Heartburn* whirrs along, not so much a novel as an appliance—an appliance whose inner workings are on the fritz. Like her first husband, Ephron assembles Jewish cuteness and crass prurience into a slick, tidy package, pitching her product to an urban upscale audience. Sample sentence: 'He was so Jewish when I dated him that he taught Hebrew school, and I, who at that point had had no Jewish education whatsoever, learned about Purim and good Queen Esther and the wicked Haman from him one night in a dormitory at Harvard while he stuck one and then two and then three fingers into me.' What makes *Heartburn*'s publication so distressing an event is not that this slapdash heap of masochism and weepy pluck has been hailed by New York critics, but that this is the sort of book that turns everybody within earshot into sniggering eavesdroppers. Not knowing that Katherine Mansfield was in part the model for Gudrun doesn't prevent a reader from plunging into *Women in Love,* but *Heartburn* makes sense *only* if you know who the principals (really) are. Not only has Ephron gleefully ripped off her own experience, but she's pirated her own journalism—an article in *New York* magazine revealed that sizeable chunks of Ephron's magazine prose turn up again in her novel, unembellished. Knocking off a novel to get even with one's friends and former spouses is a cheap enough treason, but for a writer to trash her own *language*—that seems to me the real betrayal. It's trivialization taken to its tackiest low.

Triviality is what many critics feel is most cripplingly afflicting American literature now. A few years ago, Tom Wolfe razzed American writers for ignoring the big booming upheavals on the American scene in order to luxuriate in unearned alienation or spin out the same old comic tales about wacky doings in the English Department. It's a charge that's been repeated and given different emphasis by the critic Joseph Epstein, who argued in a recent issue of *Commentary* that the scorn and contempt so many American writers express towards their country has driven them to the irrelevant fringe, where they ineffectually hoot and heckle. The common wisdom is that the writers of the most pressing significance are those who have either passed through the shadow of totalitarianism (Kundera, Solzhenitsyn, Milosz) or bear witness to the tumult of the Third World (Marquez, Naipaul); by comparison, it is argued, most American writers are fey, indrawn, petty ... dilettantish. Giving weight to the consensus is the fact that when writers like Malamud and Bellow and Styron have gone after the Big Themes in recent years, they've bellyflopped rather badly. (Norman Mailer's long-awaited extravaganza about Egypt—*Ancient Evenings*—isn't likely to turn that consensus around, for it, too, makes an ungainly splash.)

But it would be wrong to sign off on a note of resignation. *Granta* 7 served as a showcase for a hit-parade of young British hopefuls, and one could just as easily draw up a roster of young American up-and-comers (indeed, *Granta* did this and featured them in its 'Dirty Realism' issue, no. 8), a list that would also include Emily Prager (*A Visit from the Footbinder*), Ted Mooney (*Easy Travel to Other Planets*), Patricia Geary (*Living in Ether*), Mary Robison (*Oh!*), and Jane DeLynn (*In Thrall*). What hasn't emerged, however, is a *commanding* figure, someone to shake the scene by its heels. We're in the midst of a noisy lull.

Poland
Ronald Sukenick

In Lublin, listening to news on the Voice of America and the BBC World Service, my Polish companion and I heard about strikes in some factories, demonstrations in the major cities and the arrest of eight hundred people. This 'streaming' of events defines the political situation in Poland; it also defines the literary situation, a situation so unstable that the writers, whose main effort is to grasp what is happening to Poland, find themselves at a loss to keep up with it. And yet, as one well-known poet told me, 'Now there is only one subject—Poland—and what will happen to us all.'

Writers in Poland feel they are engaged in a war. Stanislaw Lem, the eminent science-fiction writer and probably Poland's best-selling author, quit as editor of a series of science-fiction books because the regime banned a translation of Ursula Le Guin by Stanislaw Baranczak, a writer in exile at Harvard who was an important figure in the Solidarity movement. Zdzislaw Najder, a literary critic who recently published an important biography of Joseph Conrad, left the country after the take-over to accept the directorship of the Polish section of Radio Free Europe, one of Poland's underground news sources. A leading journalist banned from his previous job by the junta finally found work writing for a magazine for the blind. Now everybody is trying to get the magazine, which nobody had ever heard of before. This kind of spontaneous reaction to unforeseeable circumstance seems to be the key to the Polish literary situation.

When martial law was imposed many writers and intellectuals were interned, though by mid-November, according to Writers Union and Solidarity officials, most had been released. Among the notable exceptions were Jozef Kusmierek and Krzysztof Wolicki, both journalists, and Jan Jozef Lipski, a founder of the Committee for Social Self-Defense and a literary critic who was under prosecution. Most of those released have trouble finding work, some have been suspended with seventy-five per cent pay, and others must now work freelance or get jobs writing for publications like technical journals. The Government has ordered the Writers Union and PEN to suspend all activities. One of the achievements of the Solidarity movement was, paradoxically, a censorship law that defined for the first time what could be censored and under which writers could sue, and sometimes win, if their work was capriciously censored. This law is now suspended. Under these circumstances, the second circuit, as the underground press is called, has entered a new, more secretive phase, and has succeeded in publishing, printing, and circulating a number of political, intellectual and literary magazines. In fact, an official of the Writers Union told me that now one of the second-circuit problems is to raise money to pay writers for their work; obviously a whole alternative literary establishment is getting under way.

Illegal Solidarity bulletins reportedly circulate in all areas of the country. There is a *samizdat* circulation of manuscripts. There is a creative boycott by almost all writers of all mass media and of most Government-approved magazines. All the official weeklies are being boycotted, with the important exception of the Catholic weeklies. The secular weeklies, which were able to publish immediate reactions to events, have been either reconstituted in official form or have been changed to monthlies, thus cutting down on the possibility of debating current issues. The Catholic weeklies, however, and in particular *The Universal Weekly,* publish those who can't or won't publish in the secular weeklies. Writers from the whole spectrum of opinion are finding homes in these Catholic journals, protected as they are by the church. The only Solidarity symbol I saw during my whole stay in Poland was a huge banner in the offices of a Catholic magazine, one of whose editors explained it by saying, 'This is our home.'

The junta in Poland seems to be hovering between the kind of hard-line control of culture characteristic of the regime of Nicolae Ceausescu in Rumania and the more open policy in Hungary, where writers are allowed room for a certain amount of dissent. Journalists in Poland have fared worse than other writers, their professional association having been not just suspended but completely dissolved and reconstituted by the Government to its liking. Authorities have pressured the leadership of the Writers Union to resign, though it seems to have no intention of doing so. When a book appears by a reputable writer, usually a book accepted for publication three or four years ago, it is the occasion for long queues at the book shops. Zbigniew Herbert's last book of poetry sold out in half an hour. There are no second printings.

Given the regime's attempts to control what is published, nobody knows why there are plays still on the stage that are anti-Soviet and critical of the military regime—by Slawomir Mrozek, for example. And university faculties, despite extensive firings of personnel in many areas of the country and the intimidating presence of riot police on campuses, still seem to have relative freedom in the classroom. These contradictions imply a certain amount of chaos, and chaos, under the circumstances, implies a degree of freedom.

Anything that is not published illegally, however, is subject to censorship, which theoretically includes even mimeographed materials used in universities. Here too Catholic journals have an advantage in that they have the power at least to indicate where things have been deleted by censors. Political content, of course, is the main object of censorship, but erotic material has also been known to get publications in trouble.

Poland is no stranger to literary resistance. In a country repeatedly overrun from east and west, writers developed ways of maintaining national solidarity. In the mid-nineteenth century almost all artistic life was carried on abroad in Paris. Now underground books are produced in Paris and London as well as in Poland, and many Polish writers live abroad. 'I have more friends abroad than in Poland,' the novelist Andrei Brown, a vice president of the Writers Union, told me. 'It is the destiny of Polish writers,' a poet observed, 'not to publish or to publish for one hundred people. The situation is no different now from the last three hundred years.'

The pre-Solidarity regime of Edward Gierek was almost liberal in its attitude towards writers, looking the other way when it came to illegal underground magazines. I was told more than once that under Gierek one could actually see people reading underground magazines in public, on the trams. (Those caught reading underground material in the seventies were fined, but there was no fear of arrest.) The decisive moment for the beginning of the second circuit was in 1976, when the intellectuals, who were protesting against an oppressive new constitution, joined the workers, who were protesting against price rises; this led to the formation of the Committee for the Defence of Workers (later the Committee for Social Self-Defence, known as KOR), which in turn helped give rise to the Solidarity movement. This movement fostered the climate for all sorts of underground magazines—information bulletins, literary magazines, intellectual and political journals—and books.

Particularly influential was Baranczak's book, *Those who Distrust and Those who are Self-Confident,* which distinguished writers who accepted the status quo from those who didn't. Another important book was *The Unpresented World* by Adam Zagajewski and Julian Kornhauser, which contended that Polish fiction did not present the society as it was. These two books started dismantling the propaganda language of the regime and showed, as one young poet put it, 'how the lies worked'. The slogan for the group of writers affected by these books was 'here and now', and though they couldn't publish with the official press, they did use their own names. In the current underground situation, not using a pseudonym is in itself a gesture of defiance, and among the many poets, fiction writers, editors, translators and Writers Union officials I spoke to, most were leery of my using their names.

What kind of writing is being published in Poland, either in the second circuit or officially? Since the literary situation in Poland is almost totally continuous with the political one, it is not surprising that the second circuit tends to publish a lot of documentary material in the form of testimony about contemporary events, such as memoirs and journals, not only from writers like Kazimierz Brandys, a novelist stranded in the United States by the imposition of martial law, but from soldiers and workers, presented without names but with social position indicated. Several writers and critics indicated that second-circuit literature tends to be overvalued because of its political content, but it is also clear that some important work has emerged.

Zbigniew Herbert, whose most recent work has been published in the second circuit, seems to be the most respected poet in Poland, despite the award of the 1980 Nobel Prize in Literature to Czeslaw Milosz, which itself was cause for enormous elation among Polish writers. This event allowed for the publication in Poland of many, though not all, of Milosz's books for the first time. Herbert—one of the few writers publishing in the second circuit under his own name—is currently trying to isolate himself as much as possible, according to his wife, because otherwise he can't write. In fact, the pressure of events has prevented many writers from writing at all or at best has confined their work to short projects.

The dominant style in fiction is distinctly realistic, a category that includes the writing of Kazimierz Brandys and Marek Nowakowski, a prolific short-story writer who has published ten or twelve books and appears in the second circuit under his own name.* Jerzy Andrzejewski is a seventy-five-year-old novelist who had to wait ten

* Work by Marek Nowakowski appeared in the last issue of *Granta,* no. 8.

years for the publication of his recent book of more than six hundred pages about political high life and corruption. Some of the younger novelists—Julian Kornhauser, for one—are more adventurous stylistically, but their works are not well received by those who think they should be more directly concerned with the current situation. One poet, who translated Wallace Stevens, told me that there is no place for experimental writing in Poland: 'We have to write so the man in the street can read it. One has to be simple. We like experimental writing, of course, but we can't do it.'

Wieslawa Szymborska is a woman whose poetry is traditional in form but who deals with the quotidian and politics with an especially acute sense of irony and humour, according to her colleagues. Irony is also one of the main weapons of Tadeusz Konwicki, whose recent novel *The Little Apocalypse* concerns a man who wishes to protest against the political situation by self-immolation but because of shortages can't find matches to ignite the petrol. Konwicki, whose novel *The Polish Complex* was published in the United States and Britain last year, is considered one of the more important fiction writers now publishing.

Notes on Contributors

John Berger's books include *Ways of Seeing, G,* and *Pig Earth.* He lives in France. **G. Cabrera Infante** has just completed a new novel, *Infante's Inferno.* He left Cuba in 1965 and has lived in London since 1966. **Russell Hoban** is the author of five novels, including *Riddley Walker* and *Pilgermann.* He is a regular contributor to *Granta.* **Frederic Prokosch's** 'Niagara' is taken from his forthcoming autobiography, *Voices.* **Gabriel García Márquez** won the Nobel Prize for Literature in 1982. **Mario Vargas Llosa** is the author of a number of works of literary criticism, political journalism, and fiction, including *Aunt Julia and the Scriptwriter* which was published in spring, 1983. **Patrick Marnham** has just returned from Central America. He is the author of *Fantastic Invasion: Dispatches from Africa,* and writes regularly for the *Spectator.* **Manlio Argueta** was born in El Salvador in 1935 and now lives in exile in Costa Rica. He is the author of four other novels. 'A Day in the Life in El Salvador' is his first work of fiction to appear in English. **José Donoso** is the author of seven novels, including *The Obscene Bird of Night.* He lived in exile after the overthrow of Allende, but has recently returned to Chile. 'The Country House' is taken from *Casa de Campo (Country House)* which will be published in the United States by Alfred J. Knopf, inc, and in Britain by Allen Lane in the spring, 1984. **Graham Swift** is the author of four novels. His previous contribution to *Granta* was 'About the Eel' which, like 'A Short History of Coronation Ale', is from *Waterland,* the novel he has just completed and which Heinemann publish this autumn. **David Harsent** has written three volumes of poetry, the last of which, *Dreams of the Dead,* won the Geoffrey Faber Poetry Prize. 'Pefkos' is his first published short story. **James Wolcott** is a staff writer for *Harper's Magazine* in New York. **Ronald Sukenick's** most recent novel is the *Long Talking Bad Conditions Blues.*

An Apology: In issue six, *Granta* published 'A City of the Dead, A City of the Living' by Nadine Gordimer, but incorrectly spelled Nadine Gordimer's name and printed an incomplete version of the title. *Granta* regrets this mistake and apologizes to Nadine Gordimer for the inconvenience.